the family

MARISSSA KENNERSON

full
fathom
five

(digital)

Full Fathom Five Digital is an imprint of Full Fathom Five

The Family
Copyright © 2014 by Full Fathom Five, LLC
All rights reserved.

For information visit Full Fathom Five Digital,
a division of Full Fathom Five LLC, at
www.fullfathomfive.com

Cover design by Cow Goes Moo™

ISBN 9781633700178
Second Edition

For Greg and Shepard—my boys, my heart
For Mom and Dad

BOOK ONE

Family Tree

1

The ceremony would begin in less than an hour. Neither girl had a watch or could see a clock, but they both had an innate sense of time, as did all members of the Family. There was only one clock on the compound. Its face sat impassive and oversize on a small tower in the center of the white, clapboard cottages that served as their living quarters. But they had other ways of knowing the time: the way the sun shone hot and bright at the height of morning, or how the air became moist and the mosquitoes started buzzing shortly before dinner was called. The church bells from Turrialba, the city that hemmed the compound in at the foot of the mountain, chimed faintly on the hour until darkness took hold each night.

"Almost done." Twig took a few steps back and looked over her work. She had laced Rose's strawberry-blond hair with *lluvia de oro*, buttercup-yellow orchids that looked like candlelight flickering through Rose's long, thick locks. *Lluvia de oro*—rain of gold. The Family was segregated from the rest of society, but some bits of Costa Rican culture had still managed to seep in. The twisting yellow orchid would glow in Rose's hair in the moonlight. *Perfect for a wedding night,* Twig thought. Then she felt herself blush. What did she really know about what happened on a wedding night?

She knew a little from their lessons about procreation, but not much else. She imagined Thomas would be kind to Rose. Would Twig's husband, whomever they picked for her, be kind?

"What are you thinking about?" Rose suddenly asked. "You seem far away."

"I'm sorry. I was... I was thinking about marriage." Twig was embarrassed that she had been thinking about sex and didn't want to say so out loud.

Adam's voice droned on through the intercom in the living room. "*Confess your sins daily to a sister or brother. Do not try to hide the evil that is inherent in every one of us. I will cleanse you of sin, but you must admit the truth of your nature before I can...*"

"Okay, turn toward me." Twig gently steered Rose's shoulders toward her. "Perfect," she said.

Rose smiled weakly.

"You're nervous," Twig ventured.

Even though she and Rose had shared a single bedroom with their mothers for as long as she could remember, they rarely spent time alone together. There was a slight awkwardness between them.

"I'm okay," Rose replied, letting out a big breath. "Thomas is amazing. I got so lucky. They could have paired me with Doc!" Both of the girls erupted in nervous giggles, relieving some of the tension.

Doc was a psychiatrist in his fifties, but he served as the Family's medical doctor. As far back as Twig could remember, when she had a fever or a sore throat or a beesting, Doc had taken care of it. When she was a child, she'd suffered from constant headaches. She had vague memories of lying in Doc's office with ice packs on her head. Those were lonely memories she didn't care to recall. As she got older, her headaches had faded.

Doc was also Adam's right-hand man. He was nice enough, but now that Rose mentioned it, Twig had never thought of Doc as someone's husband. He was older than most members of the Family by quite a bit, and while he was nice enough, he always seemed a bit removed. If

Twig had to give him a color, it would be gray. A cold blue-gray. Twig loved to give people colors. There was something visceral about them, something pre-speech. Sometimes a person's color came to her when Twig first met them. Sometimes she would know a person for years and still couldn't assign them a color.

She turned her attention back to Rose. "Come on. Let's get you to the mirror, and then I think we'd better get going."

Rose paused. "It's okay because it's a special occasion, right?"

"Yes," Twig reassured her. "You aren't straying. A bride is allowed to look in the mirror on her wedding day."

Twig led Rose gently by the hand out of the bedroom and into the living area of their cottage. Adam's voice became louder as they entered the room. The space was not large, but it was bright, and the big stone tiles that made up the floor helped to keep the cottage cool. The south wall had two bay windows that faced the compound and the rainforest that spread out behind it. A dining room table made of blond Cocobolo wood rested against the far wall next to an open kitchen. The rest of the room was sparsely decorated with two handmade wooden armchairs polished to a shine and a white, slipcovered love seat. The only mirror in the cottage was hung high on a wall next to a large, framed photograph of Adam. The glass on the frame and the mirror gleamed. Twig had dusted them herself that morning. She never knew when Adam might send someone to make sure the cottage and photograph were dust-free. It was best to keep the place spotless at all times. An unclean cottage or a dusty photograph meant a verbal lashing in front of the Family.

Twig dragged a chair from the kitchen and helped Rose stand on it in order to see herself. The young bride wore the same white eyelet dress that every woman in the Family wore, but Twig had gotten permission to alter it into a modest strapless gown for the wedding. She'd woven the ribbons usually used for their hair into a wide sash that she now tied around Rose's small waist. Twig sometimes taught knitting and sewing classes to the younger brothers and sisters. When it came to anything clothing- or fabric-related, the Family deferred to Twig.

Rose wobbled in front of the mirror, turning this way and that. Twig was glad she couldn't see her shoes. There was nothing to be done about the shoes. Everyone in the Family wore the same heavy, dark-brown hiking boots. They were comfortable, practical, and ugly.

Twig smiled, watching Rose admire herself in the mirror. Despite her small pangs of envy, she was happy for Rose. She could also see why Adam discouraged vanity—it could get out of control. But it was lovely to see Rose smile like this. Rose's color was definitely pink. Not a cloying pink, but a soft, creamy pink.

"You're a genius, Twig."

2

Adam was late by almost an hour, but no one dared utter a word of complaint. The ceremony would not begin until he arrived.

It was hot. The sun beat down upon them. Twig wrapped a scarf around Rose's freckled shoulders. She didn't want them to get burned. Rose had dangerously fair skin for the climate they lived in. Twig hoped Adam would come soon. Thomas stood on the stage with Doc, waiting patiently, while Twig and the other bridesmaids waited at the foot of the aisle with Rose. The Family sat in white, hard-backed chairs, fanning themselves. Throats were parched, but no one moved to hand out water.

"All rise."

Adam had arrived. The crowd seemed to lift up in one movement.

"Hello!" Adam seemed to glide down the aisle despite the subtle limp that hampered his right leg ever so slightly. Twig felt a tinge of compassion whenever she noticed Father's limp, although he told them to never feel sorry for him. It was something he was born with that had helped him become the person he was.

Adam's arms were outstretched as if offering the whole community a huge hug. He gave the wedding party a backward glance, flashing his famous smile. Twig felt chills run down the back of her neck and arms. Every single one of the girls blushed in spite of themselves. Adam clapped his hands together with a *boom*.

"What a morning! Glorious!" he beamed. Despite being hot and thirsty, everyone smiled and nodded. Adam made them feel alive with just his presence.

"Is everyone ready for prayer?" Adam boomed.

"Yes!" the Family shouted in return.

"Let's do this. I believe we have a wedding here today, right?" Everyone laughed. Adam raised his hands over his congregation. The Family raised their hands up in the air, each wanting to snatch a piece of Adam's grace, his essence.

"No country," he began. The Family took up his words. Eyes shut tight, they recited the words together. "No state." They began to sway. "No self." Their voices rose steadily, the excitement and energy building. "We are a collective, and we live for one promise…"

"And what promise is that?" Adam shouted. His white teeth gleamed. He seemed to glow, power surging from his outstretched fingertips.

"Connection, prosperity, and joy! A life with purpose, a life with meaning!" the Family retorted.

"That's right. My Family. My loves." He looked upon the group tenderly, as if he wanted to scoop each one of them up and embrace them. "I love all of you so much." Twig felt herself take a deep breath.

Doc took his place next to Adam. Adam stepped back, his gaze of affection replaced by a look of modesty as Doc began to speak. "And who can bring you these gifts of connection? Of prosperity and joy? Lead you on the path toward this life—life on another plane? Life rich with meaning?" Doc offered the questions to the crowd. "Who can save you from the pain and sickness of the outside world? Who is the Father you never had but always wanted?" The passion in Doc's voice began to rise. "Who sacrificed everything for you? Who is the Father that will never leave you?"

This last question was especially poignant for Twig. Her own father left when her mother was pregnant. Without Adam, she would not have a father. She was overcome with feelings of gratitude.

"Adam!" The crowd was almost frenzied with excitement, and, as they began to chant, the ground seemed to vibrate with the thunder of their voices. "Praise him! Praise Adam!" The Family, one hundred and eighty-six people, swayed together in a paroxysm of worship.

"Get these people some water!" Adam shouted when they'd finished.

Twig was parched, but she felt elated. It was a familiar mix of excitement and almost-nausea, an electric high that came with a gravity—subtle but obscene. Twig could never reconcile these feelings. It was just how Adam made her, and everyone else, feel.

A handful of brothers and sisters began walking around, filling the water canteens that hung from every person's belt. Twig drank gratefully.

The wedding ceremony was short and presided over by Adam. The Family erupted into applause as Thomas took Rose in his arms and kissed her for the first time. Twig laughed and clapped and then felt that small pang of jealousy again. Watching Rose and Thomas kiss sparked not only her desire to be married, but some elusive longing as well. She could see the passion and excitement between Rose and Thomas, and she wanted that for herself. It scared her, but she wanted to experience those feelings. Twig sighed inwardly. Rose really did get lucky. Marriages were arranged within the Family, and Twig had seen many first kisses fall flat. But this kiss was just how Twig imagined she'd want her first kiss to be, too. Loving. Playful.

Adam nodded his head toward the young couple in approval. His wife, Tina, sat smiling next to him, her long oval face framed with a severe black bob and a fringe of long bangs. Their daughter, Kamela, stood with Twig beside the bride. When the kiss ended, Adam cleared his throat and stood. He patted Thomas heartily on the shoulder and put his hand on the small of Rose's back for just a moment. Adam waved his hands toward the crowd to signal quiet. A hush rolled over the group immediately. He wasn't a large man, but his presence was larger than life. He was magnetic.

"We couldn't be happier for you both," his smooth voice boomed. "You two are adorable. Aren't these two adorable?" The crowd laughed and burst into applause again. Rose beamed, and Thomas turned red with embarrassment. "Let me be clear: we expect some new Family members soon!"

The group roared with laughter. Twig felt her stomach flip-flop. She looked at Rose, who was glowing as she stood in front of the crowd.

Adam clapped his hands together loudly and continued. "Now listen. The last thing I want to do is steal this young couple's thunder, but I have news."

The crowd went silent, waiting for Adam's words.

"I am going to take a new bride."

There was a collective gasp of surprise.

What? Tina and Adam had been married Twig's whole life.

Twig's eyes darted to Tina. Something quick and sharp flashed in her eyes, but her overall demeanor betrayed nothing. Something in her expression made Twig wonder if Tina was learning this for the first time along with the rest of them.

"As you know, Tina has only been able to give me one child," Adam continued. Twig felt Kamela go rigid beside her. She noticed Tina shift slightly.

Adam paused for a beat. "I need a new wife in order to bring us more Family members. I have decided to bestow this precious honor on one of our beloved daughters. An original daughter, born and raised in our Family." Adam paused. "The young lady I have chosen is smart and resourceful, and she's grown into a beautiful young woman. Be sure to wish her a happy seventeenth birthday tomorrow."

Rose gasped. Twig looked at her in confusion until it finally hit her, too.

"She is the partner I need to expand my vision for our Family," Adam continued. "To bring us closer to our peace. She's a natural-born leader. The universe has whispered its choice, and I have listened." He paused thoughtfully. Twig started to feel faint.

"When I get back from my winter pilgrimage, I am going to marry Twig."

3

Twig was suddenly surrounded. People were congratulating her and hugging her from all sides. She was so shocked, she could barely process the news. A wide grin spread across her face as she accepted the congratulations. She was getting married! To Adam! Never in her wildest dreams had she imagined herself married to Adam.

"Come here, Twig." Adam beckoned her through the small throng that enveloped her, which parted to let her go to him.

"Will you accept this honor?" Adam asked her.

Tina stood by his side. Her expression was always hard to read, but it was especially so in this moment. It suddenly occurred to Twig that Tina might be jealous. Perhaps she really *was* just finding out about this news along with Twig and the rest of the Family.

Twig's heart sank at the thought. Tina might be alone now, like Twig's own mother and Rose's mother, Evelyn. Tina was not old, but she was past childbearing years. How Tina must hate her. And Kamela... Kamela and Twig had never gotten along. They were the same age, and soon Twig would be marrying her father and living with them.

"Don't you worry about a thing." Adam tilted Twig's chin up to his face, leaning in to whisper in her ear. He felt warm, and his breath smelled like mint and apples. Being next to him was like being caught in a sudden storm—beauty, surprise, and the possibility of destruction. In a conspiratorial tone, he whispered, "I'll handle the girls." He lifted his head and flashed his brilliant smile at her. Twig felt her insides melt.

Adam always knew what people were thinking, and he always knew just what to say.

Twig stood on the stage with the setting sun reflecting in her hair, making it shine like gold. It fell in thick, butterscotch waves down her back. She couldn't help but smile beneath Adam's gaze of adoration. He pinned her with his large, black eyes. With his tanned skin and shock of black hair, his looks were arresting.

"You haven't answered," Tina said suddenly, breaking the spell. Tina stood just behind Adam. She matched him in height, somewhere around five foot ten inches tall.

"What?" Twig asked, flustered.

"You haven't given your answer," Tina said flatly.

Twig looked to Adam. No one ever said no to Adam. Of course her answer was yes.

"I'm honored, Adam. Thank you. It is a true blessing."

Her voice did not betray the nervousness she actually felt. It came out quiet and clear as a bell, a silver thread in the dusk that had begun descending around them.

"I knew you'd be pleased, Twig. Happy birthday."

4

Twig pulled her shawl closer to her body. The night was hot and sultry, but she had a strange chill that she couldn't shake. She wanted desperately to find her mother, but she hadn't seen her anywhere. Able to recede into the background during the revelry, Twig had taken a chair from the midst of the party and was sitting on the edge of the clearing, staring out into the forest. Parties were rare events saved for weddings or Adam's birthday. Usually Twig's days were packed from the moment she got up until the moment she went to bed. Exhaustion had hit her, and it felt good to just sit and look out into the darkness. Every tree in sight had been hung with lanterns, and candlelight danced all around her. Adam's voiced buzzed through the outdoor speakers. It was camouflaged by music from the party, but there all the same.

"Everyone is accepted here. In America, people are hated and terrorized because of the color of their skin, because they don't have the right clothes or drive the right kind of automobile. Here, everyone is loved equally, unconditionally…"

"Hey."

Twig jumped at the sound of someone's voice behind her.

Ryan. She felt so relieved to see him that tears sprung to her eyes. She hadn't known she'd been holding in so many feelings.

"Mind if I join you?" he asked.

Twig smiled and wiped away the sudden tears. She extended her hand, and Ryan dropped a chair down beside hers. She fingered the garland of orchids they had placed upon her neck at dinner. Ryan's normally unruly chestnut-brown hair was combed into submission for the wedding. He was on the shorter side for a guy, somewhere near Twig's height. He was sinewy—skinny like Twig but all muscle. Twig thought his angular face looked especially handsome now, softened by the candlelight.

"Congratulations, Twiglet," Ryan said quietly.

"Thank you, Ry. I'm sorry… I just feel so tired all of a sudden."

"You don't have to apologize. I noticed you didn't eat at dinner." Twig felt herself freeze just a little. She should have eaten. People were always watching, and something like that could be taken the wrong way. They were trained to watch each other, help one another to follow the correct path, to not stray…

Twig thought back to dinner. People would probably think she was just too excited to eat, which was true. Maybe no one even noticed. Either way, she knew Ryan would never report her.

"Do you want to talk?" Ryan asked. "Or just have a little company?" They both looked behind them toward the party to make sure no one else was listening. It was habit.

"I was just sitting here, thinking," Twig said quietly. "Something is bothering me, but I feel guilty about it. I don't even really want to say it out loud. You know that feeling?" The Family members were required to confess all of their doubts or sinful thoughts, and it was sometimes a challenge.

"You don't have to—not now at least. This all just happened. Maybe give yourself some time."

"You have a dad," Twig blurted out suddenly. "Sophie has a dad. Adam is the only father I have. I'm losing the only father I have ever known. This is the greatest honor I could hope for, but it is confusing. On one hand, I feel so happy. On the other hand, I just feel a little sad. And I feel bad for feeling anything but joy."

"I understand."

"You don't think I am bad for feeling this way?"

Ryan laughed softly. "No, not at all."

Ryan and Twig had managed to get away for these talks for as long as she could remember. She wasn't even quite sure how they did it. They had some strange thing between them, always knowing when there would be an opening, where the other one was, and how long they'd be there. She felt like she would die without their talks. And there was no one else she could talk to like this. No one. If she ever made a mistake and spoke to the wrong person as openly as she talked to Ryan, she would end up paying for it dearly. All of the things she loved—yoga, school, gardening—would be replaced with months of hard labor. Digging holes just to refill them. Painting buildings just to have Adam walk by and order that it be done all over again, even if it meant not sleeping for days in a row. She'd seen it happen to enough brothers and sisters. But she and Ryan had held each other's secrets for a long time now. Their friendship had formed as children, long before they knew concepts like paranoia and betrayal.

"We'll talk later, Twiggy. I just want you to know that *I* know this might be hard for you, and I am here for you."

"Hard for me in particular? Because I don't have a father?" Twig asked, suddenly feeling slightly defensive.

"Maybe, but I meant for other reasons, too. You're a little different. I'm a little different. We always have been, and you know it. Our little Sophie... She's not so different."

Sophie was Twig and Ryan's other best friend. Twig knew what Ryan meant. There wasn't the same push and pull within Sophie that she and Ryan experienced together. Sophie's parents, Farriss and Yasmine, were Elders—founding members of the Family alongside Adam. Besides Adam, Elders garnered the most respect in the Family. There were a handful of them, including Doc and a few others. While Twig loved them, she was also scared of them. They were so protective of Adam that sometimes Twig thought they found fault where perhaps there wasn't any. People got nervous when the Elders were around, fumbling with their words and maybe even saying things they didn't mean to say.

Every Family member had "lore"—a story Adam would tell that explained how that brother or sister had come to the Family. Sophie's parents had met Adam while he was traveling in Morocco, before he started the Family. They'd helped Adam find a location in Costa Rica for the compound. They'd helped Adam realize his dream.

Unlike Twig, Ryan had both his mother and father, but they were like oil and water—always fighting. Adam had arranged for them to remarry other Family members, but they all lived in the same quarters. As much as they worked on their issues at Meetings, their relationship was a tangle of tension and unhappiness.

Twig just had her mother, Avery. She never had a father, and Adam never arranged a marriage for Avery.

Ryan's voice pulled Twig back from her thoughts.

"I don't mean to be a downer. It's an honor, Twig. And let's face it: he's not ugly."

They both laughed quietly, but their laughter had a weight to it. Ryan liked boys. No specific boy in the Family, but he knew he was homosexual. Adam said it was natural for some boys to love other boys, but that Ryan could not live that way. Family members needed to live in husband-and-wife pairings so they could make babies and continue growing the collective.

"I wonder who I'll be paired with," Ryan said thoughtfully. Then he shook his head as if to clear it. "Come on, let's see if there's some cake or cornbread or something left. You need to eat. Tomorrow could be a fasting day. You never know."

"What about Kamela?" she asked warily. "She might try to poison me or something. As if she didn't hate me enough already…"

Ryan smiled, extending his hand to her. "I'll be your royal taster. Come on."

5

Eventually the party began to die down. Twig wasn't on cleanup duty, so she was free to leave. She was looking forward to falling into her bed—looking forward to sleep. But as she began to wander back to her cottage, she noticed a commotion. She turned toward the noise to see a woman being escorted through the edges of the crowd. She was dressed in civilian clothes.

A new Family member. Twig knew immediately that she was supposed to avert her eyes so she wouldn't be infected, but she couldn't help looking. Twig was used to seeing newcomers only after they had been through purification rites. This woman looked different, dazed and disheveled. Her face was drawn, and her eyes were dark and smudged with what must be makeup.

"Do not look," Twig could hear Doc saying. "You will catch the poison she's brought from the outside. She is riddled with it; it crawls all over her."

People were starting to gather around despite Doc's warnings. They began to spit at the woman, trying to ward off infection. The woman tried to look over her shoulder, but her head just lolled back. She leaned heavily into Doc. Twig wondered what was wrong with her.

"That's enough!" Doc shouted. "Move out of the way!" Doc and the woman drew closer to where Twig was standing. Twig wanted to move, but she couldn't seem to make her feet move forward. She was fascinated. Before she knew it, they were standing right in front of her.

"Twig," Doc snapped.

"I'm so sorry," Twig stammered and turned away sharply. She avoided looking, but everything about the woman assaulted Twig's other senses. Her perfume, which might have smelled nice at some point—oranges and vanilla, maybe—was now stale and mixed with the scent of sweat and something sharp and metallic.

"Twig, I need your help. Follow me," Doc said urgently.

"I don't—" Twig hesitated. She didn't want to become infected.

"Now! Come with me," Doc barked. "Move!"

Doc put the woman's arm around Twig's neck. "Hold her." Up close, the woman's stench was so strong that Twig nearly gagged. She didn't want to be unkind, but her first instinct was to drop her.

"Doc," Twig pleaded. "I don't mean to be disobedient," Twig rushed to get the words out, "but I don't want to become corrupted—"

"What?" Doc looked at Twig with irritation. Perhaps he hadn't heard her.

"Become like her. I-I'll be infected, I—"

"Adam will perform purification rites on you. You will be fine," Doc said hastily. "Now please just hold her." Twig felt anxious and nauseated. Doc knew what he was talking about. He did this all the time, and he was okay. She would just have to trust him.

"Leave! Go back to your cabins!" Doc shouted at the crowd, waving his free arm up and down as if he were fanning a fire. The brothers and sisters started to back off.

Twig thought of Rose and Thomas and hoped they had already gone to sleep. She hoped they didn't see this. It seemed like a bad omen on their wedding night. Twig struggled to keep the woman upright. She was wearing shoes with high heels and was quite a bit taller than Twig.

"Come on." Doc and Twig began to carry the woman together toward Doc's cabin. Soon it was just the three of them.

"I'm going to be sick," the woman said.

Twig held her up as she vomited onto the ground. Twig had to fight to keep from throwing up herself. When the woman was finished, Doc opened his cottage, and they managed to get her inside. They laid her on Doc's cold, metal examination table.

"I'll be back in a minute. I need to get a few things," Doc said gruffly. Twig looked after him helplessly. She wasn't even supposed to look at the uninitiated, and now Doc was leaving Twig alone with her? Twig felt sick and twisted up inside.

With shaking hands, Twig got a pillow and laid it beneath the woman's head. She wet a cloth and wiped the woman's mouth, then pulled her hair, which had traces of vomit in it, away from her face. The woman's eyes were closed. Twig began to feel sorry for her; she seemed so helpless.

"It's okay," Twig found herself saying quietly. "It's going to be okay."

Doc came back and threw a dress, a bra, and a pair of underwear at Twig. "Wash her and change her into our clothing."

"But, Doc, I—" Twig felt completely overwhelmed and alone. "How long do I have before Adam needs to perform purification rites, Doc? I'm scared," Twig admitted.

"He'll be here soon. Now please, Twig, just get her cleaned up. Normally Tina would do this, but I can't find her."

Tina. The engagement. Twig's stomach twisted further. She worried she wouldn't be able to keep herself from vomiting. Doc left the room again, shutting the door behind him. Twig wished he had left it open.

She looked around for supplies. Maybe if she hurried, she could get out of there and find Adam. She wondered how much time she had before the infection would set in and harm her. Doc didn't seem concerned, but he also seemed so distracted and agitated. Twig didn't think he was really paying attention.

The room had a sink, and Twig found towels, soap, and cotton balls.

She located a small tub of shea butter and wiped some under her nostrils to help with the smell and staunch her own nausea.

The woman seemed to be sleeping as Twig removed her shoes. Her feet were swollen and red, blistered. Twig felt bad for her, but she also couldn't help feeling disgust. Regardless, she was going to be Adam's wife, and she would have to begin acting like it. This is one thing she could do: help this woman get on their path, right here and now.

She began to wash the woman's feet with warm water and soap, rubbing them to get the circulation going. Finally, she wrapped them in towels. "You'll know peace soon. It's going to be all right," she whispered.

She worked quickly and tried not to think, desperate to keep her mind off the revolting task in front of her. Still, she continued to gag while she washed the woman's face and sponged the vomit out of her hair. Twig couldn't help noticing that the woman had a pretty face as she used cotton balls to wipe the makeup from her wide-set eyes. Twig wondered if she was Asian and where she had come from. Adam brought people from all over the world to their Family.

Twig had to prop the woman up against her own shoulder to remove her dress and then covered her with towels as she cleaned the rest of her body. She kept glancing at the door, hoping Adam would come soon. Twig squeezed her eyes shut and gritted her teeth when she removed the woman's underwear, exotic and purple, and flung them into Doc's metal trashcan. When she bared the woman's breasts, Twig felt embarrassed for both of them.

Finally, she was finished. The woman was dressed like one of them now—all in white. Soon she would be one of them.

Twig began to scrub her hands with the hottest water she could stand.

The woman opened her eyes. She looked at Twig and began to shake. "Where am I?" she asked, quietly at first. "Where is Adam? Who are you?" Her voice became shrill and desperate. Twig didn't know what to do.

"Don't hurt me," the woman said. "Adam will explain who I am—"

And then he was there—Adam—standing in the doorway. He wasn't looking at the woman, who was quickly becoming hysterical, but at Twig. He rushed to her and kneeled in front of her. "Are you okay?" he whispered.

"I don't know," Twig said quietly. "Please, Father." Twig began to cry quietly. "Please, I don't mean to be disrespectful, but please, I don't want to be infected."

Adam laughed lightly in response. "You dear girl. Wait for me outside. I will perform purification rites on you. You will be just fine. I am so proud of you." Twig felt herself blush with pride.

"Adam?" The woman was looking down at him with a strange mixture of relief and confusion. "Adam, honey?" she slurred.

"Be quiet," Adam said to her sternly, ushering Twig out the door.

"But, Adam, I don't understand."

"Twig, please wait for me right outside."

"Adam, please," the woman pleaded.

"Be quiet," Adam repeated coldly, still looking at Twig.

"I would never let anything happen to you," he said soothingly. "Don't you know that?" Twig nodded.

"I want you to leave now, but wait for me outside. I will come perform purification rites when I am finished here. Don't talk to anyone but Doc. Stay with him."

Twig nodded again and then ran toward the door. As she moved to close it behind her, she could hear Adam speaking to the woman.

"It's okay, sweetheart," Twig heard him say in a new tone. A tone of affection. "Everything is going to be okay, darling."

Twig stopped for a moment to listen, feeling sick to her stomach again. Why was he talking to her like that? He spoke to her as if he adored her. Twig felt a small claw of jealousy brush up her spine, but she forced it aside. Of course Adam would be kind to this woman. He was saving her from a life of darkness and ignorance.

"Close the door, Twig." It was Doc. He was sitting there in the dark. Twig didn't say anything in response. She shut the door and walked past him to the front door of the cottage. She opened it and let the night's warm air wash over her.

They stayed like that for a long time—Doc sitting in the dark and Twig standing in the doorway trying to rid her lungs of whatever poison she'd breathed in while cleaning the woman.

"What's her name?" she finally said out loud, not turning around.

"Anna." It was Adam. Twig hadn't heard him come out. "Her name is Anna. You will get to know her tomorrow. I will introduce her to our Family. She is ready now."

"What was wrong with her?" Twig asked, turning to face him. She had so much to learn now that she would be Adam's wife.

"She is a very troubled young woman, Twig. But that is in the past. Her new life starts tomorrow. Come on. We need to gather some witnesses, and then I can begin the ceremony."

For a panicked moment, Twig thought Adam meant their wedding ceremony, but of course she quickly realized he meant her purification ceremony. She was so tired. Why else would the idea of marrying Adam make her panic?

6

For the second time that day, Twig stood on the stage. About forty brothers and sisters surrounded her, all in a circle. The mood was serious; infection could be fatal. If one member was infected, it could spread. The disease of the outside world started in the mind and then worked on the body. Despite their fear, witnesses had been easy to gather. The Family's curiosity about their new member seemed to override their fear of infection.

"Please kneel." Adam touched Twig's shoulder, and she fell softly to her knees. There was still no sign of her mother. Twig figured she must be in bed by now, though she wished she were there with her. She thought about asking Adam if she could go get her, but then decided against it. The more Twig kept Avery away from Adam, the better. But she felt so alone. Neither Ryan nor Sophie was among the group that had gathered.

Adam grasped both of Twig's shoulders firmly. "I am going to lay hands on you now, Twig," Adam's voice fired into the night. The witnesses watched in awe. He laid his palms around her head and began to hum. It was quiet at first and then increased in volume. He pressed harder into her head as his voice grew louder. "Flow into my hands, poison. Like a serpent's venom, I draw you out of this innocent. Come out of this pure young girl. Come play with someone your own size. COME OUT!"

Twig felt lightheaded. Family members were humming and swaying.

"It burns," Adam said, holding his hands in front of him. "Doc, get me water. It burns! How this poison from the outside world burns my hands!"

Twig looked up at Adam with concern. He was holding his hands out for everyone to see. She wondered if he had gotten all the poison out of her. Doc ran to Adam with a bucket of water, and Adam plunged his hands into it. Twig thought she saw smoke rise out of the water and imagined she heard sizzling sounds. She wondered if she would be okay now.

Without a word, Adam walked off the stage. Twig, still on her knees, looked up at Doc.

"Come on, Twig," he said to her. He offered her his hand. "It tires him when he does a healing." Twig nodded and took Doc's hand. She was overcome with tender feelings for Adam. How much he did for them. He was always helping someone, always giving his time, his wisdom. There were rumors that he never slept.

"Am I okay now?" she whispered to Doc. She noticed everyone was staring at her.

"Good as new." He turned to the rest of the group. "Now get to bed, everyone. I want to see every one of you on time for breakfast tomorrow. Go."

Twig had questions. Had she been infected? Had something from the outside world been inside her? Was she safe now? Doc had said "good as new," but the crowd of people still stared at her as she headed to her cottage. No one made a move to accompany her or help her. She felt ashamed, tainted. She had seen this happen before to other members of the Family, but she had never been on the receiving end. But Doc had said she was as good as new. *Good as new.*

Twig ran after Doc, grabbing at his arm.

"Yes, Twig, what is it? You should get some sleep."

"Yes, yes, of course—I just… What was it, exactly?"

"What was what?"

"I'm sorry," Twig stammered. "I just don't understand. Was I poisoned? Like a snakebite? Like venom poisoning my body?"

"Worse," Doc said, staring down at Twig. "Like venom entering your spirit. Much more insidious. It enters by way of your spirit and eats away at your soul."

Twig felt confused. She didn't understand, but she could tell by Doc's tone that the conversation was over.

She repeated the words to herself as she made her way back to her cottage and into bed. *Good as new. Good as new.*

7

Twig slept deeply. When she woke, a cloudy, pink dawn was beginning to peek through the night's curtain of ink. If she wanted to paint before breakfast call, she'd have to get up now. She thought about turning over and getting just a little more sleep, but it was her birthday, and she had a special painting planned for today.

She put on her dress and wrapped a thin, knitted sweater around her lean body without waking her mother or Rose's mother, Evelyn. Rose would stay with Thomas's family now. Evelyn was not Twig's favorite person, nor Avery's. She was tough, and Twig was not looking forward to life in the cottage without Rose to soften things.

Twig looked down at Avery sleeping peacefully, just as she had been when Twig returned the night before. As much as she wanted to wake her and tell her everything that had happened, Twig let her sleep. Peace and sleep were two things that often eluded Avery.

Twig piled her hair on top of her head and pinned it up. The cottage was completely silent save for the soft murmurs of sleep and the odd creak as Twig moved about. She stopped in the kitchen to grab a roll from a basket on the counter and drink a glass of water from the sink. As an afterthought, she removed the rolls from the basket and slipped it over her arm, then tiptoed out the door and shut it without making a sound. She was practiced at this. A feeling of guilt pulled at her stomach. She pushed it aside, but it remained in the background like Adam's voice over the intercom.

"Always remember that you are nothing without your Family. At times we tend to think that we alone know something important, that we've figured some things out. That maybe we're just a little better than our sister or our brother…a little smarter. These sorts of thoughts begin to separate you. They are the first warning that you are headed for trouble. These thoughts are lies. Trust me, you are nothing without your Family. Repeat this to yourself like a mantra. Say it in the shower, as you fall asleep at night. Teach it to our children. 'I am nothing without my Family.'"

It was going to be a beautiful day. The sky rested in shades of purple and gray above the mountain range behind the rainforest. On a clear day, steam could be seen erupting from the Irazú Volcano, the highest volcano in Costa Rica. Twig had always longed to visit the volcano, but leaving the compound was forbidden. Thomas made trips into Turrialba for supplies, and Family members were allowed to explore the rainforest in groups or even pairs of two if they received special permission, but those were the only exceptions. Men stood guard twenty-four hours a day at the entrance, where a small road dead-ended into the compound. Adam said the guards were only meant to keep people out, and his teachings kept people in. Twig could not remember anyone leaving the Family, ever.

Adam's teachings, his love, his care, and his rules *did* keep the Family in. For the most part, Twig enjoyed her life. Her days were spent learning or creating, strengthening her physical body or intellect. Together, the Family had built and maintained a vegetable garden that brimmed with abundance, and they were able to harvest almost all of what they ate. They had a small pineapple plantation. Adam sold the pineapples in the cities to pay for things they needed. Twig believed in the Family's mission toward peace. She believed the way they lived could serve as a model to change the world.

The world. Twig knew what lay outside of the compound. Adam regaled them with stories. Rape, murder, vicious poverty, war, and disease.

Evil, sadness, pain, and nothing else. Twig thought about the woman from last night, Anna. The state she'd been in when she had arrived. What happened out there to make someone like that? Would Twig have become like that if Adam hadn't healed her?

And yet, still, she couldn't help wondering. How could the Family really change the world if they never left the compound? Adam left a few times a year to spread the word, but he was only one man. Couldn't they do more? Adam could protect them from infection. Couldn't they go out in groups? Be living examples of the power of the collective?

Twig looked up at the sky. Soft streaks of pink and orange hinted at the sun's impending rise. They'd had a reprieve from the rains the last few days, but the heaviest were still to come. Twig continued to pad her way toward the rainforest, leaving the clearing the Family had created many years ago to build their homes. She breathed a little easier as she entered the protection of the rainforest. Palm trees soon towered above her, their *pejivalle* fruit hanging in thick, orange clusters. Large lemon-yellow butterflies landed on her hands and shoulders.

She was quickly enveloped by the lushness of the forest. Geckos darted across her path. The leaves beneath her feet became a soft sea of green, wet and vibrant. She carefully placed the most colorful leaves in her basket as she went, occasionally glancing behind her—more out of habit than actual fear that anyone had followed her. Members of the Family did not give up their sleep. They didn't get much of it, so they would usually stay in bed until the minute before breakfast call.

The sun was just beginning to fold into the valley when Twig arrived at a small glen hidden by interlacing branches. There was a wide stream where water bubbled over white rocks. She loved the sounds of the rainforest; the first impression of silence giving way to the gentle gurgle of water, the scurry of life in the surrounding green… Twig sat down on a big, flat rock and took in a deep breath.

"Happy birthday to me."

Only Adam's birthday was truly celebrated. People might wish her a happy birthday throughout the day, but that would be all.

She began to take the leaves from the basket, smoothing them and sorting them by depth of color. She had been trained her whole life to use action as a weapon against unwanted thought. Adam had taught them what he called the Thought Test. *Examine every single thing that comes into your head. Does it drive the Family forward? Will it help the Family? Anything else is individualism.*

Individualism: the very evil that infected the world outside the Family.

If any Family member's thoughts were impure, they were supposed to banish them or confess them. But how could Twig not have confusing thoughts today? The memory of the day before had the strange force of a dream. She'd been so excited to hear that she would be marrying Adam, but then doubts had crept in. How could she marry the man she'd always looked to as a father? Twig always had trouble expressing herself in Meetings, always struggled with thoughts she wanted to keep to herself. She liked to escape to the rainforest to be alone—these things were forbidden in the Family. As Adam's wife, she would need to be the perfect Family member; mother of the collective. She wouldn't be able to keep anything to herself or escape from scrutiny.

Then there was the woman last night and the purification ceremony. What if she was infected and Adam hadn't gotten all of the virus out? What if people treated Twig like she was sick and wouldn't come near her? Twig wanted to scream. She knew she wasn't supposed to think about this stuff on her own, but she couldn't talk to anyone about it. She felt like she might explode. How was she supposed to deal with all of it?

She would make a painting. She would chase the thoughts away with action. Distract herself.

When the leaves were finally sorted to her satisfaction, Twig pinned her dress up around her thighs and waded out to the middle of the stream.

She carefully laid the leaves down in a thin ribbon of color where the stream stood still. Deep greens gently became sage and then burst into hot yellow-greens. Purple leaves the color of figs with waxy, red veins cooled into muddy browns and finally greens so dark they almost seemed black. A perfect painting made from nature. The current started to seduce the leaves away from Twig. Her thoughts continued to beckon for attention with a similarly unavoidable pull.

Twig wished she had a camera. They were strictly forbidden on the compound. She only knew about them from her classes and the slides they studied. Usually, letting nature take the leaves away was part of the process, but today she wanted something to mark the moment. Everything was about to change. She would be Adam's wife. Last night with the woman was just a preview of what life might now be like for her. She made her hands into a frame and cocked her head to the side. *Click.*

The leaves dipped and bobbed away from her.

Did her marriage mean the end of her private self for good?

She sensed movement behind her before she heard it. Footsteps. Her heart caught in her chest. Being out in the forest like this on her own was strictly forbidden. She'd been doing it for the last year, but she'd never been caught. She couldn't run or hide—she was knee-deep in water.

Sophie came through the trees holding a thermos and a picnic basket. "Happy birthday, Twiglet," she whispered nervously. Twig let out a deep breath. This was very unusual; Sophie never broke the rules.

"You scared me! What are you doing here? Did you follow me?" Twig's heart was racing. In the Family, even children told on their parents. It would not be surprising for one friend to betray another. They were supposed to betray one another to prove their loyalty to Adam. "Is that coffee?" Twig added, trying to sound friendlier.

"Yes and yes." Sophie smiled anxiously. "Now that I'm here, get out of that water and come break bread with me." She spread out a small blanket and unpacked a meal of warm croissants, cheese, and oranges. "You really should not come out here alone. What if you get caught?"

The girls bent their heads over the food and said, "Praise Adam."

"You're right," Twig said. Sipping her coffee after a bite of flaky croissant, Twig looked up at Sophie. Sophie's eyes were full of light, a warm brown with specks of gold and copper. Her skin was the deep brown of honey. She had a sweet round face and a head of curly, dark-brown hair. She looked like a doll.

"Don't forget to make it look like you haven't had breakfast yet at call." Sophie looked around nervously. Her hands were shaking.

"I won't. Promise. I'll eat another whole breakfast." Twig cut a piece of cheese and smiled at Sophie.

Sophie was suddenly silent. Twig watched as she tossed an orange up and down, seemingly deep in thought.

"Hey, congratulations," Sophie finally said, quietly.

"Thanks," Twig replied modestly.

"How do you feel?"

"I'm kind of in shock, to be honest."

"But you're okay?"

"I guess so," Twig said. She didn't want to lie to Sophie, but she couldn't talk to her the way she talked to Ryan. She had to keep it simple.

"Can I ask you something, Twig?" Sophie suddenly whispered.

"Sure," Twig answered. "Anything."

"Well, I know things will be different now, but before last night, did you ever think of…well, of leaving?"

Twig froze. "What?" she asked in surprise. She tilted her head toward Sophie, waiting for some kind of explanation. This was not something Family members talked about. Sophie had never said anything like this before. She didn't sneak out to the rainforest alone and paint with nature either, but talking of leaving? It wasn't even a consideration. It was one of the worst crimes Family members could commit against Adam.

"Well, I mean, did you ever think that maybe this isn't the life for you? Did you ever want to live the life we hear about in people's lores?"

"Where is this coming from, Sophie? Are you unhappy? Can I help you?"

"Me?" Sophie put her hand to her chest in surprise. "No! I'm not unhappy, I was just wondering."

Twig was suspicious. This kind of talk was absolutely forbidden. Had Adam and Doc sent Sophie this morning to test Twig? To see if she had been infected after all? Sophie wouldn't have a choice. She'd have to do it and report back.

"Sophie, really, why are you asking me this?" Twig tried again.

Sophie just shrugged her shoulders. "Forget it. Forget I asked."

"Okay," Twig said. She was happy to let it drop. Maybe she was being too paranoid. Maybe Sophie was just making conversation. Sophie never got a chance to talk like this.

"But you never answered me, Twig," Sophie pressed. She obviously wasn't going to let it drop.

"No. No, I've never thought of leaving, Sophie."

She hadn't. Twig certainly wasn't perfect, but she had never thought of leaving. Besides, it really was the only answer she could give. Even to her best friend.

The air between them was heavy. Twig felt bad, but it felt very unnatural to have Sophie there. She wanted to wrap up their breakfast and get back.

"Maybe you should be more careful now. Now that you will be Adam's wife," Sophie said suddenly.

"You're right," Twig said thoughtfully. She wasn't sure why Sophie had come this morning, but she could tell Sophie's warning was genuine.

Twig felt depressed. Sophie was right. Once she was married to Adam, moments like these simply wouldn't be possible. She would no longer be able to sneak out here and paint. And painting was like oxygen to Twig.

As they walked home, Twig unpinned her dress and let her hair spill over her shoulders and down her back. Neither one of them said a word.

"Do you want to go straight to breakfast?" Sophie finally asked, breaking the silence between them.

"I want to make sure my mom is up," Twig said.

Sophie nodded in understanding. She smiled warmly at Twig.

For the moment, Twig had to push everything else aside. Her only priority right now was to get her mother to breakfast call on time.

Unfortunately, when Twig went back to her cabin, Avery wasn't there. Twig sighed. Avery had struggled to be a part of the Family for as long as Twig could remember. Throughout Twig's childhood, Avery had been constantly humiliated and assigned impossible tasks that required hard labor.

It's her own fault.

That's what Adam would say, time and time again.

Until she learns to control herself—control her moods—this is what life will be like for her. It doesn't have to be this way. She is a selfish, petulant woman who needs to be reined in. Her commitment is to her sadness, to herself, when it should be to the collective.

Mostly, Avery was just quiet and wanted to be left alone, but she did have mood swings—swings from deep sadness to anger. Her sadness made her withdrawn and listless. It made it difficult for her to fulfill her responsibilities to the group, difficult to bathe and eat and sleep. Her anger made her defiant and nearly always got her into trouble with Adam. Twig had a habit out of trying to chase the pendulum of her mother's moods—anticipate which way it would swing next.

"What's going on?" Twig whispered as she took a seat between Sophie and Ryan at breakfast.

"New girl," Sophie said, lifting her chin toward the center of the circle where Yasmine, Sophie's mom, was approaching. "Meeting before breakfast." She leaned in toward Twig conspiratorially. "My mom told me she's from America."

"I helped bring her in last night," Twig whispered. She felt important sharing this information with Ryan and Sophie.

"What? Really?" Sophie said, raising her eyebrows in surprise. "How did that happen?"

"Quiet, everyone," Yasmine addressed the group.

"More later..." Ryan said, nodding his head toward Yasmine, who was starting the Meeting.

"It's time to begin." Yasmine had to clap her hands together several times. It was a very large group, and no one could wrangle them like Adam could. People stamped their chairs on the floor to signal quiet.

"Let's give our newest member, Anna, a big, warm round of applause." The room thundered with applause. "Anna, welcome!" Yasmine flashed a warm smile toward Anna, who smiled shyly in response. She looked so different from the night before. Without the clothes and makeup, standing awake and alert, Twig was surprised to see how young she really was—maybe only a few years older than Twig. She looked uncomfortable but much more put together than she had the night before. Several people walked up to her and gave her an embrace, which she accepted stiffly. Twig, Ryan, and Sophie stayed in their seats, watching.

"Please tell us who you are. Tell us your story," Yasmine prompted.

"I'm not sure what to say. I'm sorry," Anna said.

"First of all, you never have to be sorry again. That's the beauty of being here, of being one of us."

Anna covered her face with her hands. "I'm embarrassed," she admitted. "I'm not very good at speaking in front of a crowd."

"Please, dear. Don't think of us as a crowd. Think of us as your Family. Why don't you start by telling us about your upbringing?"

"Okay," Anna agreed with a small nod. "I was raised in a very strict Korean family," she began. The group nodded encouragingly as she spoke. "There was a sort of prescribed path for me from early on: school, good grades, medical school, become a doctor, and get married."

"That must have been really difficult. Such intense pressures were put on you as a child. It also sounds to me like no one listened to what *Anna* wanted," Yasmine said thoughtfully.

Anna laughed and shook her head. "No. What I wanted didn't really come into play. I mean, my parents loved—love me, they—"

"They love you with conditions," Yasmine corrected her sympathetically. "They love you if you twist yourself to become who they want you to be."

"Yes, I guess you could say that. Adam keeps telling me that." Anna looked thoughtful for a moment as she turned the idea over in her head.

"May I say something?" Farriss, Sophie's father, rose from his chair in the circle to speak.

"Of course, darling." Yasmine smiled at him.

Farriss looked at Anna with warmth in his eyes. "You are so brave, Anna. You are so brave, and I can sense the power of your spirit." He looked around. "Can everyone feel it? Wow!" People nodded their heads and laughed. Anna smiled shyly in response.

"You are very special, Anna. Do you know that?" Yasmine had taken Anna's hand. "You are unique. Powerful. It is palpable." Anna looked at the floor. Yasmine continued. "Look at me, child. I know you haven't been told this enough in your life, but you are so special, Anna. And you have been chosen to become part of something bigger. Chosen to become the person you were meant to be in this life. And you heeded the call. Special and brave! Those are the words I would use to describe you!"

"I'm sensing that there's something on her mind. She looks doubtful," Evelyn said in her brusque way.

"Is that true, Anna?" Yasmine asked. "You can say absolutely anything to us. We are your Family now." Yasmine squeezed Anna's hand again and bent her head to look into Anna's eyes. "Anything."

"Well, it's just that… I don't think my parents were all bad. I think they really love me and care about me," Anna said tentatively.

"No, sweet one, they don't." Farriss frowned as he imparted this truth to her. Twig felt bad for Anna. That must be hard to hear. "They love you with conditions. That's a perverted kind of love, but it's all you have ever known."

"Until now," Sophie chimed in. She was just like her parents. Twig smiled. Now Anna would know true, unconditional love.

"Yes, until now," Yasmine agreed. "It will be an adjustment, life without them. But you'll come to see how necessary it is to escape their influence. They will just try to draw you back into that life. It's all they know. They are ignorant. It's not their fault. It's just how they were raised."

Suddenly the doors to the dining hall slammed open. Adam walked in. He was obviously angry and was dragging Avery by the hand behind him.

Oh no. Twig felt her entire body go rigid with fear. *Mom, what have you done now?*

Avery looked furious as well. Her gray eyes seared into Adam. He looked back at her with such venom, Twig was afraid he might strike her.

"Anna, Yasmine, out of the circle. You," Adam nodded to Avery, "in." He gave her a slight shove as she passed him and sat in the one of the chairs Yasmine and Anna had just vacated. He turned back to Anna. "Anna, I am deeply sorry to have your time interrupted. We will continue this later. You have my word." Anna nodded, but she looked a little lost. Yasmine took her gently by the hand and led her out of the circle.

"Now," Adam boomed. Twig held her breath. Ryan moved his thigh closer to hers in a gesture of silent support. Adam lowered his voice and spoke coolly. "Avery, I would like you to tell your brothers and sisters what I had to wake up to this morning."

Avery glared at him.

"So help me, Avery—" Adam growled.

Twig wanted to get up and sit next to her mother. *Be agreeable, Mom. Don't make it worse.* Twig silently willed her mother to calm down and obey.

Avery looked at Twig for a moment and caught her eyes. Twig wanted to convey her love to her mother, but she didn't want to be disobedient. She tried to keep her expression neutral.

Avery turned to Adam. "I went to your cottage this morning to ask you to reconsider marrying my daughter."

9

Twig's eyes widened with surprise. She nearly let out a laugh of awkwardness and disbelief. Why would her mother do that?

"You do not question my judgment. Not you and not anyone in this room." Adam looked around in warning. Everyone was dead quiet. "Damian, go get my case."

Damian, a Family member in his early twenties, hopped up and left the dining hall. Adam looked around for a chair, and someone brought him one. He took it and placed it so that he sat nearly knee-to-knee with Avery.

Damian burst back through the door, breathless. He handed Adam a small black case, which Adam laid on his lap. Twig noticed Adam rub his bad leg. Everyone looked on. It seemed as if the whole room was holding its breath.

Adam snapped the case open and removed a large, gleaming pair of scissors. Twig gasped.

Adam looked at Avery. He studied her, then turned and picked Twig out of the crowd. He pointed the scissors at her. "Cut it all off. Every strand. And as your mother's hair falls to the ground around her, so may her poisonous ideas, as well as her insolence and her attitude and, most importantly, her misguided notion that *she* knows what's best for you."

Twig stood and slowly approached. Avery had gorgeous hair—blond and thick and impossibly long. For as long as Twig could remember, Avery had asked Twig to braid it or put flowers in it, to twist it up, create some pretty style, brush it before they went to bed. Trivial as it might seem, this ritual between them meant everything to Twig.

"Twig." Avery didn't miss a beat. "It's okay, Twig." Avery grabbed onto Twig's hand, and Twig could feel her trembling. She wanted to scream. She had no choice. It never got easier watching her mother get punished, and now it would be by her own hand.

Physical punishment purifies the soul. Used sparingly and responsibly, physical consequence bleaches out old patterns of behavior.

Twig knew this, but she had never had to administer any sort of punishment to anyone, let alone to her own mother.

Adam held out the scissors to Twig. She took them obediently and stood over her mother, filled with dread. She wanted to put her lips on top of Avery's flaxen head, whisper in her ear how much she loved her, but she couldn't. Her only loyalty was meant to be to Adam, but at this moment she felt torn. Maybe this was the lesson that would finally make Avery learn to be agreeable and obey: the path to harmony. Still, Twig wished there were another way. And sometimes, though she'd never revealed this sinful thought, Twig wondered if Avery couldn't control herself at all. Like she wasn't the one in control of her moods or actions. Maybe.

"It's better if it's you, Twig. It really is."

"Avery, not another word," Adam scolded.

Twig cried quietly as she lifted a piece of Avery's hair with tenderness. She winced at the sound the blades made as they severed Avery's hair from her head. She wished she could mute the sawing, snapping sounds.

The Family sat unusually silent around the spectacle. When she finished, Twig set the scissors down on the ground.

"Now shave her." Adam stood, holding a razor.

Twig was going to throw up. She gathered her dress, darted out the door, and began to run from the compound toward the forest.

"Twig!" Adam ran after her.

Twig ran faster, but Adam was athletic and quickly overcame her. He took her into his arms. Twig sobbed and beat at his chest. "She doesn't know what she's doing! She can't help it. Why do you keep punishing her?" Twig was out of control. She knew she would be punished for talking to Adam this way, but she couldn't help herself.

"Shh. Shh." Adam tried to comfort her. He stroked her hair and held her closer. "It's okay. Calm down, darling."

Twig took a deep breath, her sobs beginning to subside within the tightness of his embrace. She cried quietly into his chest. "Maybe she's sick? Maybe she has a virus from before? From before she came here?"

"It's okay," he cooed. "It's going to be okay. It's for her own good. You'll see. Imagine the peace she'll have when she learns. She'll find her joy again, and we will celebrate when she does. We will honor the beautiful woman she is."

Twig wanted to hate him in that moment, but his words soothed her. She felt herself calming despite trying to hold onto her rage. It seeped away from her.

"Better?" he asked.

Twig looked up at Adam. His black eyes glimmered as he took her in. "You've become so beautiful," he murmured.

Twig looked down, embarrassed. Adam held her tighter.

"It's okay. I'm going to make everything okay." Twig felt his lips touch her head. He pulled her even closer and ran his hands up her back. His lips were close to her ear. "So beautiful," he said, his voice suddenly urgent.

Twig froze.

His lips moved to her neck. His body was hard, pushing against her. Was he trembling? Twig felt claustrophobic. He moved his mouth to hers, pressing urgently. She quickly pulled away in shock and fear.

He recovered himself. "Twig, I'm sorry." And then he recovered even more. It wasn't like Adam to apologize. He smiled. "Everything will be okay. You'll see. Just trust me."

Twig stood wide-eyed, just staring at him. What just happened? He kissed her. Her first kiss was supposed to be with her husband—*after* they were married. It was supposed to be loving and playful—at least, that's how Twig had dreamed it would be.

"Are you okay now?"

"Yes," Twig muttered. She wanted to get away from him.

"Do you believe me?" Adam asked her.

Twig was silent. She didn't know what he meant.

"That everything is going to be okay?"

"Yes. Yes, of course I believe you, Father," she said quietly.

"Good. Now please go back and shave your mother's head. And tell everyone there will be no breakfast today and that they can thank your mother for that."

10

Twig moved through the rest of the day in a haze. She couldn't wait to take her favorite horse, Sapphire, out for a long run. They always rode in a group or at least pairs of two, but galloping on Sapphire always left her room to clear her head despite the company. Afterward, she would brush Sapphire's coffee-brown coat until it gleamed and feed her carrots and apples by the handful.

Farriss was at the stables when Twig arrived. He loved the horses, and even though, as an Elder, he didn't need another position within the Family, he was the stable lead. He had been for as long as Twig could remember. Most roles rotated every month, but Farriss never gave up the care of the stables and horses. Twig grabbed an apple from one of the food baskets, rubbed it on the skirt of her dress, and took a big bite. She let out an audible sigh. She felt lighter just being near the horses.

"Congratulations are in order, aren't they, dear?" Farriss' voice was velvety. Twig loved the sound of it.

"Yes, thank you, Farriss," Twig said quietly. Twig turned away and fed the rest of her apple to a big white horse with a mushroom-gray muzzle named Candy. Twig liked Farriss. It was hard to look him in the eye and pretend nothing was wrong.

"You know you can always come talk to me or Yasmine. It will be a big responsibility, being Adam's wife, but I have complete faith that you will rise to the occasion."

"Yes." Twig nodded humbly. "Thank you."

"She's ready for you." Farriss nodded toward the stall where Sapphire slept. "The group is already out there," he added.

Twig began gathering grooming supplies and headed off toward Sapphire's stall.

"Don't forget this," Farriss said, throwing Twig another apple, which she caught with one hand.

Twig walked to Sapphire's stall and pulled on the cotton tights she'd sewn for riding beneath her white eyelet dress. She couldn't bear riding sideways in her dress, so she'd made the tights. All the women and girls wore them now when they rode. The men and boys in the Family wore white button-down shirts and dark-blue jeans. Twig had asked many times if the girls could be permitted to wear jeans, at least for some of their activities. So far the answer had been no. But now that she would be Adam's wife, maybe she could convince him to change this. She brushed the thought away to revisit later.

Twig saddled up expertly and pulled herself onto Sapphire with ease. Twig's frame was slight, but her body was strong from years of yoga. Twig trotted out of the shade of the stables and entered the clearing. Buoyed by the fresh air and her love of riding, she grinned and galloped forward, her long hair streaming behind her. It looked dirty blond in the afternoon light.

"Hey, beautiful girl," Ryan said as Twig pulled Sapphire up beside his horse. Twig blushed. "Come on, princess. I know it's your birthday, but let's get going."

Twig saw Avery sitting atop a sweet but serious yellow-haired stallion named Phoenix, Sophie at her side.

"Mom?" Twig couldn't believe her eyes. She couldn't remember the last time she and Avery had gone out on a ride together, and, after this morning, she hadn't expected to see her mother for the rest of the day. She must have made the effort for Twig's birthday. Twig was deeply touched. She looked at Ryan and Sophie, and they smiled back at her.

"Race you!" she challenged. The four of them tore out toward the forest, catching up to the rest of the group.

11

The trees stood tall, stamping the blue sky with dark-green silhouettes. There were eight of them on horseback, including Twig, Ryan, Sophie, and Avery. Ryan tore off in a blaze of dust. Ryan's color was orange: bright, clear, and fiery. He was the strongest rider among them. He looked so able and grown up as he flamed ahead of her. A flicker of excitement ran through her, settling in her breasts and giving her the chills. It's not that she had feelings for Ryan. Not those kinds of feelings. It was just the whole picture: Ryan, his horse, and his confidence, the light of the sun, and the sudden dampness in the air. It was inspiring.

Twig thought back to Rose and Thomas and their kiss the day before. She thought about Adam and how he'd pressed his mouth against hers. Would it always feel like that—awkward and slightly wrong? Could she imagine kissing him back? Did she want to? If she was really honest with herself, did she want to be with him that way? She loved him. She loved him deeply. He was gorgeous and charming, and, truth be told, exciting. But to lie with him? The thought terrified her and made her a little sick.

Twig could have kissed Ryan a hundred times. It was forbidden before marriage, but they'd had opportunities to do it in secret. Ryan just didn't exude that kind of energy toward Twig, as close as they were. They hugged, but it wasn't sexual.

Adam said there was nothing wrong with Ryan's feelings, that they were natural for him, part of his fabric. It was a roll of the dice whether people came out homosexual or heterosexual, but when he came of age, Ryan would have to change. The Family needed heterosexual couplings for procreation, and that was that. Adam said that if he didn't strictly enforce this rule, they would die out. He simply couldn't recruit enough new members to keep them thriving as a group. If you lived in the Family, you needed to be in a heterosexual coupling—period.

But then there were sisters like Avery and Evelyn, who were both single. The logic didn't quite click for Twig. Why hadn't Adam remarried her mother or Evelyn? Were they too old to make babies now, so it didn't matter? Would Tina soon join them?

Evelyn was a miserable woman, but she was 100 percent committed to the Family—committed to Adam. According to her lore, Evelyn had lost her husband in a war between the United States and Iraq. She was pregnant with Rose at the time of his death. That was when she joined the Family.

Neither Rose nor Twig had fathers. They didn't ever talk about it, but it was something they shared, and it was why their mothers were housed together. Twig's father left Avery when he found out she was pregnant, which is when Avery joined the Family. Evelyn and Avery were the only two single women over the age of eighteen in the Family, and for reasons Twig did not know, Adam had never remarried them, not even when new members joined the compound.

"Come on, Twig!" Ryan yelled. Twig dug her heels into Sapphire, and the horse obediently sprinted after him.

They rode for an hour and then circled back. It was still warm and humid, but the sky had turned a threatening gray. The group formed a tight cadre as they ambled back to the stables. Everyone chatted casually, laughter bubbling up from the pack now and then.

"I'm going to walk Sapph over to the stream for some water," Twig said.

She steered Sapphire away from the group and headed toward a wide stream that lay to their right. The water was frothy with the turbulent current. As Twig and her horse neared the stream, she felt raindrops on her head. Sapphire stuck her black, velvety muzzle in the water and began to drink. The raindrops came harder and faster. Twig loved the rain; she wasn't fazed when it started to come down in sheets.

She thought she heard someone calling her name. Twig pulled Sapphire's reins to steer her back toward the group, but Sapphire resisted. She had become interested in something in the grass. Suddenly, a flock of birds emerged from the trees. Their wings snapped loudly, like clothes on a line pulled taut in the wind. The sound startled Twig. The birds disappeared into the sky, which had turned gunmetal gray.

"Come on, Sapph. We'd better go. It's getting a bit wild out here." Sapphire continued to resist. She began to snort and scratch one of her front hoofs on the ground.

"What is it, girl?" Twig leaned sideways to try to get a look at what was upsetting Sapphire. The rain made it hard to see, and Sapphire was so agitated that she wasn't responding. Twig was just about to pull harder on the reins, to demand that Sapphire come with her, when she saw what was happening. By then, it was too late. The horse had put her muzzle into a hive of bees that must have fallen from a tree. Sapphire reared up as the bees swarmed. Twig tried to hang on, but she was in the wrong position. She felt a sharp, unnatural twisting in her back as she was thrown from the horse.

She heard screams.

Everything went black.

12

Twig looked down at her light-brown pony with its shaggy, white mane and long, white bangs. The girl in front of her rode a white pony with big, black spots. They were riding slowly around a ring. Six impeccably groomed ponies carrying six elegant children dressed in party clothes.

Twig looked down at her frothy, raspberry-pink party dress. A tulle ballerina skirt parachuted around her small body.

"Livvy! My birthday girl! My baby girl!" A tall young man with warm, golden skin and prematurely gray hair held Twig carefully atop the pony, making sure she didn't fall. His eyes, like bright-green marbles, were full of love. They were magical eyes.

"Daddy!"

Twig saw her mother outside the ring. She was dressed in a fitted, strapless, chocolate-brown dress. Avery's hair was almost platinum, buttery, blond, and pulled up in a high ponytail. A beatific grin spread across her gorgeous, tanned face. Twig wanted to go to her.

"Mommy!"

"Just another round, Livvy. Then you can go to Mommy."

13

A sharp pain in Twig's arm shot into her consciousness. Her head throbbed. She was parched.

"Mommy?" Twig was barely able to utter the word. Her mouth was so dry despite the rain pelting her. She didn't know where she was, and she was in a lot of pain. She was so dizzy.

"Twig, I'm here. Everything is going to be okay." Twig thought she heard her mother, but she wasn't sure.

"Mommy, I want Daddy. Where is Daddy? I want my daddy!" Twig had begun to scream. A panic was setting in that she couldn't control.

Commotion. People swarmed around her, creating a canopy and blocking the rain. Twig couldn't see the sky. She wanted desperately to see the sky. She wished the people would move, give her some air. She felt like her lungs were collapsing. She couldn't get a breath.

"Doc is coming! He'll be here in a minute," Twig heard someone shout through the rain, through the pain in her head, her arm.

Twig tried to crawl deeper into Avery's arms. She was terrified. She didn't know any of the people she saw crowded around her. "Where's Daddy?" she sobbed.

"Shh, shh," Avery cooed. "It's okay, baby. Everything is going to be okay." Avery's voice sounded panicked. Twig thought it sounded like Avery was crying. She never cried.

"Mommy, just take me home. Where are we? Take me home! Now!"

"What happened?" Another man's voice that Twig didn't recognize.

"She got bucked off Sapphire," Twig heard her mother yell into the rain. "She's shivering, Doc. Why is she shivering when it's ninety degrees out? She doesn't know where she is. We have to get her to a hospital!"

The man came closer. "Get away from me! I want my daddy!" Twig screamed, and Avery pulled Twig closer.

"What do we do, Doc?"

"Mommy, I can't breathe. Please help me, Mommy."

"Doc!" Avery's voice teemed with urgency.

"She's breathing, Avery. She's breathing. She's in shock from the fall, and she's having a panic attack. But look, she's breathing."

"What the hell is going on here?" Another man's voice, furious. Twig clung even tighter to Avery.

"Adam, we need to get her to the hospital. She had a bad fall. She's completely disoriented and doesn't recognize anyone besides Avery. She's having some sort of amnesic episode."

Twig felt like she was going to pass out again. The man called Adam kneeled down next to Avery, and Twig's head popped up. "You get away from me!" she shrieked. "All of you get away from me! Mommy, help me. Why won't you help me?"

"Adam, we don't have much time," Doc said. "I'm going to sedate her."

Twig felt herself slipping away again.

"Can't you treat her here? Give this a little time to see what happens?"

"She could have severe brain damage, and she could be bleeding internally. Adam, she could die. We need to get her to the hospital. Now. If we don't hurry, we might lose her."

Those were the last words Twig heard before she slipped into unconsciousness.

14

"Thank God they brought her in. They look Amish or something."

"Sorry, doctor? Amish?" Twig heard a woman's voice respond.

Twig felt fuzzy but wonderfully calm. She kept her eyes closed. It felt like too much effort to open them.

"Right, you wouldn't know that reference. They...never mind. Listen, her father said they're Costa Rican, but I don't buy it. I was born and bred in the States, a dyed-in-the-wool Texan. I know a group of expats when I see one."

The man stopped talking, and the room became quiet.

"The CT scan shows a subdural hematoma. I want her on Mannitol and Keppra IVs to prevent any seizing. She was very lucky. Let's keep the oxygen going for the night. She should be fine, but I want to take every precaution. We'll do another CT scan in the morning, and I want a follow-up CT next month." The man paused. "Pretty girl."

"Yes, doctor."

Twig wondered whom they were talking about.

She let her eyes flutter open. She was in an alarmingly white room. A very tanned man with white-blond hair, maybe in his fifties, stood near her. He wore a white coat and stared at a clipboard. A younger woman with warm-brown skin and shiny black hair pulled into a bun stood next to him, looking at the clipboard over his shoulder. The woman was dressed all in white with a small white hat fixed into her hair. They didn't notice Twig looking at them.

Twig was too tired to be scared. She just wanted to sleep. The pain was gone, and she just wanted to go back to sleep. She felt as if she was floating.

"I want her here overnight. There's something about this crew. I just can't shake the feeling that something is..." he tapped his pen on the clipboard, "...not quite right with them."

The man and the woman looked up from the clipboard toward Twig.

"Look who's awake," the man said with new warmth in his voice.

Twig smiled out of a habit of politeness and fell back to sleep.

15

Twig was dreaming of steam. Irazú, the volcano. She'd finally made it. She hovered above the huge basin filled with swirling clouds of white vapor. This high up, with the mouth of the volcano gaping beneath her, Twig had never felt so powerful.

Then voices began lifting out of the steam, pulling at her. Doc. Avery. Adam. Twig felt herself being dragged into the volcano, the steam climbing out of the stone basin to envelop her. She tried to push it away, covering her face.

"Twig. It's Mom. It's okay."

Something was on her face. Twig tore at it.

"It's okay to remove the mask," said a man's voice that Twig didn't recognize. Avery removed the mask from Twig's face as Twig squinted, trying to open her eyes fully.

"Mom, where are we?" Twig was scared and thirsty. Her head was swimming.

"Twig, you had an accident, but you're okay. We are at a place called a hospital. This man is a doctor. He is helping us."

A man in a white coat stood at the foot of Twig's bed. Twig gripped Avery. *An outsider.*

"But, Mom," Twig started to say, but the man began to approach Twig, and she gasped. She began to hold her arm up to tell the man to stop, but she was attached to some sort of tube. She started to feel faint.

"Okay, let's slow this down," the man in the white coat said.

"Twig, do you know who I am?" Adam was suddenly at Twig's side.

Twig squinted at Adam. "Of course," she whispered. "Father, I don't understand. Why are we...?" The man in the white coat laid his hand on Adam's shoulder.

"Why don't we give her a little room, give her a moment with her mom." Adam glared at the man's hand. He quickly removed it.

"We can come back in a few minutes," Doc added.

"But she might fall asleep again. I need to talk to her."

"Adam!" Avery said, exasperated.

"Okay, okay." With a tense smile, Adam stood up. "Twig, I'll be right outside the door. I'll be back in a few minutes, okay?"

Twig nodded, completely confused. "Is this man okay?" she asked Adam. "Is he safe?"

"Yes," Avery said. "Yes, he is helping us. He is a good man."

"Well, I don't know if he's a good man, but he seems to be a good enough doctor," Adam said, his voice as tense as his facial expression.

Doc steered Adam toward the door. "We'll be right back," Adam said, his eyes boring into the doctor.

"Intense guy," the doctor said once Adam and Doc left the room.

"You don't know the half of it," Avery answered. Twig was shocked that Avery seemed comfortable with this man.

"Let's start over. Twig, I'm Dr. Young. Are you in a lot of pain?"

Twig nodded, but the effort made her head throb. Her body was aching and sore. "Can I have something to drink?"

"Let's start with some ice chips."

Avery quickly began to spoon a chip of ice from a pea-green plastic pitcher near the bed. She held it to Twig's mouth. Twig took it gratefully and sucked on it. She took a deep breath, feeling calmer.

"What happened to me? What kind of accident? Am I okay?" As Twig spoke, her anxiety began to grow again.

"Yes, you are absolutely okay—"

"She's never been to a hospital before, Dr. Young. She doesn't know what any of this is."

"I understand," Dr. Young said warmly.

He seemed…nice. Twig tried to match this man to the descriptions of the demonic people she knew lived in the outside world. Had Adam purified him before she woke up?

"What is this?" Twig held up her hand. There was a needle pricking out of it, which was connected to a small tube. It was then that she realized her other hand was in a cast. She began to cry a little bit, feeling completely overwhelmed. "What happened to me?" she sniffed.

"Like your mother said, you had an accident. You fell off your horse, Twig. You bumped your head pretty good, and you sprained your wrist. You must be tough, though, because from what I hear, it was a nasty fall. That's all that happened." Dr. Young paused. "Now, it was a severe sprain, so I want that cast on there for about three weeks."

"But why this needle? Why am I here? Is Sapphire okay?" Twig began to look around the room while Avery fed her another ice chip. Everything was foreign. The sheets in the bed were stiff and itchy. The lights were blinding and a strange shade of greenish-yellow. Hard, cold-looking tile covered the floor. The walls were painted a sterile white and looked oddly glossy.

"Twig, we were giving you oxygen to help you breathe. That was the mask. It was temporary, and you don't need it anymore. This wild-looking tube coming out of your arm is called an IV. It's how we are making sure you get enough water, and it's giving you medication. I can take that out soon, too. Okay?"

Twig nodded. She was beginning to feel more comfortable with this man. He seemed kind. "But is Sapphire okay?"

"She's fine, Twig," Avery said reassuringly.

"Now, I'm not going to lie to you," Dr. Young continued. "You took it pretty good on the noggin." Avery was shaking her head at the doctor. "Head," he corrected himself. "You hit your head hard when you fell, causing a very small bleed called a subdural hematoma." Twig felt her stomach tighten with fear. "But," the doctor continued, sensing her alarm, "it was minor. How are we doing so far?"

"Will I have brain damage?"

"No, dear. Your family did the right thing by bringing you in right away. You're going to be fine. You are going to have to rest and take some medication for a while, but you are going to be fine. I hear you like yoga."

Twig nodded.

"In about three weeks, when you get the cast off, if you're feeling well, you can go back to light yoga. And I want you up and about in the next two weeks. How does that sound?"

"Okay," Twig said tentatively. She was scared. Scared for her brain, scared of the hospital and of the doctor, even though he seemed so nice.

"In the morning, we are going to repeat the CT, which is a scan that lets us see what's going on inside your head, and I am going to need to see you back here in a month to do another scan."

Twig heard Avery sigh.

"Will that be a problem?" the doctor asked, glancing toward the door.

Avery was silent for a moment. "No, I don't think so."

Dr. Young eyed Avery. "Listen, I am going to give you my card. If there is a problem, please call me."

Avery nodded but didn't say anything. Twig noticed how unhappy she looked.

"Are you okay, Mom?" she asked. Avery looked at Twig and grabbed her hand. "I'm fine, Twig. Let's just concentrate on you."

"Can I sleep now? I'm very tired."

"Of course," the doctor replied.

16

Twig woke to the sound of people arguing.

"Another night? You said it was a small bleed. This morning's scan was fine." Doc was speaking with Dr. Young.

Adam was furiously pacing back and forth in the confines of the small white room. One hand seemed permanently lodged in his thick, dark hair. Twig had no idea how long she had been sleeping.

"I need to make sure it is resolving and not getting worse. I also want her here for observation. She's still in danger of seizures, and I need to make sure she responds to medication."

"That's ridiculous," Doc said dismissively.

"The girl has had brain trauma," the doctor answered sternly.

"Look, I am a doctor," Doc explained. "I can take care of her. If she has any problems, I'll bring her back. Please discharge her this evening."

"Exactly what kind of doctor are you? Where did you get your degree?"

"I am a doctor of psychiatric medicine, and I got my degree at the University of California, San Francisco—not that it is any of your business."

"Hmm," the doctor said, unimpressed. "And can I assume you've been keeping up with your CEUs?"

"How dare you!" Doc glared down at the doctor. Dr. Young was shorter than Doc, but he was sturdy and impressive with his white beard and tan, weathered skin.

"She's awake," Avery said, coming to Twig's side.

The two men stopped arguing, and Adam stopped pacing.

"How long have we been here?" Twig asked. There was no window, and she couldn't tell if it was day or night. For the first time in her life, she had no idea what time it was. "I'm hungry," she suddenly said. She felt better.

The whole room laughed with relief.

A woman in a white dress and small, white hat entered the room. It was crowded already, and one more person made it stuffy and uncomfortable. "I'm Marianna," the woman said, smiling brightly at Twig. Twig flinched as the woman came up behind her and adjusted her pillows. Another outsider. But no one was telling this woman to stay away. Twig looked at Adam. He looked exhausted; he didn't even seem to notice the woman.

"Out, out." Marianna had an accent. Despite her fear, Twig liked the warm sound of the woman's voice. "I need to clear the room."

"Just a moment, Marianna." Adam's voice dripped with charm when he addressed her. He sat on the edge of Twig's small bed. "Hello, dear."

"Hi," Twig answered. "Can I have something to drink?"

Dr. Young nodded.

Adam brought a small cup with a straw to Twig's mouth. She took a sip and shut her eyes. It was juice, and it tasted so good. "Thank you," she said.

"We're going home soon, okay? This nightmare will be over soon, and I'll take you home."

Twig nodded. She felt antsy. She wanted to go home.

Everyone except for Marianna and the doctor left the room. Avery, Doc, and Adam went to get some food at Dr. Young's insistence. "Your mother and father haven't left your side," Marianna told Twig. "They love you very much."

Twig forced a smile. It felt indescribably strange and more than a little scary to be left alone with these two strangers. She kept telling herself that she was safe. Adam would not have left her alone with them otherwise.

"Can I get up?"

"How does your head feel?" Dr. Young asked her.

"Good," Twig said. She laughed a little. "I thought it was going to hurt for the rest of my life. How long did I sleep? A long time? No one will answer me."

"You slept a good twelve hours. Exactly what you needed. It's noon," said Dr. Young. "Marianna is going to take you for a walk."

"Oh, I don't know." Twig eyed the door. "Maybe I should wait for my mom." Twig was terrified of what lay outside the small, stuffy, white room.

"Doctor's orders. It will be good for you. Just a lap around the hallway. You'll be back before your family returns from the cafeteria, and then you can eat. I'll be back this evening to check on you. You're doing great. I'm pleased." Dr. Young patted Twig lightly on the shoulder and then left the room.

Marianna helped Twig out of bed and to the bathroom. It felt good to stretch her legs. When they came out of the bathroom, Marianna helped Twig into a wheelchair. "We'll start with this," she smiled.

"Marianna, please wait. I'm scared. I really can't go out there."

"It's okay, dear. I'll be with you. I won't let anything happen to you."

"But infection—" Twig blurted. She hadn't meant to say it so bluntly. She didn't want to insult Marianna. This was Marianna's world.

"Infection? You will not become infected."

"But the people out there? The virus. I'll be corrupted... I really should wait for my Family."

Marianna knelt down beside Twig. "What virus, *mi chiquita?* Tell me what virus you are afraid of." Marianna's eyes were full of concern.

Twig paused. She didn't want to be mean, but she had to speak the truth. "The virus of the outside world. The virus people carry."

"I see." Marianna smoothed Twig's hair. "There is no one big virus, *mija*. There are small viruses: the common cold, the flu, etcetera. There are contagious diseases, of course, but not everyone carries them. Most people are pretty healthy."

She must be lying. Of course she would be lying. Twig wondered if she should scream for someone to help her.

"I can see that you don't believe me. Wait here for a moment."

A few moments later Marianna returned with Dr. Young. He closed the door behind him.

"Twig, I want to ask you a few questions."

"Okay," Twig nodded.

"You believe—I mean, you have been taught—that the world is infected with a contagious virus? Is that correct? Do I have it right?"

Twig nodded. She felt a combination of embarrassment and fear. She gripped the arms of the wheelchair to stop from shaking.

"I see." Dr. Young held his chin in his hand. "Jesus, I need a biology textbook."

"Sorry?" Twig asked.

"Listen, dear." Dr. Young paused to look at Marianna. "If we were in the States, I'd be calling social services right about now." Marianna looked back at the doctor blankly. "All right, all right, I'll get to the point. Twig, there is no one big apocalyptic virus out there. Not yet, anyway."

"Doctor," Marianna coughed into her hand.

"Right. There are serious diseases, but… Well, now, let me ask you this, Twig: how do you suppose this one worldwide virus gets transmitted from person to person? How does one catch this super virus?"

Twig was quiet. She was mortified and confused. "I don't really know,

Dr. Young. By looking at an infected person? By touching them or talking to them?"

Dr. Young squinted his eyes at Twig. His look was full of compassion. "I wish we had more time, dear. There is a lot I'd like to tell you. But I'll tell you the basics. I'll tell you what you need to know to give you peace of mind on your jaunt around the hallway." Dr. Young winked at Twig. "Sound good?"

Twig nodded. She could at least listen to him. There was no harm in that. He had healed her head.

"What do you know about biology? About cells? Does the term 'nucleic acid chain' mean anything to you?"

Twig shook her head. She wanted to slink away. She felt so stupid.

"It's okay. It doesn't matter. Here's the bottom line: everyone gets sick from time to time. You've probably had a cold before, correct?"

"Sure," Twig said. "Of course."

"Okay. That, my dear, was a virus."

Twig looked at the doctor skeptically.

"There are several ways viruses can spread." Dr. Young held up his finger. "One: direct contact. Touching, kissing, someone coughing on you. Getting bitten or scratched by your pet, if they are carrying something. A mother passing a disease to her unborn child. Not," Dr. Young looked Twig in the eye, "by looking at someone. And not by just talking to someone. Unless they sneeze on you." Dr. Young pretended to sneeze. Twig laughed in spite of herself. "You with me so far?"

Twig nodded. It was hard to take in everything he was saying, because if he was telling the truth, then someone else was lying. Many, many people were lying. Or maybe they didn't know. Maybe Adam was confused.

Dr. Young held up two fingers. "Two: indirect contact. Someone with the flu touches a doorknob, and you touch that doorknob and then rub your eyes, wipe your nose, or touch your mouth before you wash your hands. Even then, many times you would not become infected. It depends on the state of your immune system in that moment."

Twig did not know what an immune system was, but she nodded again anyway.

"Now, this last way is closest to what you're talking about with your worldwide super virus. It's called particle transmission." Dr. Young was speaking very quickly now. Twig was trying hard to concentrate on what he was saying. "Very tiny disease particles travel through the air, and a person can breathe in these airborne germs and become infected. Now, there are bites and stings and food contamination and all of that. Listening to me, you're probably wondering how anyone manages to stay alive. But we do. And modern medicine and vaccinations help."

"Twig? Are you okay?" Marianna took Twig's hand. "Is this all new information for you?"

"Yes," Twig said quietly. "I was taught that you could catch…well, character traits, too."

Dr. Young and Marianna looked at one another with concern.

"Well, that's a question for philosophers and theologians, but you don't catch immorality the way you catch a disease, if that's what you mean," Dr. Young said.

Twig was stunned. She stared wide-eyed at the doctor and Marianna, trying to take in everything they were saying. It seemed too complicated to be lies. "They must not know—the Elders, Adam. They must not know any of this," Twig muttered, mostly to herself.

"If your friend Doc actually has a degree from UCSF, he knows this and a lot more, Twig. I'm sorry, but you've been lied to." Dr. Young touched Twig's cheek tenderly. "I need to go now, Twig. Please use this information as you see fit. Keep it to yourself, if need be." It seemed as if he was about to say something else but then thought better of it and just shook his head, turning to leave.

"Wait. Dr. Young? Can I ask you something?"

"Of course."

"What is a vaccination?"

"The fact that you are asking me that makes me think you haven't had any. That doesn't make me very happy."

"Well, our Father does do these things…these rituals." Twig wondered if she was saying something she shouldn't. Something that was secret to the Family. But maybe if she just explained to Dr. Young and Marianna, they would understand. "He has healing powers. Powers in his hands. I don't know how it works exactly, it's hard to explain, but he can heal people, and he can protect people from the outside—" Twig stopped herself. "From getting sick."

"I see," said Dr. Young. "Well, I'm not sure about all that, but I can answer your question. When we vaccinate, we inject you with very small amounts of treated microorganisms that give your body immunity to the disease we are vaccinating for. Okay?"

Twig nodded, pretending she wholly understood what he was saying. "Okay. Thank you."

Dr. Young left the room.

Twig felt as if she'd been punched in the stomach. She felt foolish. Embarrassed. Ignorant. Betrayed. And also, guilty. Why would she trust Dr. Young and Marianna? What was wrong with her? And yet she *did* trust them, for some reason. At the very least, they had just planted a serious seed of doubt in her head. She had to think this over.

"Shall we go?" Marianna whispered.

Twig nodded. She knew she was taking a risk, but now, right now, might be her only chance to see what the outside world was really about.

Marianna wheeled her out into the hallway. Twig's eyes popped open.

People, so many people. Some were dressed in the same white dresses as Marianna's. Others had on long white coats like Dr. Young. The people dressed in white whizzed past her along more glossy white walls that seemed to stretch on forever. They faded into a blur of activity. Twig was used to people dressed in white, but there were other people, too. Fat, skinny, very old, very young. Her heart beat wildly in her chest. She was scared and ready to make Marianna turn back, but no one even seemed to notice her. She expected people to be doing terrible things—shouting profanities, being violent—but she saw none of that.

What she did see fascinated her—things she had heard about and imagined but never encountered firsthand: makeup painted garishly over faces, tight clothing, and high-heeled shoes. Jeans and comfortable-looking sweatshirts with hoods. Black hair bleached blond. Elegant-looking women with big, shiny purses and tights tucked into riding boots, sunglasses pushed on top of their heads. Old men with beautiful sweaters, tan slacks, and shiny loafer shoes. Some people's clothes looked new, and some looked old and tattered. Some people looked clean and well cared-for and others, heartbreakingly neglected. Twig forgot about her cast and her pain. Her fear soon turned to something else: curiosity. Fascination. She wished Ryan were here to see this with her.

"Okay, you pick the song."

"Katy Perry, 'California Gurls.'"

Twig looked up in the direction of the voices. A guy and a girl were standing a stone's throw from her down the hallway. They seemed to be about Twig's age and both had the same warm, light-brown skin and dark-brown, curly hair flecked with amber. Their eyes were a beautiful shade of green. Most of the people in the hospital seemed to be Latino, but these two looked as if they were a mix of black and white.

"Sister, surely you jest."

"Brother, I do not. It's catchy. Either you can dance, or you can't."

71

They looked like biological sister and brother, but everyone in the Family called one another brother and sister, too, so Twig couldn't be sure. The boy was on crutches, a cast covering one of his feet. He was gorgeous.

"Cute," Marianna whispered in Twig's ear, stopping the chair to let Twig watch for a moment. Did Marianna know she had never been off the compound? No, she couldn't know that. But it seemed like Dr. Young and Marianna were conspiring to give Twig a chance to look around the hospital. Maybe that was crazy.

"All right, Hazel. You're killing me, but all right. You know I like a challenge. Got your iPod synched?" The boy was playful. Twig had no idea what he was talking about, but she liked listening to him talk to his sister. It was like they were playing catch with their words.

"Synched. Do you mind if I film this? On crutches and grooving to Katy Perry? This goes right to Facebook."

Without looking up, the boy answered, "Negative."

"Please?" the girl asked.

"Deal's off if you mention Facebook again."

Twig watched as the two of them stuck tiny white globes in their ears and clipped whisper-thin silver machines, smaller than matchboxes, onto the pockets of their shorts.

The girl had on cut-off jean shorts, and her legs were muscular and thin. Her hair was pulled back from her face with barrettes. Her eyes glittered green. The two looked so much alike that they could have been twins. And they looked healthy. Really healthy. These did not look like people who were infected with a virus. These two looked nothing like Anna had that night. In fact, so far she hadn't seen anyone who looked like Anna had when Doc brought her in. Twig continued to watch as the boy started to push his chin out and move his rib cage and shoulders from side to side. Twig heard Marianna giggle beside her. Twig looked up at her, and Marianna gave her a sweet smile and gently stroked her cheek.

Twig gathered that the pair was listening to music, but she had never seen anything like the small devices they used. The boy began to put on a real show. He stuck his crutches out in front of him and used them as extended hands, pushing them back and forth, moving up and down. It was so rhythmic that Twig could almost hear the music. The girl watched, her arms crossed with mock disdain, bopping her head smartly, shoulders dipping and rising.

The boy *was* cute. Marianna was right. Twig studied him as he danced. They hadn't noticed her sitting there, so she could just look. He was muscular, like the girl, but taller. His smile was infectious. Twig loved watching him. He was dressed in khaki shorts and a bright-orange T-shirt with a white logo that looked like a record album. That was how the Family listened to music at home—record players. Not often, though, and nothing that would make someone move like that.

The girl started to sing. "*California gurls, we're unforgettable…*"

"Oh… Here comes Snoop," the boy said. He started to raise his crutch again, but he slipped. The crutch escaped his grasp and went clattering toward Twig. It landed at her feet.

"Oh!" Marianna giggled. She took a step back away from Twig.

The boy began to hop toward his crutch. The girl took the globes out of her ears and went to help him, but when he noticed Twig, he put his hand up to stop the girl.

"I got this, Haze," he said, smiling up at Twig, who was trying to lean down to help him retrieve his crutch. He spoke a little too loudly because the globes were still in his ears.

They reached the crutch at the same time, and their hands touched. Twig felt a bolt of electricity go through her. His skin was so soft. She removed her hand immediately, embarrassed. What was she doing? What if Marianna and Dr. Young were wrong or deceiving her? She hadn't thought about it; she had just reached out on instinct.

She noticed the boy's cheeks turn a slight pink. He placed his crutch under his arm, righted himself, and extended his hand again.

"Uh… I'm Leo," he said.

Twig paused for a moment. *Corruption. Evil.* The words slammed into her brain, but they slipped away just as quickly. She didn't feel anything but good coming from this boy.

You've been lied to. She heard Dr. Young's words echoing in her head.

She stuck her hand out. "Twig," she offered.

"Twig," Leo repeated. "I like that. It's different. Hey, sorry for almost knocking you out with my crutch. We were just messing around," he said.

Twig smiled awkwardly. "That's okay. It wouldn't have been the first time." Twig touched her forehead with her long fingers.

"Ouch," he said. "Are you okay? What happened?"

"I was dancing to Katy Perry on top of my horse, and I got bucked off." What was that? It just came out. Twig began to turn red.

Leo looked at Twig quizzically, his eyebrows knitted, his perfect lips pushed out while he considered what she had just said. Then he grinned.

"You are *so* messing with me."

"I am." Twig smiled back. This was fun!

"I like that," Leo said quietly. "But what really happened? And, you don't *really* listen to Katy Perry, do you?"

"I don't even know who she is," Twig admitted in a more tentative voice.

That's an understatement, Twig thought to herself. Sometimes Adam played classical music for them or strummed some songs on a guitar. There were the few records, classical and folk, for special occasions like weddings. But that was it. Anything else rotted the mind.

Leo suddenly noticed Marianna. "I'm so sorry," he said. He looked up at Marianna and stuck his hand out. "Leo," he said with a smile. "Forgive my rudeness." Marianna stepped forward to shake his hand.

"Mucho gusto. Yo comprendo. I understand," she said, smiling and glancing down at Twig.

"So, what really happened to you?"

"I really did fall off my horse." Twig admitted, frowning slightly.

"Ouch," Leo said, wincing.

"Ahem." The girl cleared her throat behind Leo.

"Oh!" Leo stepped aside to introduce her. "Twig, this is my sister, Hazel. Hazel, this is Twig, horsewoman extraordinaire."

Hazel offered a warm smile, extending her hand to Twig. Twig reached forward in her chair, and Hazel came closer. They shook hands.

Hazel held Twig's hand for a moment. "You're a pretty little thing," she said.

"Me?" Twig answered, feeling disheveled after her ordeal and awkward in her hospital gown and papery robe. Hazel looked so grown up and polished. "You are gorgeous! Both of you."

The flush returned to Leo's cheeks. Hazel looked at her brother.

"Leo, you're a mess. Thank you, Twig. Lee, I'm going to go find Mom and Dad. I want to get out of here. Twig, it was lovely meeting you."

Hazel mouthed something to Leo and then sashayed down the hallway away from them. Leo nodded after her, a slight smile playing on his lips.

With Hazel gone, Twig's stomach had become a swarm of fluttering butterflies. Leo didn't have just one color. He was a rainbow. She didn't know what to say. She expected Marianna to whisk her away at any minute.

"Can I ask you a question?" she finally forced the words out of her mouth.

"Yeah," Leo said sweetly. He leaned toward her.

"What is that?" Twig pointed to the small silver machine.

"This?" Leo looked surprised.

"Yes."

Twig winced a little, she was sure she had just confirmed herself as a space alien in his eyes. Leo noticed her embarrassment.

"It's an iPod nano. It plays music."

"It's so little."

"Yeah, I'm surprised you haven't seen one. Want to try it?"

Twig shook her head. "No, no. That's okay, really. I'm sorry; I shouldn't have asked."

"Please," Leo said gently. "Give it a try. If you'd like to."

Twig looked up at Marianna. Marianna smiled, nodding and urging her on.

"Okay," Twig said shyly.

Leo hopped to Twig's side. He began to hand Twig the small globes, which he called earbuds, but the cords wrapped around her cast.

"Let me," Leo said.

He leaned on one of his crutches and gently pushed Twig's current tangle of blond hair behind her ears. Twig shivered at his touch. She tried to stay still, but she felt as if she was going to fly out of the chair. Leo placed the little buds in Twig's ears as carefully as if he were handling glass. Suddenly, he took one out and looked at Twig seriously.

"Wait, you just had a head injury, didn't you?"

"Yes." Twig nodded.

"Okay, I'm going to play something super mellow and super low. Another time I can really show you what this is all about."

"Okay," Twig whispered, thinking she especially liked the idea of there being another time.

"Hey, where do you live? I mean, you look American, but if you don't know what a nano is…"

Twig thought about how to answer this question. She decided to go with the simplest answer.

"Near Turrialba."

"No way!" Leo beamed.

That smile.

"We're staying in Turrialba. I'm from the States, but we're traveling for a few months before school starts. I deferred until the spring," Leo explained. He paused for a beat and then went on. "We came here to learn Spanish, chill, and take surf trips on the weekends." Leo looked in the direction of his casted foot. "Thus the foot. Surf spill. I'm getting my cast off today."

Twig had no idea what "deferring until spring" meant or what "surf trips" were—she assumed something to do with water—but she liked listening to Leo talk, and she was amazed that he was staying in Turrialba. She'd never been there, but it was close to the Family's compound. The States certainly were not.

"I hope this doesn't sound lame, but you're really cute." Leo looked bashful as he said this. All of his earlier dancing-bravado had disappeared for the moment.

Twig beamed. She couldn't help herself. She felt this strange, happy lightness just from being around him.

"Look, do you have an email or a number?" Leo asked.

"What's going on here?"

Adam. He had snuck up from behind them.

Twig had completely forgotten about him, about Avery and Doc. She had been so absorbed in the moment. Twig stared up at Adam. He looked furious.

Adam glared at Leo with quiet venom, waiting for an answer.

"Get out of here. I'll take her back," Adam spat at Marianna.

"It's okay, sir. I will take her."

"Go," Adam said, taking a deep breath. He looked like he was about to explode. Twig glanced up at Marianna. She wanted to apologize for Adam. For the first time in her life, she felt embarrassed of him. She had seen him when he punished people, but this was different. All of his vitality and charm was gone, as if he'd turned them off with a switch.

"Oh, hey, man. I'm Leo. I was just talking to Twig about Turrialba." Leo stood a good two inches taller than Adam. He leaned carefully on his crutches and offered his hand. Adam looked at it but didn't take it.

"Son, Twig doesn't know anything about Turrialba."

Twig cringed. What would Leo think of her? That she was lying? She had no way to explain. She just sat there, silent, wishing she could say something. Adam was humiliating her.

Avery and Doc walked up at that moment. Leo softly nodded his head toward Twig. Twig didn't know what Leo was thinking, but he seemed to get the point that he wasn't welcome. Twig's stomach clenched. She so badly wanted to tell him she didn't feel that way, and he seemed to read her thoughts.

"Nice to meet you, Twig," Leo winked at her sweetly.

"You, too." Twig's voice was barely audible. She knew she shouldn't say anything, but she couldn't let him go without saying good-bye. Adam glared at her, and Twig put her head down.

"I'm going to take off, go find my folks and Hazel."

Leo nodded politely at Avery and Doc. They nodded back at him. Twig was grateful to them for showing Leo some graciousness. She felt a mixture of fear and anger toward Adam at the moment.

Leo pivoted around on his casted foot and hopped down the hallway in the direction Hazel had gone a few minutes before. Twig watched him go. Before he turned the corner, he looked back at her, his expression conspiratorial. Twig pressed her lips together to keep from smiling.

Adam stared after Leo with disgust. Twig cast her eyes back down to avoid Adam's gaze.

"Unbelievable. This is exactly how these people are. Taking her out here. Exposing her to this sickness. We need to get her back to the room. Now."

Adam was glaring at Doc and Avery, as if Twig being out here in the hallway was somehow their fault. He glanced at a watch on his wrist that Twig had never seen before.

"Damn it," he hissed. Twig flinched. Adam *never* used profanity. That was a sign of infection, but wasn't he protected from that?

He pulled a small phone out of his pocket and held it to his ear. Telephones had never been a part of Twig's life. Like cameras, she knew they were out there, but she had never used one. Twig wondered what else Adam had up his sleeve. Doc looked at Adam with concern but stayed quiet. Adam pressed a button and then waited a few seconds.

"Did you make the transfer?" he barked into the phone. "Good. I will call you tomorrow, and we can discuss the rest."

Adam pressed a button and ended the call. He stuffed the phone back into his jeans.

Twig thought Adam seemed tired despite his fury. His face was drawn. It was the first time she'd ever seen anything even resembling vulnerability in him. She was surprised he had let her see him talking on the phone. Was it because they were engaged?

Engaged.

Suddenly, the word felt like a prison. All she wanted to do in that moment was run after Leo and see his big smile, hear the warmth in his laughter again. But this was her Family. How could she feel that way? She sighed out loud without meaning to.

"Let's get her back to the room. She needs to sleep." Doc misinterpreted Twig's sigh for pain or fatigue. She felt all that, of course, but she was being kept afloat by some new feeling she had never experienced.

"Hold on." Adam held up his hand to Doc. "Doc, Avery, give us a minute." Doc and Avery nodded and walked a few steps away. They both looked exhausted.

"Listen, honey," Adam began. "You must think I'm being a jerk."

Adam kneeled down and took Twig's hand in his. He looked into her eyes and removed a piece of hair from her forehead. Twig noticed his touch felt comfortable and kind, but it didn't move her the way Leo's had.

"Twig, you've had a big couple of days: the engagement, the fall, leaving our home for the first time. I want you to know that I understand. I get it. It's exciting. It's scary. It's novel for you."

Twig just nodded. She wasn't sure what to say—what was *okay* to say. She was on the verge of confessing her conversation with Dr. Young. Adam was back to his usual, powerful self, and it made her want to open up and say everything she was thinking. She was about to when he spoke first.

"But there's something you need to know." Adam began to stroke Twig's hair a bit too hard. The comfort went out of his touch. He slid his hand into the neck of her hospital gown and pressed his thumb against her collarbone. "You are mine now. Talking to that boy was a sin, and it was dangerous. It is my job to protect you, to teach you. If you hadn't just had an accident, you would be punished." Twig felt him press the edge of his hand harder into her collarbone. It hurt, and she was scared.

Adam removed his hand and began to stroke her cheek. A tear escaped Twig's eye. "You poor thing. You're exhausted. I'm sorry, darling, but I am responsible for you. I love you more than you could ever know. If I seem harsh, it is because you are so special. It is my job to guide you." He looked at her with his powerful eyes and smiled. "Do you understand? Can you accept that?"

"Yes," Twig said dutifully.

"You may be questioning things right now, my darling. That's normal for your age. But soon you and I will become one. After our marriage.

I will show you things you've never dreamed of. Your questions will be answered. Your faith will become unshakeable." Adam brought his lips close to Twig's mouth. "I will be a gentle teacher."

And suddenly, Twig knew he wouldn't be. She could feel the brutality of his nature just below the surface. She could feel the harshness that she had seen on his face when he'd spoken to Leo, when he'd grabbed her the morning of Avery's punishment. She wanted to gag as he put his mouth on hers; it was more punctuation than kiss.

He pulled his head away and looked at her. She forced herself to smile.

"I'll get you to your room now. I want you to know you are safe. Talking to that boy could have been fatal, but because I just cleansed you the other night, you will be fine. You are protected from exposure."

Twig searched his face. How could she tell if he was lying or if he just didn't know any better? He seemed completely sure of what he was saying. Why would he make something like this up? Why terrify everyone?

To be the cure. He made up a disease so he could be the cure, our savior. So we would be completely dependent on him, and never leave him.

Even as the thought occurred to her, Twig couldn't make sense of it. Why would Adam want a community of people completely dependent on him?

"Enough of all that now. I love you, my beautiful, young bride. I love you with everything that I am. I don't know what I would have done if something had happened to you." He stared deeply into her eyes. She felt hypnotized, unable to look away.

"Let's go get you some rest now."

Twig nodded. Internally, she felt pulled in so many directions that she could not speak.

"All right," Adam soothed. He stood behind her wheelchair and began to push her along the hallway and back to her room.

17

Twig woke with a start. She heard shouting. People were shouting. She was in the wheelchair again. Had she fallen asleep in the chair?

She was moving. Twig looked up and saw that Avery was pushing the chair. Fast.

"Mom, what's going on?" Twig was groggy. They had given her pills for her pain before she went to sleep. "Mom, slow down." She was scared she was going to fall out of the chair onto the floor.

"I'm so sorry, honey. I can't. It's going to be okay."

"Please, señora! Please, stop!" Someone was running after them, but Twig couldn't turn around to see who it was. Was she dreaming?

"Mom, what are you doing?"

"We're leaving."

"What? Why? Mom—I think I'm going to be sick." Who was leaving? She and Avery?

"I am so sorry, Twig. Just hang in there."

The hallways were empty except for her and Avery and whoever was chasing them.

"Señora, please. Please." A man in a white uniform overtook Avery and Twig. He stood panting before them, a clipboard pressed to his chest. "Señora. You can leave—that is your choice—but please, if you don't sign these papers, we can lose our jobs."

Avery stopped. Her eyes were darting everywhere. "Please, I can't," she said quietly. "Please just let us by. I'm sorry, but you have to get out of our way." Avery tried to steer past the man, but he didn't budge.

"It is for our liability. Please."

Avery looked down the hallway again. Were they running away from Adam? Twig's heart soared. She wouldn't have to marry him. Avery snatched the clipboard from the man. He handed her a pen. She scratched something onto the paper.

"Señora, gracias. I thank you."

"We have to go. Please, move!" Avery threw the clipboard back at the man.

The man moved aside, and Avery continued her sprint down the hallway. They finally reached a pair of swinging white doors and burst into the night.

And then Twig saw them: Doc and Adam in the Family's white van. Waiting for them. Her heart dropped.

"What took you so long?" Adam hissed as he slid the back door of the van open.

They hadn't been running away from Adam. They'd been running to him. They were running away from the hospital. Twig wanted to cry. How could she have thought otherwise? Where had the power of those thoughts come from? She felt sick. What if anyone had known what she was thinking?

Avery was icily distant on the way home, obviously deep in thought. She and Twig sat shoulder to shoulder in the back of the van, but Twig could feel Avery slipping away. Their stay at the hospital was the most time Twig had ever had with Avery. She would cherish the memory of her care. Now they were going back home, and Avery was disappearing back inside her sadness.

"How long is the drive home?" Twig asked quietly. She had seen the van coming and going from the compound, but she'd never actually been in it. She assumed they had used it to bring her to the hospital, but she had no memory of the ride.

No one answered her. She drifted in and out of sleep.

* * *

"Something's wrong, I think we've been followed."

Twig woke to Adam's voice. She stayed quiet, listening.

"What do you mean?" asked Doc.

"Those two cars behind us, they've been following us for at least twenty miles."

"Are you sure?" Doc whispered. Adam just looked at him in response. "Okay, okay. What do you want to do?"

"We can't lose them now; there's nowhere to go. The guards can keep them out of the front entrance. That's not a problem. But that doesn't mean they won't try to infiltrate from the forest. Everyone needs to be woken and brought to the dining hall. We may be under some sort of attack."

Twig felt Avery groan quietly beside her. Twig looked at her, but Avery just tilted her head back with her eyes closed. Who would have followed them?

Suddenly the compound's front gates came into view ahead. Doc accelerated, and Adam opened the van's windows and began to shout at the guards to open the gates. "We're under attack!" he screamed. "Close the gates behind us!"

Twig felt her body tighten. This had happened before. People had come and surrounded the compound, but they had never been able to get in. Maybe they'd just wanted to scare the Family. Adam said a lot of people hated them for what they stood for.

Twig grabbed Avery's hand as Doc slid the van's back door open to help Avery get Twig out. Adam was screaming orders to the guards. Twig looked for cars trying to enter the gates but didn't see any. They must have gotten a good lead on them.

When Twig was safely out of the van and leaning on Doc for support, she heard Avery say very quietly to Doc, "Tonight of all nights, huh, Doc? What luck."

"Just get Twig to the dining hall," Doc said in response. "Try to make her comfortable."

"I can't just get her to bed? We can bring a guard and wait this out in our cottage. She needs to rest, Doc."

Doc took a closer look at Twig. Chaos was starting to erupt around them. The whole place was coming alive with lanterns and people running back and forth, screaming instructions to one another. Adam had disappeared into the crowd. "Do you feel faint at all, Twig?" Doc asked Twig.

"Kind of," Twig answered. Doc took a deep breath.

"Just get her there. We'll make her comfortable, Avery."

"Will she be able to sleep, Doc?"

"You know that's forbidden during a raid. Just go. Do what you can to keep her comfortable."

Avery nodded her head angrily but silently. She didn't seem scared, just angry. "Can you walk, honey? I can get someone to carry you."

"I'm okay. I just need to lean on you."

Soon the dining hall was packed with the entire Family. People rubbed their eyes, looking confused and scared. Tables and chairs had been pushed aside to allow them to sit in a giant circle on the floor. Adam stood in its center. When he was sure everyone was there, he began to speak.

"Family, we are under attack. I know some of us have been through this before and made it out, but I think tonight might be different. I have the guards surrounding our perimeter, but our attackers might have more manpower and more weapons than we do.

"If this is the end, there are a few things I want to say: first of all, I want every single one of you to know how loved you are. I want you to know that you all have shown me that you are worthy of my love. I have dedicated my entire life, my existence, every part of my being to you. Would I do that if you weren't worthy?

"If we do go tonight, we'll go together. We'll go having lived a true life. A life full of integrity and meaning. We will be soldiers, dying upon the sword of virtue."

Twig tried to focus on Adam, but she was starting to fall asleep.

"Twig," he said sternly. "Do not nod off. We must all stay vigilant tonight. If anyone nods off, they will pay for it. Only the children may sleep in their parents' arms." Adam took a seat in the circle near Twig and Avery but not next to them.

"Now, does anyone know how this attack might have happened? Any clue? If you have any information about one of your brothers or sisters or even any suspicions, speak up now."

Suddenly, the sound of gunshots filled the air. Twig and the others jumped. Adam lurched up and dashed outside. Everyone looked terrified. People held hands; parents soothed their little ones. No one said a word.

A few moments later, Adam came back in. "It's okay. The gunfire came from our men. They saw something and fired warning shots. Everything is okay for now. Whatever or whoever it was has been deterred for the moment." Twig could hear small sounds of relief.

After that, it was quiet for a while. Adam paced. He kept going back outside, then returning and giving reports. An hour, maybe two hours passed. It must have been three or four o;clock in the morning. Several people were struck or spit on for nodding off. Twig saw people trying to keep their loved ones awake. Subtle nudges or coughs. She herself leaned against Avery's back, and Avery had to pinch Twig hard several times to keep her awake. Avery was watching Twig with vigilance. Twig's head hurt, and she was groggy, but she was managing somehow. Her fear mixed with her pain medication was keeping her strangely wired and very nauseated. She had been through these nights many times before, and the guards were always able to keep the attackers out. She was more scared of being punished for falling asleep.

A young woman walked to the middle of the circle. She opened her mouth to speak, and Twig realized who she was. Anna. Her hands were shaking. She wrung them together as if trying to twist out her fear. "Father," she said softly. "I have something to say."

Twig held her breath. Newcomers were dangerous when they first arrived. They were strongly encouraged to report any wrongdoing in order to gain Adam's trust. If they didn't have anything to share, then they would be punished themselves. Many newcomers would make something up before offering themselves for punishment. The whole room knew this. Everyone waited with baited breath to see what she was going to say.

"Father, it was me. It was me who brought on these attacks."

Adam approached her. "Continue," he said.

She looked down at Adam's feet and kneeled before him.

"Speak," he said softly.

"I was just tired. So very tired. The work in the fields the last few days, the heat and lack of sleep—"

"If I didn't know better, I would think you were complaining, Anna," Adam said sweetly. He got down on one knee and raised her chin to face him. "You wouldn't be complaining, would you, dear?"

"Ada—Father—I," she took a deep breath. She was trembling with fear. "I don't mean to complain, I'm sorry. I just—I know it is my fault." She began to cry.

"Tell us," he said gently, prodding her to continue. "Whatever it is, confess it now."

"I wished I hadn't come here," she finally sobbed. "In my mind, I wished I had never come. Wished this place would burn to the ground... Forgive me. I was just so tired. I missed home. It's all so new, I—"

"That's enough." Adam silenced her. He stood back up, looking down at her with disgust. Convulsing with sobs, Anna grabbed at Adam's shoes. He was so angry, Twig was scared he might kick her in the face. Twig was wide-eyed, staring at the poor young woman. She forgot her own pain and fatigue, watching the agony that was ripping through Anna.

"So it was your treacherous thoughts that have brought the enemy out tonight?"

"Yes," Anna said quietly.

Twig's conversation with Dr. Young popped into her head. She suddenly felt suspicious. People around her began to stand. They looked angrily at Anna, ready to attack. Adam held up his hand.

"You were brave to admit this," he said to Anna. "But if we are infiltrated tonight, of course you will never be forgiven. You will be responsible for the deaths of all those you see around you." Adam let his hand drop, and people started swarming around Anna. They began to kick her, spit on her, pull her hair. Twig watched Adam walk across the dining hall and go outside again, leaving Anna to the crowd.

With a sudden impulse to help her, Twig moved to get up, but she was too dizzy to stand. What would she have done, anyway? Anna fell into a fetal position on the floor, balling her hands into fists to protect them as people stepped on her fingers. She covered her face, holding her head in her hands, curling inward as she took the abuse. Before today, Twig would have hated witnessing this, but on some level she would have thought it was a necessary evil. She had believed Adam when he said punishments like this ultimately healed people. But Dr. Young had planted a seed of doubt that was quickly taking root in Twig's head.

What if there were no attackers outside? What if these rituals, these punishments, were just meant to scare people? Just like the virus. She was tired and in pain. She didn't know what she was thinking; she couldn't trust herself right now.

But in this moment—whether it was because of what Dr. Young had said, or her lack of sleep, or the pain medication—she couldn't bear watching this beating. She began to shake and didn't try to fight it. She let her body go into tremors. Tremors of doubt, tremors of fear, tremors of anger. She let it all radiate from the core of her being until it spread through her whole body, shaking her violently. She writhed on the floor.

"Doc!" Avery screamed. "She's having a seizure!" The crowd turned away from Anna to see what was happening. "It's from her head injury; she's having a seizure!" Avery screamed. Doc ran to Twig.

"Lay her on her side," he shouted as he moved through the crowd toward them. Avery pushed Twig onto her side, making sure she didn't roll Twig onto her cast and injured arm. Twig let herself be pushed. She continued to act out the convulsions. It felt freeing, and it was working. She could tell Anna was no longer the center of attention. She felt Doc press her lips and jaw open with his long, cold fingers. He held her teeth apart. Having his hands near her mouth shocked her. She wanted him to stop, so she let the tremors subside. She kept her eyes shut as Doc and Avery tried gently to revive her.

"I'm okay," she finally whispered. "I just need to sleep. I just need sleep." Doc was putting pills in her mouth, and Avery carefully made her swallow them with water. They held her mouth shut to make sure she took them. Somewhere between faking and genuine fatigue, sleep finally overtook her.

18

Twig woke up the next morning, her head and body aching. She was in her own bed. The room was bright with warm sunlight but eerily quiet. She had the horrifying thought that everyone else had died last night, and she was the only one left. She nearly laughed with relief when Rose entered the room a moment later.

"How are you today?" Rose said kindly, her eyes red-rimmed.

"What happened last night? The attack? Is everyone okay?"

"Yes, yes. When the sun came up, Adam came and got us. They went away. Nobody was hurt."

Twig thought of Anna. "The new girl. Is she okay?" Twig asked.

"She is. Adam held her for a long time after the…" Rose paused. She lowered her voice to almost a whisper. "…the beating. He told us he was proud of her for her honesty. That she was brave." Twig nodded. She wanted to change the subject all of a sudden. The whole thing made her feel sick.

"Thanks for being here for me, Rose, but where's my mom?"

"She was on breakfast duty, but she never came back," Rose whispered, frowning. "Doc told my mother and me to take care of you for the day. That's all I know." Twig felt her stomach plummet with loneliness at hearing that her mother wasn't there.

"Oh! Speaking of Doc, you have to take your medicine, and you have to eat," Rose said suddenly. "He'll be by to check on you today." She left the room and returned with some pills, a glass of water, and a small meal of applesauce and broth. Twig was exhausted by the time she got some of the food down.

After her small meal, she fell back asleep. She was in and out of consciousness all day. Each time she woke up, she was given a pill. She asked for her mother, but Avery was never there.

When Avery did finally return to the cottage, it was night. Twig felt more awake than she had all day.

"The great goddess decides to grace us with her presence," Evelyn muttered, leaving the room as Avery came in.

"Hi," Avery said softly. "How are you? Doc said you had a good day. No more seizures." She sat on the edge of Twig's bed.

Twig frowned at her and bit her lip, which had begun to tremble. The pills and the pain were making her so weepy. "Where were you?" Twig asked quietly. She wanted to tell her mother about faking the seizure, but right now she wanted to know where she'd been all day. Why she had left her.

"I'm sorry. I just got caught up in the day," Avery said loud enough for Evelyn to hear as she smoothed out Twig's blankets in a gesture of tenderness.

You got caught up in the day?" Twig said, tears starting to fill her eyes. "How could you leave me all day, Mom?" Twig asked, starting to sniffle, feeling sorry for herself.

Avery looked around before she leaned closer to Twig and whispered, "They said I had to perform my duties today, that I couldn't stay with you. Doc said if I decided to disobey I would be punished, and that would mean even more time away from you."

"Oh, Mom," Twig groaned.

"How are you? How are you feeling? I was dying not being able to get back here to you. They made me stay after dinner and write an essay about the evils of capitalism. I'm keeping it together pretty well, wouldn't you say? If it weren't for being worried about you, I would have buckled for sure with everything that's happened in the last few days."

The last few days. Avery spoke as if everything had happened to her and not Twig, but Twig knew what she meant. Avery was doing her best, and she probably hadn't slept for forty-eight hours now that Twig thought about it. Avery wasn't used to being needed, and Twig wasn't used to needing her.

"I'm going to be really honest with you, Twig. As you know, I am not naturally maternal or great at nurturing other people, but I am trying. I want to be here for you. Please know that. Sometimes I want to be a better mother, but I get stuck. It's like I'm behind a thick curtain, and I can't get to you. I know it doesn't make sense," Avery said softly. Her face was drawn with fatigue.

Twig studied her mother. She was happy she was getting some sort of explanation. Usually Avery just retreated into one of her moods and that was that. Twig had to live with it.

Twig's anger was fading. She was relieved to have Avery back, and she was very happy that Avery had performed her duties today without getting punished.

Avery leaned very close to Twig, pretending she was going to kiss her. "When you get the cast off, I'm going to take you somewhere. No matter what happens until then, just know we have that date. Okay?"

"A date? Okay," Twig said quietly. She would have been more excited and curious, but sleep was overtaking her once again. "Mom. I have a lot of questions about a lot of things," Twig mumbled.

Avery put her finger to her lips. "Shh," she said, gently stroking Twig's forehead. Her touch was so soothing, and Twig couldn't fight the pull of sleep. Her questions would have to wait.

19

The next afternoon, Rose and Thomas came to get Twig to take her to a Meeting. She had been asleep when they came.

"Adam said it's just the thing you need." Thomas smiled at Twig.

She'd only been home from the hospital for one day. She couldn't even walk by herself yet. Rose helped her get out of bed and dressed. Twig had a bad headache.

"Can I have one of my pain pills before we go, Rose?" Rose was brushing Twig's hair. Avery and Evelyn were out performing their duties.

"Adam said no more pain pills. He said they are very addictive and that you've had enough of them," Rose said, not unkindly.

"Oh," Twig said. She took a deep breath. "Can I have a cold wash-cloth and a glass of water? Do you mind, Rose?" She could get through the pain, but she hoped he would not take her anti-seizure medication away before she finished them. The idea of a *real* seizure terrified her.

"Of course not!" Rose hopped off the bed and went to get Twig a glass of water and a washcloth.

Fifty-seven of the Family's children and teenagers, ranging from ages twelve to eighteen, sat in chairs spread out in a giant circle. Yasmine oversaw the youth Meetings. "Before we begin," she started, "Twig, how are you feeling? Adam and Doc said you are doing great."

Twig smiled and nodded. "I'm okay," she said quietly. She couldn't openly contradict Adam and Doc, but she would hardly say she felt great.

"Fantastic. Way to make a speedy recovery. So, who would like to begin today?" Yasmine asked, addressing the group.

Twig knew what was going on: Illness was often thought of as laziness, and laziness was not tolerated. People were supposed to bounce back as soon as possible. Tough it out whenever they could. Infections caused by the outside world virus needed to be treated by Adam. For everything else, any sickness that was picked up in daily Family life was something you should be able to fight off with your mind. And if you didn't, if you became really sick, you had failed. Doc always helped as much as he could with his medicines, but ultimately, the choice to be healthy was yours.

"I would." Kamela stood up. She smoothed her dress and put her dark hair behind her ears. "I have a problem with Twig. I would like to make sure that she is not carrying the outside world virus. I don't know where they took her when she fell, but I for one need to be reassured that she is not going to infect all of us. Did you see her the night of the attack? It was like she was possessed by demons." People in the group nodded, signifying they shared Kamela's concern.

"Okay, excellent. Thank you, Kamela. I'm glad you voiced something we are all probably thinking. I have verification from Adam that Twig is perfectly healthy and that her health has not been compromised in any way. She is safe to be around. Now, Twig, Kamela, please enter the circle." This time, Twig did not feel ashamed the way she had when Adam had performed healing rights on her. Instead, her mind was churning. How was the outside world virus supposed to work, anyway? Why wouldn't she have caught something at the hospital? Adam said she was safe because he had purified her a couple of nights before. So did his ceremonies serve as vaccinations, like Dr. Young had spoken about? For how long? A few days? A lifetime?

Twig stood up slowly. Her head was still pounding. She kept trying to take deep breaths to stop the pain. She rubbed her scalp with the hand that wasn't casted. Ryan came to her side. "Let me help you. Are you okay?"

"Thank you," she whispered.

"I think she will need a chair," Ryan appealed to Yasmine.

"Of course. Please bring one for yourself, too, Kamela," Yasmine said. Once the girls were seated, Yasmine looked at them expectantly. "Confessions, please. Twig, Kamela, please begin."

"That is why I am up here," Kamela said angelically. "I have been having very unkind thoughts toward my sister Twig." Kamela widened her eyes to feign innocence.

"Go on," Yasmine encouraged her.

"I think Twig thinks she is better than everyone else. I think she is a tramp who seduced my father to take him away from my mother. I am so sorry to use this language, Family. Forgive me, but I must speak the truth."

"Does anyone else share these feelings?" Yasmine posed the question to the room.

"I think Kamela should be punished for talking like that. Twig is going to be our new mother." There were so many onlookers that Twig couldn't tell who had spoken.

"I agree with Kamela." That voice was unmistakably Kamela's best friend, Schuyler. "I hate how Twig acts so innocent, but she seduces Kamela's father when she's not looking."

Before Twig could defend herself, Caleb, a pimply, fifteen-year-old boy, spoke. "Kamela is no angel, and she is definitely not as smart or as caring as Twig." Twig was surprised to hear anything remotely nice come out of Caleb's mouth. Usually his contributions to meetings were mean and provocative.

The room erupted into arguments comparing Twig to Kamela.

Suddenly it seemed as if everything about the two girls was up for discussion. Voices shouted across the room. Twig slumped into her chair and hugged herself. She pushed her nails into her arms to distract herself from the pain in her head.

"Fantastic!" Yasmine cheered. "Get it out. Get all of these feelings and resentments out." She punched her arms in the air to encourage them.

The screaming continued and escalated.

And then Kamela was the only one screaming. Standing over Twig, shrieking, "You seduced my father! How could you?" Kamela started to cry. Everyone was silent.

"Twig, I think this is a really good time for you to confess your sins," Yasmine said quietly. Twig wanted to strike out at Kamela, make her go away. But more than anything, she wanted to get back to her bed. She wanted to diffuse the situation and leave. She took more deep breaths to calm herself and then began to speak.

"Kamela, I honestly don't know what to say. I know this is hard. Hard and weird and…" Twig paused.

"Just admit what you've done, Twig. Stop acting like you're a perfect angel."

"You do sound sneaky, Twig," Yasmine said. "Just say what you're thinking. A minute ago you looked like you wanted to push Kamela away. I sense anger there. Did you want to push her away? Did you want to hit your sister, Twig? Speak the truth."

Twig looked at Kamela. She had weaved different shades of pink ribbon through her coal-black hair. It looked like something Twig would do. Twig briefly imagined the two of them stacking rocks into sculptures and crushing red clay to paint their toenails. Too bad they couldn't be friends.

"I didn't seduce your father," Twig finally said, plainly and quietly.

"You cold witch!" Kamela shouted back.

"Fine, here's my truth," Twig said. She was beginning to tremble with anger, but she kept her voice low and even. "Don't my feelings count? Don't they even though I'm not shouting them or screaming them? It doesn't make them less sincere."

The room was still silent, all eyes now on Twig.

"Continue, Twig," Yasmine said.

"I am not being sneaky. I am trying to tell Kamela that I understand how awkward this is for her. For both of us." Twig turned to face Kamela directly. "We have grown up together, and now I am supposed to marry your father. I sincerely apologize for the pain this is causing you." Kamela rolled her eyes at her. "No! Don't do that," Twig said, still quietly but with force. "He chose me. You can make up all the lies you want about me being a tramp, but he *chose* me. I did not do anything wrong."

"You must have seduced him. You must have." Kamela started to cry.

"Did you seduce Adam, Twig?" Yasmine asked.

"No!" Twig said. "I don't even know *how* to seduce someone!"

Twig thought about Leo. Had she flirted with him? If she had, she knew she had never done *that* with Adam.

"But that's just it, Twig." Kamela's voice was cooler now. "You float around here like you're better than everyone—"

Twig interrupted her. "Why would you say that?"

"She's crazy like her mother is," Schuyler chimed in.

Twig thought Schuyler was an idiot, but that comment still hurt.

"It's not that you think you're better than everyone else." Sophie was speaking now. Twig's head snapped toward her. Was she taking Kamela's side? "It's more like you—like you just act differently, beat your own drum. That's it! You march to the beat of your own drum." Sophie looked pleased with herself for finding these words. Twig quickly glanced at Ryan. He was shaking his head and looking at the ground. Twig knew Sophie meant well, but she was not helping.

"I need to talk about the other night. The night of the attack." Ryan's voice pierced the tension in the air, like a dove's song.

"Ryan, we can do that, but I'm not sure the girls are through," Yasmine said softly.

"Girls? Are you through?" Ryan asked, looking from Twig to Kamela.

"I'm done," Kamela said through tight lips.

"Yes," Twig added, thankful for his distraction.

Ryan began to speak, sharing his fears that the attackers could come back at any time. As Ryan spoke, Twig's heart went out to him. He was genuinely disturbed by the events of the other night.

But Twig was not. She didn't think there was any real threat. There was something weird about Avery's comment to Doc. She hadn't seen any cars following them when she had stolen a look. The part of her that had been conditioned to love and revere Adam hated herself for thinking he was lying, but in her heart she didn't believe there had been any real danger. She didn't know the details, but she suspected Adam had been behind it, had orchestrated it in some way.

And then there was Anna. Now that she thought about it, Twig was suspicious of Anna's confession. Anna was from the outside world. If Dr. Young was right and infection couldn't be transmitted through thought, then how could Anna have brought on an attack through her thoughts? And if Anna had just come from the outside world and knew the truth about infection, she would know that thoughts are just thoughts. Did Adam make her come to him with a false confession?

There was no way to get any answers. She would just have to push these thoughts deep down inside and forget about them if she could.

Twig turned her attention back to Ryan as Yasmine and the others asked him questions and responded to what he was saying. She wondered if Ryan fantasized about leaving. Now that she had left the compound, she could imagine there might be more possibilities for him on the outside. Maybe he could live life as a homosexual and find a partner who felt like he did. How alone he must feel at times. She wanted to reach out to him, say these things to him, but they had decided a long time ago that they wouldn't out each other at Meetings, even though that's exactly what they were supposed to do. Instead, she just kept her eyes on him, sending him silent strength.

20

Slowly, Twig began to feel better. Physically, that is. After a week, the headaches became less frequent, and her head began to clear. They hadn't taken away her anti-seizure medication when they'd stopped her pain pills. Though she'd been faking, it was nice not to live in fear of having a seizure. Doc said he was pleased that she had not had another episode and that the threat of seizure would cease after a month. She knew she wouldn't be going back to the hospital for another CT scan. She would just have to have faith that Doc knew what he was talking about.

After two weeks of a very modified schedule (which included more regular sleep than she could ever remember experiencing), she began to slowly resume life on the compound. She wasn't yet sent to work in the fields and was given a lighter schedule of classes and lectures. She helped groom the horses, especially Sapphire, as best she could but wouldn't be able to ride until her cast was off. She went to yoga and just lay quietly on her back, head propped up, breathing. Listening. Listening with new ears. Despite her best efforts to stop it, the seed of doubt inside her had managed to grow into a tree of complicated questions. It had flowered into a new habit of questioning. Questioning everything.

"The biggest problem with the United States, besides racism, is capitalism. Capitalism is its church. Capitalism disgusts me like nothing else. Citizens of the U.S. are lazy. They build nothing. And then they consume in a mad attempt to fill the emptiness inside them. For the same amount

of money that could house a family for a month, a woman of privilege will buy a pair of shoes and let an underprivileged family starve. She'll do this month after month. These people build nothing. They plant nothing. What they grow is pain, starvation, and insurmountable debt. In our Family, if one person eats, everyone eats. If one person starves, everyone starves. We are a collective."

Ever since she'd returned from the hospital, Twig noticed she was having trouble listening to Adam's voice on the intercom. She found herself analyzing what he was saying. He spoke about the United States a lot. And it was never good. Leo and Hazel were from the United States. They were unlike anyone she had ever known. Would Hazel buy a pair of shoes instead of feeding a family?

In the few weeks that passed after her accident, Twig noticed the Family begin to treat her differently. Everywhere she went, people congratulated her on her engagement. They told her she was truly blessed. That she was a blessing herself. They went quiet when she entered the room, a little like they did for Adam. Some people even seemed a little scared of her.

Other people were angry. She received little shoves here and there. Little insults. Subtle, hardly noticeable. Nothing she could quite confront them about. Not that she would. But she could feel their anger.

During those few weeks, Twig felt isolated. She still hadn't had the chance to really talk to Avery, to ask her any one of the questions on her growing list. There just wasn't an opportunity. They were never together for long enough. If Twig had a little pocket of time, Avery was nowhere to be found. If they were at the cottage at the same time, Evelyn was there, too. She was comforted by Avery's promise of their date. She might be able to talk to her then.

* * *

Finally, the day arrived for Twig's cast to come off. Twig sat in Doc's waiting area, scanning the room as she waited for him to come out of his office. The walls were decorated with pencil drawings of anatomy. Twig looked at the images and thought about drawing. She used to draw more. All she had available was graphite. Sometimes she would create dust from leaves and flowers to add color, but she had stopped doing that long ago and started her "paintings." Twig wondered where these drawings came from and what Doc's life had been like before he came to the Family. Doc's lore was missing from the Family Tree. Twig had never really thought about it until now, but Adam had never told Doc's story.

After Adam had met Farriss and Yasmine, they had set up a small Family unit in New York City. Twig liked to think of the three of them there. Adam said they had lived in a place called Greenwich Village. Yasmine would describe wonderful cafés that had chairs on the sidewalks. She said she'd loved to watch people go by while they indulged in French pastries and big cups of coffee or hot chocolate. Twig could picture a young Yasmine. She imagined her in a pair of old jeans with a yellow silk scarf braided into her wild afro of dark, curly hair. A city-girl version of Sophie.

Adam had met Tina in New York. She'd been a journalism student at one of the universities there. Sadness fell over Twig as she thought about Adam and Tina, recalling how they met. Adam used to drape Tina with compliments about her intelligence and political awareness, telling her how impressed he was by her. Tina would blush. She was genuinely in love with Adam and always had been. In fact, it seemed as if they had both been so in love with each other. What happened? Twig wondered if she herself would have fallen in love with Adam if they had been the same age when they met; if Twig had been a graduate student in Manhattan, had her own apartment and her own life; if Adam had draped her with compliments about her intelligence rather than grabbing her neck. *"You are mine now."*

"All right, Twig. Come on in. Let's take a look at that arm." Doc had opened the door to his office.

Twig looked around. Usually, a woman named Maya came to get her when Doc was ready for her. Maya was always in the room during examinations. Twig had never really been alone with Doc.

"Where's Maya?" she inquired.

"I needed her to run an errand. She should be back any minute now," Doc answered, waving Twig toward his office. "Do you want us to wait for her?"

There was something in Doc's tone that made Twig think the only answer was "no." She would have preferred Maya be there. She had so many questions about Adam and the Family, and Doc was part of those questions. Having someone else there would have made her more comfortable.

Twig tried to smile. "No. It's okay. I'm ready to get this off and get back to yoga."

Doc nodded. "Of course. No downward dogs for you for a while, though. Don't put weight on your arm for another month."

Twig sat on the cold metal table covered in white paper. She was aware of Doc watching her.

"Can you take off your sweater?"

"I can just push up the sleeve. Is that okay?" Twig answered casually. Now she really wished Maya were here.

"I'm worried I'll cut your sweater when I cut the cast off."

"Oh," Twig replied. "Of course." She needed Doc's help because the arm of her sleeve was a bit too narrow. He came close to her and helped her work the sweater over her cast. Twig was aware of her arms and neck, which were all suddenly exposed. Doc's hands were freezing, and he smelled faintly of medicine.

Doc quickly became absorbed in his work as he used a pair of surgical scissors to cut off the layers of fiberglass and plaster in her cast. She no longer felt his gaze upon her.

"That was a lot of excitement, wasn't it?" Doc continued to cut and did not lift his eyes as he spoke. "We never really had a talk about it."

"What's that?" asked Twig.

"The announcement of your engagement, the accident, and then the hospital." Doc continued to look down.

"Oh. Yes. Yes, it was," Twig answered.

Doc stopped cutting for a moment and looked up at Twig. He parted his thin lips and smiled.

"How are you feeling about your engagement, Twig?" Doc finished cutting off the cast and carried it to the small silver trashcan across the room. Twig hurried back into her sweater before looking at her wrist; it was pale and had a purplish-green hue. She held it gently in her other hand and turned it over tenderly. "Just needs a little sun." Doc had returned and was by her side. He looked down at her.

"I'm okay. My head is spinning a bit—figuratively speaking." Twig was trying to be genuine, but this was the first time she had spoken to Doc since she had talked to Dr. Young. She hadn't even seen Adam since the night they'd left the hospital. He hadn't been around lately, and she had been glad for this. She didn't know how it would feel to be around him with the way she had been lately—so full of doubt and questions. She feared he would sense it.

Doc laughed. "How is your head, by the way?"

"It's been good. No headaches for the last three days," Twig answered. Everything in her wanted to ask Doc about her follow-up scan, the one Dr. Young had insisted occur after a month, but she was scared. The question sat in her throat, unable to come out. Would Doc see the question as her questioning his judgment?

"So tell me about this spinning." Doc motioned for Twig to join him and headed toward a large oak table that served as his desk. He took a seat in a big chair behind the desk. The chair made him seem even taller and skinnier. Twig sat in one of the chairs facing him.

Twig knew she couldn't divulge too much, but it might be nice to talk to someone about things and maybe get some perspective—step back into the Family process of openness a little bit. Hiding her feelings all the time was exhausting. Maybe Doc was genuinely concerned about her. He had been very helpful the night of her accident. Of course, she could never talk to him about what she had learned from Dr. Young. If he knew that she harbored any doubt about Adam's teachings, she would be punished. If he knew she suspected that he and Adam might be liars—well, she didn't even want to think about what they would do to her. Not only that, but she could be seen as a threat. What would happen if they *were* lying, and she exposed the truth? She doubted that anyone would believe her, but what if they did? Would the other members of the Family simply feel betrayed? Would they try to leave? No—they wouldn't believe her. Twig wasn't even sure what she believed herself. Many of the Family members had joined the collective after years on the outside. Wouldn't some of them know? Maybe they'd tucked the truth away. Twig couldn't help thinking that maybe it was Dr. Young who was in the wrong.

But Twig *could* talk to Doc about her engagement, at least in a way. "Well, getting married seems so adult," Twig said, testing the waters a bit.

Doc nodded. "Indeed. And where do you see yourself in terms of adulthood?" Twig frowned. Doc considered for a moment. "Let me say it another way," he added. "If life is a big journey that begins in childhood and moves through adulthood and beyond, where are you on that journey right now?"

Twig thought about Doc's question. It was an interesting way of framing what she'd been feeling lately.

"I'm a citizen of childhood with my bags packed, and I'm about to cross the border into adulthood. No, wait, that's not quite accurate. I've taken trips into adulthood, met the people, eaten some of the food, but I still live in the other village. Maybe something like that." Twig shrugged shyly.

Doc's eyes remained sober, but he smiled. Twig wasn't sure if he was just socially awkward or if he was thinking one thing and saying another.

"Okay, and how do you like this new village and its people and its ways?"

Twig took a deep breath. The adults in her life all seemed a bit nuts lately, if she really thought about it.

"It seems complicated."

"How so?" Doc pressed. This is what he was looking for. Any kind of criticism or doubt. She had to be careful.

"Well, one minute Adam is happily married to Tina, and the next she's supposed to step aside, and I'm supposed to marry him." Twig knew she was out on a limb here.

"And how do you feel about that?" Doc's voice was deceptively neutral, as if he had no investment in how she answered either way, but Twig knew better. Doc worshipped Adam. She put her guard back up.

"Well, Adam knows best, so I feel good about it," Twig said. "It just takes some getting used to."

"Right. Yes of course. Good, good." Doc held his chin between his index finger and thumb. "Now, Twig, what does marriage mean to you?"

The question took Twig by surprise. So much so that she answered honestly, without reservation.

"It means love. Two people who love each other decide to join together in order to pursue and create the life they want to live, together. It means the power of two."

"That's a very romantic vision of love for someone who has grown up seeing arranged marriages." Doc's tone was curious, not critical.

"Is it?" Twig responded. It had just come out of her naturally. But what he said made sense. And now it made sense why her engagement didn't feel right any longer. There was no choice for her, and at this point, no love. Now that she thought about it, she couldn't imagine ever loving Adam like *that*. In her vision, two people created their life together. Adam had already created his life and now was forcing her to fit into it.

"Just one more thing, Twig." Doc was drumming the fingertips of his long, pale hands on the table. Twig was relieved he wasn't pursuing his current line of questioning.

"Sure," Twig said.

"What about San Jose, the hospital?"

"What about it?"

"The boy you were talking to."

Twig felt her stomach clench. Leo.

"Adam already talked to me about that," Twig said quietly.

"I know, I know. Humor me."

"Well, I met him and his sister in the hallway. They were nice," Twig answered.

"That's all? Nice?" Doc furrowed his silver eyebrows, raising one slightly above the other. "Did that surprise you?"

"I was pretty out of it. I didn't really think about it," Twig lied.

Doc chuckled softly and pulled back in his narrow seat. "Okay, Twig. Okay. I think that's enough for today. Is there anything else you want to talk to me about? Anything else about that night? Now's the time."

Oh, yes! One more thing! I almost forgot… I want to talk to you about how disease is really transmitted. I want to talk to you about the cellphone Adam carries and who he called on it. His watch and why he had one.

"I'm good. Thank you, Doc," Twig said instead. "And thanks for this." She held up her wrist. She started to get up out of the chair. Doc remained seated.

"You're welcome, Twig. Now, remember what we talked about. You can always come to me."

Twig walked out of Doc's cottage and let out a big sigh. She was glad to be out of there. If she hurried, she could make meditation before the Meeting. She needed it. As she quickened her pace to cross the compound to the meditation room, she passed Maya working in the garden. Twig put her newly exposed wrist behind her back. She didn't want Maya to know she'd just been to see Doc. She stopped and cupped a big purple orchid to her nose, inhaling its perfume.

"I love this smell," she said.

Maya stopped working for a moment and pushed her hat back on her head.

"I know. They are beautiful. I can still picture how you did Rose's hair for her wedding. We should all go around every day with flowers in our hair like that, dontchya think, honey?"

"Yes," Twig agreed enthusiastically. "No nursing our wounds today?" she asked casually as she fingered a vine of tomatoes.

"Nope. Doc gave me the day off. Thought I'd just work out here and enjoy the sunshine for a change."

"Sounds wonderful." Obviously, Doc hadn't wanted Twig to know that Maya wasn't coming into his office today.

Twig wasn't surprised.

21

The plan was to meet Avery at the stables. Before they'd gone to bed the night before, Avery whispered to meet her there after lunch. Avery would secure permission from Farriss for the two of them to ride out together. Twig didn't know where Avery would take them, but as she walked toward the stables, she realized that she felt better than she had in a while. Her belly was full from lunch, it was hot but not impossibly humid, and while her wrist looked small and weak, it actually felt fine.

When Twig reached the stables, no one was around. The air was moist but not unpleasant. She went to Sapphire's stall to wait for Avery. Adam's voice crept through the sawdust and the hay.

"They play God. They use drugs and technology to decide when and if to have children. I know this is disgusting, but you need to know these things, Family. They go into the mother's protective, sacred womb, and they kill the unborn! You need to know what lies outside of our perfect world."

"You look good, Sapphy." Twig ran her hand gently down Sapphire's velvet muzzle and put her head on the horse's massive neck. Sapphire pressed back into Twig, returning the hug. "Farriss is taking good care of you."

"Hi, Twig." Avery had walked up behind her.

"Hi, Mom." Twig cupped Sapphire's muzzle between her hands, and Sapphire licked her with her big, pink tongue.

"Ready?"

"Ready. Where are we going?" Twig whispered.

"I'll tell you on the way. Come on."

"Are we still riding?"

"Definitely. It's a ways away, and we can use the horses as an alibi if we need one."

"Alibi?" Twig croaked. "Are we doing something we shouldn't be, Mom?"

"We are."

Twig frowned. "Maybe we should think this through…"

"It's okay. I'm going to take Bill Evans," she said, pointing to a horse a few stalls down from Sapphire.

The name made Twig giggle and distracted her. "I can never get used to that name."

"Come on. I'll tell you where it comes from." The two women walked the horses out of their sleeping stalls and saddled them.

"Just act natural," Avery said, looking around in her seat as they walked the horses away from the stables and into the forest.

"Okay," Twig said, feeling very unnatural all of a sudden.

To distract her, Avery started speaking. "I'll tell you why this horse is named Bill Evans. There once was a jazz musician named Miles Davis. He made an album called *Kind of Blue*. If you cared about jazz music at all, you knew it." Avery stopped speaking for a moment, looking wistful. Twig wished she knew what memories were running through Avery's head. She wished she could watch the movie in her mother's mind for a moment.

"What's jazz?"

"Eek. How do I describe jazz? Hmm…" Avery squinted her eyes. "It started in the south, the southern United States, in the black communities. It's a little bluesy—which means nothing to you, of course…. It's earthy and rhythmic and about improvisation, and it's filled with horns and pianos, and…I'm not doing it justice at all."

"It's okay," Twig said. "It sounds interesting. Did you like it?"

"Yes, very much. It takes incredible talent to play jazz music, and there's a whole *feeling* that goes with it. It can be moody and sexy or complicated and intellectual. Anyway, Bill Evans played piano on *Kind of Blue*. He's an amazing musician. A poet, really."

"So Farriss named a horse after him?"

"Farriss loved jazz and knew everything about it."

"Why do you think Adam doesn't want us to listen to jazz?"

They were deeper into the rainforest now. Twig felt her dress begin clinging to her as the air became wet and heavy. Still, she felt like she could breathe better. It had been a month since she'd been out here. She'd missed the colors, the textures. Avery seemed to be considering Twig's question, or how much she wanted to offer in answer to it.

"It's too provocative. Or he thinks it is," Avery finally said in response to Twig's question. Then she laughed. "It's ridiculous. I mean I can see his point—rock makes you want to get it on."

"Mom!"

"Sorry." Avery was laughing. "I just haven't had a conversation about art in so long. Guess I got a bit carried away. Anyway, maybe jazz is too much about individualism and improvisation for Adam. Although, it requires so much collaboration, too. Who knows? Really, who knows?"

"I didn't know you knew so much about music, Mom. That's really cool." Twig thought of Leo and Hazel and their iPod nanos and dancing.

"Well, I always loved music. I don't know that I really know so much about it. Not like some people." Avery's wistful look returned. This time Twig wondered *whom* Avery was thinking about.

They rode on in silence for a while, both absorbed in thought. They maintained a good clip.

"We're here."

Twig looked up, sorry she'd been daydreaming when she could have been asking Avery more questions. They were standing outside what looked like a tunnel made of overlapping and interlacing tree branches. The foliage was dense and the tunnel wet with vegetation.

"Where are we?" Twig asked.

"I want you to meet someone," Avery answered.

"*Someone?* Who? I don't understand."

Avery took a deep breath. She seemed nervous. "Look, you know I've had a hard time, Twig."

Twig nodded.

"Well, I wouldn't have made it if it weren't for this person."

"Mom, what are you talking about? Where are we? What is this?" Images flashed in Twig's mind: Family members screaming at her, her hair in the blades of Adam's silver scissors. Being locked in a room with no food or company for days. "Maybe we should just turn back." Twig was scared.

"Just follow me." Avery said.

They steered their horses toward the tunnel and disappeared into the strange dripping world of greenery and twisted foliage.

22

The tunnel led to an open field. The ground was yellow with a combination of flowers, leaves, and weeds. The field was expansive and bright with sunlight. The forest seemed to part for this land of yellow and light. A small house made of dark, stained wood and large glass windows stood at the end of the field. It looked like a piece of art, modest but stunning. It was highly stylized compared to the white clapboard cottages where the Family lived.

Avery spoke first. "This is where I go—where I have gone for a long time."

Twig gasped. "It's beautiful."

"You sneak out in the mornings. Well, I sneak out when I can, too. And this is where I go when I do."

"And sometimes you get caught." It made sense now why Avery was always getting punished.

"Yes, but they never know where I've gone. They just know I've not been where I'm supposed to be. There aren't many cracks to slip through in our lives, as you know. But to this day, they don't know I come here."

"Do they know this place exists so close to the compound?"

"No," Avery said plainly.

"How could this be here? How did you find it? Who lives here?" Questions spilled out of Twig. She was equally shocked by the beauty and strangeness of the place as she was by finding out her mother had some sort of secret life. "Do you have a lover?"

Avery laughed. "I wish. No. Come on, she can help me explain."

She? What was going on? Avery had a relationship with someone from the outside world? A person who lived almost under the nose of the compound?

"I will say one thing," Avery began. "When Adam said he was going to marry you, I felt helpless. You're just a kid. You're so defenseless against him. I've been wracking my brain trying to think of something I can do to help you. Openly defying Adam was not helpful," Avery gestured to her shaved head, which was covered in a light layer of stubble, "so I'm bringing you here."

"How will bringing me here help me?"

"I don't know that it will. I just had to do something."

Twig didn't say anything in response. She was stunned. She followed Avery as they walked their horses to the back of the house. There was another, smaller sort of cottage and a corral where they left Sapphire and Bill Evans, their noses submerged in giant silver bowls of water. Twig followed Avery along a path that led to the back door of the house. Either side of the path was flanked by a small, well-tended vegetable garden. Twig noted that whoever owned the house had a strong sense of color. Even though the materials from the house didn't seem local, they complemented the woods.

"Mom, is this safe?" Twig suddenly thought of Adam's teachings about the outside world, the people in it. A few weeks of doubt couldn't erase a lifetime of his preaching.

"Yes. We are safe here." Avery's voice was tender. "I wouldn't take you somewhere that wasn't safe. I mean—" Avery paused.

"What?" Twig pressed.

"Nothing. I didn't mean anything, Twig. Come on." Something hung heavy in the air between them, but Twig decided to let it go.

Avery knocked gently on the door, then turned the knob and walked in. She was obviously welcome here. Suddenly, she stopped and turned around. Twig nearly bumped into her. Avery grabbed Twig's good wrist.

"Twig, you have to promise you will never tell another soul about any of this."

"Okay." Twig nodded in agreement.

"Twig, you have to know how serious and how dangerous this is."

"Dangerous? I thought you just said it was safe."

"It's safe here, yes. But by bringing you here, I'm putting you, this person, and myself in jeopardy. But I think it's important. I wouldn't have brought you here otherwise."

Twig hesitated. This was too much. What if Adam was right? What if Avery had been deceived by this person? And even if Adam was wrong, what would he do to them if he found out? Twig wanted to get back to the safety and sureness of the compound.

"Please, Twig, I'm sorry. I'm confusing you. It's okay. You just can't tell anyone." Avery paused. "It's just that he can be extremely persuasive, Twig."

"Who?"

"Adam. He can be tricky and very convincing. I don't think you know exactly who you're dealing with when it comes to Adam." Avery took a deep breath. Twig copied her.

The back door opened into a big kitchen. The delicious smell of something baking filled the air, piquing Twig's curiosity. It didn't smell like the food they cooked on the compound. These smells had colors to them.

Twig leaned around Avery to look into the room. A large wooden table with a metal top sat to their right. It was littered with large books with glossy paper covers and stacks of magazines. The floor was covered in some sort of gray concrete and mopped to a shine. Heavy, colorful woven rugs were thrown here and there. On the other side of the kitchen sat two armchairs covered in a bright pink-orange fabric with oversize white roses embroidered throughout. Cerulean-blue silk pillows were placed on each of the chairs. Yellow and purple wildflowers sat in a bowl on a small table between the chairs. Twig gasped in astonishment. She wanted to run her hands over everything. It was perfect. Beautiful and cozy. How could all of this be here? It was so close to the world she knew, but so different.

"Twig?"

Twig's fears were disappearing by the second, the room was so inviting. "Can we go in?"

Avery eyed her. "Gran?" she called out.

"Coming, darling. I'll be right there," answered a voice from somewhere inside the house.

Avery looked back at Twig and smiled nervously. "I'm actually excited about this. I can't believe it's happening. I've wanted you two to meet for so long."

Twig felt like she was dreaming. This whole scene was so unbelievable, so strange.

A moment later, the most elegant woman Twig had ever seen entered the room. Twig judged her to be somewhere in her late sixties. Her hair was pearl white and cut into a neat bob that framed her face. Her eyes were extraordinarily large and black. Looking at this woman, a familiar feeling, one of almost déjà vu, passed over Twig.

She was dressed in a crisp, navy blouse and dark-blue jeans tucked into amber brown riding boots. Tortoiseshell bracelets dangled from her wrists. She was taller than both Twig and Avery, and thin, but not frail. She looked at Twig and smiled warmly.

"Twig."

"Hi," Twig said shyly. Who was this person? How could she live so close to the compound, but be so totally different? How had Twig never come upon her before?

"Twig, this is Gran. My, well, my savior...in a way."

The woman laughed at this. "Oh, Avery. Don't be silly. You flatter me." She crossed over to Twig. Her bangles made music when she extended her hand.

Twig looked at Avery, who nodded. Twig thought again of what Dr. Young had said about disease. Like Leo and Hazel, this woman looked perfectly healthy, vibrant even. Twig accepted Gran's hand. Copper. Warm. The hand of someone who'd been through a lot and decided to see the beauty in life—to take the good with the bad. Gran's color was copper. They held hands for an extra beat and looked at one another. Gran's eyes began to glisten.

"My God, it's good to meet you, darling."

"I don't know who you are, but it's really good to meet you, too." Twig laughed. "I'm not going to lie, this is strange." But somehow, Twig didn't feel afraid. She felt excited.

"I understand," Gran said thoughtfully. "It's not everyday you meet an old recluse in the woods. Why don't we have a little something to eat before we talk?"

Twig and Avery nodded. Gran guided them into the two armchairs. Twig examined the silk pillow. The fabric was exotic. A memory of the night she'd had to bathe Anna pierced through her head suddenly, making her feel slightly nauseated. That silky purple underwear—the only other time she had seen fabric like this. She shook off the memory and looked again at Gran's pillows. She wished she had fabric like this to work with. She wondered where it came from. It was how she imagined textiles from Morocco might look. Twig wondered if it had been hard for Yasmine and Farriss to leave a place with treasures like this.

Gran brought them tea in bright-green cups lined with gold. Twig felt like she'd fallen into some wonderland of color and texture. She was surrounded by glass and wood. The late afternoon light poured in through the kitchen windows in golden and lavender rays.

The three women sat quietly eating small plates of black beans that tasted of lime juice and some spice Twig didn't know. Gran also served a sweet corn mixture that was full of tomatoes and cilantro. It was delicious.

"Avery, how are you today, darling?" Gran spoke first.

Twig looked at her mother.

"I'm okay, but we don't have that much time, and I want to explain things to Twig."

"Of course," Gran answered.

"How do you two know each other? How did you meet?" Twig asked quickly.

Avery took a deep breath in and let it out slowly. She looked at Twig with her piercing gray eyes. "Let's start with why I've brought you here. That's the easiest thing to explain."

"Okay," Twig said gently.

"When Adam said he was going to marry you, I was blindsided. I still can't believe it." Avery paused. She seemed paralyzed with anger at the memory.

"Avery," Gran leaned forward and touched Avery's hand lightly, encouraging her to continue.

Avery drew in another long breath. "Our world has been so shrouded in secrecy. I'm not used to talking to you, Twig."

For some reason, that hurt.

"I mean talking *openly*," Avery backpedaled, "without thinking about everything I say. I'm always worried a piece of information will put you at risk."

Twig knew what she meant. She felt the same way, and if she was honest with herself, it was why she kept hesitating to tell Avery about her conversation with Dr. Young.

"Like I told you before, I felt helpless," Avery continued. "Speaking to Adam on your behalf did not work. Introducing you to Gran, though it's a risk, feels like the only thing I can do. The only thing I can do to…" Avery stopped, considering her words. "To help you find your way."

"Find my way?"

"I can't say much more. Gran has helped me and cared for me when all *the Family* offered was reproach."

Twig had never heard Avery say "the Family" with such disdain.

"She does everything from making sure I eat to washing my hair." Avery laughed nervously, her eyes darkening only slightly at the mention of her hair.

"Mom, this is crazy." Twig stopped and looked at Gran. "I don't mean to be rude, but I just don't understand. How did you two even meet?"

"That's a story for another time, Twig." Avery waved away the question. "I just thought that maybe we'd leave someday. Somehow. Maybe when you turned eighteen."

Twig's eyebrows shot up. *Leave?* She felt a strange mix of nausea and hope. Her mind flashed back to the hospital: Avery running, pushing Twig's wheelchair down the glowing white hallway.

"But now that's not possible. Adam wants you. He's not going to let you go."

"Leave, Mom? Why didn't you ever mention that to me before? Why didn't you talk to me before?" Twig was getting heated. It was a lot to take in.

"I couldn't. I—" Avery looked overwhelmed. "You just have to take some things on faith right now. I can't say any more."

"You sound like him. Just now, you sounded just like him," Twig said sadly. She wanted an explanation. A real explanation of where she was, who Gran was, how she and Avery had met.

Avery became as still as a stone. Twig immediately regretted what she had said. She felt Avery's pain in her own chest. She always had to walk on eggshells with her more than everyone else, and Avery was her mother.

"Mom," Twig started to backpedal, but Avery stood up and started to walk away from her.

"I'm fine, Twig. This was a mistake." She was obviously not fine. Her shoulders held a closed-off energy, and she looked as if Twig had stuck her. Like she might cry. Avery was just so sensitive, and Twig never knew what would hit her the wrong way and cause her to freeze up like this. But there were other times when she didn't seem sensitive at all. She seemed tough and capable of taking care of herself. She was a landmine, and Twig still didn't know how to traverse the territory with ease. Twig looked to Gran.

"Listen." Gran stood up and walked over to Avery, who was looking out the window awkwardly. "What do you think about giving Twig her present? We can talk more the next time you two come." Twig had noticed the light getting darker. They would have to go soon.

"I think that's a great idea." Avery nodded and brightened a bit, turning back to them.

"A present?" Twig added softly. Presents were a bit of an alien concept to Twig. The Family did not exchange gifts, but that didn't mean she wasn't happy to get one.

She was calming down. She felt bad for what she had said to Avery, comparing her to Adam. And truth be told, this was all very exciting.

Avery and Gran led Twig back outside, bringing carrots for the horses. It was warm and sticky outdoors compared to the cool of the kitchen. Twig felt something bite her arm and brushed off a small bug. Gran commented that she was dressed too warmly. She said you get colder when you get older.

"Well, first you get warmer," she laughed. "Then you get colder." Twig thought she must be referring to menopause. They had learned about it in school when they were taught about a woman's menstrual cycle.

There weren't any elderly people in the Family, yet—the collective was still too new. Doc was the oldest member, and he was only in his early fifties. When Twig thought about it, she realized some women would start to get hot flashes very soon. Rose's mother, Evelyn, came to mind. And Tina.

Gran skipped ahead to the small house near the horses. She opened the door and waved them in. As Twig entered, she gasped.

It was an art studio—and not just any art studio. The space was an airy, open room. The wall that faced the back of the property was practically all glass, like the windows in Gran's kitchen. Bookshelves containing every art supply Twig could imagine, most of which she had never actually seen, lined the walls. Baskets held tubes of paint, sketchbooks in every size, blue-and-white china cups filled with brushes. Twig held her hands to her mouth. She'd never really painted before. Not with *actual* paint. There were cups filled with pencils and markers. It was so organized. Twig squealed. There was a whole shelf just for different kinds of paper.

Near the window sat an easel, and at its feet lay a big roll of canvas.

"My friend Daniel will teach you how to stretch the canvas for your paintings. I haven't got a clue." Gran was standing at the door with Avery. They were both smiling. "He can teach you about the supplies, too."

"Do you like it, honey?" Avery had her lower lip between her teeth, a nervous gesture.

"Like it?" Twig began to spin around with her arms in the air. "I LOVE IT!" She ran toward Gran and Avery and threw her arms around them. They laughed. Her joy was infectious.

"I love you, Mom!" Twig blurted out. Avery laughed, but Twig felt her mother stiffen a little bit beneath her arms. Big displays of affection were not Avery's thing, but Twig didn't care. She didn't feel hurt. She knew Avery was trying. The gift of the art studio said everything.

"I hate to do this, but we really need to get back."

Twig snapped out of her reverie. Of course they did. How long had they been gone? She looked outside. Her happiness had distracted her, but now her worry and anxiety came back full force. She heard the *click click* of Gran's bangles as Gran pushed up her sleeve, revealing a thin black watch.

"It's four thirty."

"We'll *just* make dinner. I shouldn't have let us cut it this close."

Twig sighed. "I don't want to go…"

"You'll come back. As soon as you can."

They said their good-byes. Twig embraced Gran one more time. She smelled of lemons and something wonderful and spicy—maybe her shampoo or soap.

"Come on, Twig." Avery's voice was serious now. "We've got to get back on time."

Gran stood by while Avery and Twig mounted the horses. They waved good-bye, and the two women rode across the yellow field toward the tunnel of leaves and branches. When they emerged on the other side of the tunnel, it began to rain.

Twig's muscles tightened. She felt a flash of fear, like she had the moment before her accident.

"Are you okay, Twig?" Avery called after her.

Twig felt her stomach dropping. She almost felt dizzy with fear.

I've been riding my whole life in the rain, she thought to herself. *Sometimes it rains every day for months. I've got to get a grip. Think about the new studio. Think about the paint. If we miss dinner call, I could lose all of it.*

"I'm okay," Twig called back to Avery.

"You sure?"

"I'm sure."

Twig kicked her heels into Sapphire, and the horse broke into a run.

123

23

When they got back to the stables, the rain had stopped. They knew they made it before dinner because Farriss was still there cleaning up. Twig and Avery slid off their horses, relieved.

"Cutting it close, ladies," Farriss admonished them, looking in the direction of one of the stalls.

Adam emerged. "There you are, ladies," he added with levity. He was in a good mood.

Twig sucked in a breath but gave him her brightest smile. Her heart had begun to pound in her chest at the sight of him.

"I'm sorry! We were having so much fun." Did he know where they were? Was there a chance that he may have followed them? Her brain ran wild trying to figure out some excuse.

"Good, I'm glad. I'm glad to see both of you out and about. I hear you've made a complete recovery, Twig," Adam said. There was nothing suspicious or angry in his voice. Twig felt herself relax a bit. Maybe he really believed that they had just been out for a ride. Why wouldn't he? In a way, going to see Gran was not so different from her morning excursions. The only difference was that the stakes were higher.

"Yes, I have." Twig feigned lightness by holding up her wrist and twirling it. "I just have to go a bit easy on it."

This was the first time Twig had seen Adam since the night they had returned from the hospital. He looked good, rested. She had never wondered before where Adam went when he went away. He had been so distant, so public, before announcing their engagement. But their lives were tied together now. She wanted to ask him where he had been, but she didn't dare.

"Twig, may I walk you to dinner? I want to ask you something," Adam asked sweetly.

Twig forced herself not to look at Avery as Adam helped her off Sapphire. Twig noticed how careful he was with her. He touched her as if she might break. When Adam was sure she was steady on her feet, he let her go. Twig smiled at him, appreciative of his tenderness. Her fear that he had followed them began to dissolve. How do you make sense of loving and worshipping someone your whole life, only to find out they might be a liar or a fake? Can you love someone and hate them at the same time? Love them and doubt them?

Avery walked off without saying good-bye. Adam took Twig's arm and led her away from the stables and back toward the compound.

"So how are you, kiddo?" Adam asked.

"I'm pretty good." Every time Twig opened her mouth, her heart beat faster. Did he know where they'd been?

"Yeah?" Adam was charming. There was something about being next to him that made Twig begin to soften, relax just a bit, let her guard down. This was exactly what Avery had warned her against.

"Yeah." Twig smiled sweetly. Could she walk this line? Get to know him and keep her guard up at the same time? Be herself on some level but watchful on another? Twig tried to determine his color, but it was a blur, as always. That must mean something.

"What are you thinking about?"

"What? Right now?" The question startled Twig.

"Right now. What are you thinking about?"

"Your color." Out of all of the thoughts in her head, this one she could say out loud.

"My color?"

"Yeah. I can't figure out your color. You're a mystery to me."

He grinned. "Explain." He had a gorgeous smile.

"Well, when I get a sense of a person, it manifests in a color. Sometimes I get it instantly," she thought of Gran earlier, "and sometimes it comes later. But with you, it just hasn't come."

"I like that. And it makes sense that I can't be made."

"Made?"

"You can't blow my cover. It's cop terminology."

"Cop?"

Adam stopped walking for a moment and looked at Twig. "You're so young," he marveled. "I mean, you are only seventeen, of course, but I mean something else. We've kept you so pure. You are not corrupted by the media of the outside world."

Twig felt slightly uncomfortable. "Can you explain, Father? 'Cop'? 'Made'?"

Adam tossed his dark head of hair back and laughed lightly. He was in a *really* good mood. "A cop is a policeman—a enforcer of the law. When a policeman goes undercover and someone discovers his true identity, people say he was 'made.'"

"So are you undercover?" she asked with much more confidence than she felt.

"Ah. Touché." Adam began to walk again, folding his arm around Twig's. "Am I undercover?" Adam thought for a moment. When he spoke, his tone was serious. "Twig, you're going to be my wife. You're going to see sides of me no one else sees. But I've also got a Family to lead. I'll be honest: there are parts of me you won't see, that no one will ever see. That's the reality of leading."

"That sounds a bit lonely," she answered honestly. It also sounded ominous—not exactly her vision of marriage. She felt chills on the back of her neck.

"I'm okay, but you are a dear to care." He winked at her. "Listen. We can talk about this more another time. I know that sounded a bit scary and mysterious. Don't worry," he smiled. "Mostly, I am an open book."

Open book. No one she knew was an open book. Not even her own mother.

"So listen, what I *do* want to talk to you about today is this: I want you to go on the weekly supply runs with Thomas," he said, his beatific grin spreading across his face. "Are you pleased? This means I am trusting you with a great deal of responsibility."

"What?" Twig was shocked. Thomas went into Turrialba once a week to get staples they couldn't grow or make themselves.

"You've been outside of the compound now, Twig. I know you can handle yourself."

Twig nodded but didn't say anything. Did he know about her talk with Dr. Young? Had he set up that conversation to test her? Was this part of that test? She should say something right now. This was her chance. But what if he hadn't planned Twig's conversation with the doctor, and Dr. Young had acted of his own accord? She should ask Adam some question about the outside world virus, show him her fear of it. Except…her fear was wearing off. Too many people she had met lately were not infected, and they lived outside of the Family. "Is it safe?" she blurted out. "To go outside the compound that much?"

Adam smiled warmly. "My little lamb, I will prepare you. We will keep you safe. You dear, little thing. Of course this would scare you. I should have been more sensitive." He looked at her with adoration. "Yes, you will be safe. We will take every precaution to ensure your mental, physical, and spiritual safety. You will be my soldier, going out into the world on my behalf. I'm proud of you, Twig."

Twig let out a big sigh of fake relief. She laughed tentatively along with him, hoping she was convincing. She noticed now how he dictated the tone and mood of any conversation.

Turrialba. Twig began to contemplate the possibilities. She might run into Leo if she went to Turrialba. She had thought about Leo a lot since she met him at the hospital. The truth was, she couldn't stop thinking about him.

"See, the thing is, Twig—" He had become serious, his mirth evaporated. "If you're going to be my wife, I need to know I can trust you. What better way to have you prove your devotion to me than to send you into the outside world each week—and have you return to me every time?" Adam put his arm around Twig's shoulders and squeezed. "Can I trust you, Twig?"

"Of course," she said automatically.

"Good."

Could he trust her? Her loyalty, which had always been to the Family, to Adam, was splitting off in various directions. It was becoming apparent that loyalty to Avery meant peeling off from Adam, at least a little bit. And Twig felt her own agenda forming. She wanted to see Leo again. She wanted to talk to Hazel, listen to their music, see their clothes. She wanted to go to Gran's as soon as possible and try out all of those art supplies. Did she really no longer want to marry Adam? She thought of all she would be turning her back on and the extreme punishment she would incur if she decided to take a stand against him.

This was a dangerous dance. She would never completely know Adam—he had said as much. There would always be secrets between them. So perhaps he could trust her about as much as she could trust him.

Adam took Twig's hand in his. "Is this the one you broke?"

"Yes."

Adam held her wrist steadily in one hand and stroked her palm with the other. The roots of the Family were in his touch. People would follow this man. He exuded power and authority. His touch made her want to curl up and go to sleep. She thought about the electricity of Leo's touch. How it made her feel excited and alive.

"Does that hurt at all?" he asked.

"No," Twig murmured.

"Now, what are you thinking about?" Adam ran the back of his fingers down Twig's cheek. Such an intimate gesture. Twig wanted to run away. It was too much. It was all too much. What if Tina walked by right now? Or Kamela? Would this always feel so deviant? So wrong?

"That I'm going to be late for dinner."

Adam laughed, removing his hand. "We wouldn't want that."

24

When Twig went to bed that night, she instructed her body to wake up at 4:45 a.m. She could get to the stables in the dark, and by the time she was riding, the sun would be up to light her way to Gran's. Her plan was to go straight to the studio and work. She didn't know the rules of going to Gran's house, but something told her there was only one:

Don't get caught.

The ride to Gran's was uneventful. The main house was dark save for a few porch lights. Twig let Sapphire out in the pen near the studio and gave her some water and a few carrots. She found herself desperate to go to the bathroom. She was ready to go outside if she had to, but hoped she had overlooked a bathroom in the studio.

The studio was unlocked. She walked in and turned on the various lamps that decorated the small room. There was a tiny bathroom that could have been mistaken for a closet near the kitchen. It contained a toilet, a sink, a basket filled with toilet paper and small washcloths, and a wastepaper basket with a fitted lid. Gran's plumbing was no different from theirs, it seemed.

Twig went to the kitchen after washing her hands and switched on the wall light. There was a basket filled with muffins and a package of coffee. A small note was placed in a coffee filter.

Heard you're an early riser. Enjoy. —G.

Twig held the note and smiled.

As the coffee brewed, Twig looked around at the supplies. She squeezed a bit of paint out of its tube and onto her finger to sniff it. The paint touched her nose, and she quickly ran to the sink to wash it off. She couldn't go back to the compound covered in paint.

She ran her hands over the big roll of canvas and then the different papers, choosing one and fixing it awkwardly to the easel. While squeezing tubes of acrylic paint onto a big wooden slab, she marveled at the color selection. Ah! The colors she could invent. She had dreamed of this—of actually painting with real paints and not with leaves or crushed clay. She ran paintbrushes over her fingertips, noticing some were stiff and coarse, others soft and bushy.

With her coffee in one hand, she began to use a palette knife to carry the paint onto the paper. Placing it randomly, smashing it around, getting to know its texture, how it moved, what sort of stain it made… There was no plan. She put her coffee down and chose a brush. She was focusing now. She pushed the color along beneath the bristles, sensing how the tooth of the thick paper absorbed the paint. She started to make circles, adding light, bringing shapes forward, adding darker colors to make others recede. The rhythm reminded her of Leo, of his music and his tapping crutches. She was dancing.

Time and place disappeared. She was made for this.

An image was emerging. It was coming fast. Twig traced the shape of a small horse with her brush and then filled in the body. People. Bright green grass and a big, imposing house in the background. Twig put her fingers to her head, which had begun to ache slightly. Her stomach dropped and her mouth became dry. She thought about stopping. But she didn't want to stop. The painting was pouring out of her. The pink tulle of a young girl's party dress. The gray of a man's hair, his big smile and tanned skin. Shimmering gold shoes. Then

Avery, chic and smiling. A cigarette held between her long fingers.

Tears streamed down Twig's cheeks.

She put the brush down and backed away from the painting. She remembered now. She'd seen this scene the day she'd fallen off Sapphire. It had just been flashes, but she'd seen this man, this house, and this younger, worldlier version of her mother.

Twig put her hands to her mouth. She had been off the compound long before the day of her accident. She had been to this place in the painting. She *was* that little girl in the frothy dress with the glimmering shoes. She had lived in that house. That big, brick house. She remembered it.

Or did she?

The emotions the painting evoked began to subside, and reason grabbed at her. She lost her sureness of the moment.

She looked at the painting again. It was such a clear depiction. How could she have painted that if she'd never been there? How could she have painted it, period?

The sun began to warm the room. She had to go.

She scratched a note and left it in place of Gran's.

Thank you for breakfast...
for everything. Back as soon as possible.
Love, T.

Twig rinsed the coffee cup and pot, leaving them to dry on a towel beside the sink. She stuffed a muffin in the pocket of her sweater. Her heart was beating rapidly and her head still hurt, but she had to keep moving. She began switching off lights.

She eyed the painting, the paper thick and still wet. She picked it up and carried it gingerly as she left the studio. Sapphire whinnied with happiness at the sight of her. Twig ducked behind the studio and set down the painting beneath a small overhang of roof in order to protect it. It wasn't much, but it would have to do. She didn't want anyone to see it.

The lights in the kitchen began to glow. Twig didn't have time to stop. She still had to get Sapphire back before breakfast. She saw Gran's pretty white head at the window. Twig made a writing sign with her hand and nodded toward the studio. She pressed her hands together and bowed toward Gran in a gesture of gratitude. Gran nodded back in understanding.

Twig and Sapphire tore through the woods toward the compound. Twig worried for a moment about her head and her wrist but pushed ahead. A seizure might not be worse than being late.

When Sapphire was safely situated in her stall, Twig stumbled away from the stables, smoothing her hair and twisting it into a bun. There was nothing she could do about the rosiness in her cheeks from riding. She could always say her head had begun to hurt. In fact, she should have some excuses at the ready in case she was late. She pinched her wrist between her thumb and index finger and turned it gently, worried that she had pushed it, but it seemed to be standing up. There wasn't any soreness. She should ice it just in case. She didn't want to be in a cast again. She wouldn't be able to ride...or paint.

Twig saw Ryan and Sophie at their table when she entered the hall for breakfast. She grabbed a tray and filled it with food, suddenly hungry. She hadn't managed to eat Gran's muffin. It was still stuffed in her pocket. She chose an empty seat next to Ryan and sat down.

"I'm sensing some untoward morning behavior," Ryan whispered while scooping up a spoonful of oatmeal.

"What's giving me away?" Twig responded, trying not to move her lips and staring with sudden interest at her fingernails.

"Oh, a certain *je ne sais* Twig."

"That's all?"

"That's all."

Sophie had been talking to Rose and Thomas and only then looked up at Twig. "Morning, Twig."

"Morning, Sophie," Twig answered casually.

"Oh, Twig!" Rose suddenly said, realizing Twig had joined them. "We both need to talk to you." Rose pointed to herself and then to Thomas.

"Okay," Twig said, curious. "Together?"

"No, actually," Thomas said. "For different reasons. Can you stay for a minute before yoga this morning?"

"Yeah. I can't do half the class right now, anyway. But I should let Teacher know."

"I'll tell her. I'm assuming this has been approved?" Sophie asked.

"Yes." Both Thomas and Rose nodded. "We can just talk here after everyone leaves," Thomas suggested.

"Sounds good." Twig had had enough moving around for one morning.

"Hey," Ryan nudged Twig. "I miss you."

"I miss you, too." Twig squeezed Ryan's hand under the table.

"How 'bout a walk soon? Tomorrow? Before dinner?"

"Nothing I'd rather do," Twig answered, and she meant it. It had been too long since she'd caught up with Ryan. She felt far away from Sophie, too, but that might be best right now. She didn't want to jeopardize Sophie in a way that she knew she didn't have to worry about with Ryan. Ryan could take care of himself. Too much information might both upset Sophie and put her in a bad position. And sadly, Twig just didn't trust Sophie right now.

A loud noise suddenly boomeranged through the dining hall. A man named John, a father of young children, had dropped his tray. His dishes and the tray itself had clattered to the floor with a *bang*. Everyone stared for a moment. He held up his hands, blistered and bleeding, as if for explanation. He seemed to be frozen with fear and dazed with fatigue. Ryan stood up and went over to him. He helped him to a chair and then went back to pick up the dishes and the tray, bringing them over to where John was sitting. Twig looked at Sophie. They both wanted to help, but it was best not to call more attention.

Ryan righted the dishes and cleaned John's utensils with his shirt. Twig knew John could not go get another serving of food. He'd have to manage with what didn't spill. Ryan patted John on the shoulder and came back to their table. *He'll learn now*, thought Twig, recalling Adam's teachings. *Wherever he went astray, he'll be different now. He will be better for this.*

But inside, her stomach burned.

Soon enough, the breakfast crowd cleared out. Thomas and Rose sat across from Twig. She was glad for the distraction. The incident with John, though small, left a heaviness in her heart.

"So." Thomas rubbed his hands together. "Adam said you're going to be part of my supply team. Well, now it's a team. Before it was sort of a one-man show." Thomas smiled at Rose and Twig. "Anyway, I'm glad to have a new partner."

"Thank you, Thomas," she said humbly. "I'm a little nervous, but I'm happy to help." She had to speak to Thomas as if she was speaking to Adam. Anything she said to Thomas would surely go right back to him. She was sure Adam would use Thomas as his eyes and ears when it came to Twig.

"Okay. Good." Thomas stroked Rose's hair with his large, freckled hand and smiled lovingly at her. They were really cute. Twig couldn't help remembering Leo brushing her own hair off her forehead at the hospital. She felt a shiver run through her body.

"We'll start one week from today." Thomas smiled warmly at Twig. "We always leave after breakfast, but we'll pack sandwiches. It can be a long day, and we can't eat anything that hasn't been purified first."

"Okay," Twig nodded, thinking about the meal she had shared at Gran's. "What about us? Do we need to be purified before we leave and after we come back?"

Thomas looked grave and shook his head. "Adam said because he laid hands on you recently, you are fine. I have received special blessings to protect me on these outings. Adam will tell us when we are in danger of infection again."

Twig couldn't help but wonder why her purification had the power to last some open-ended amount of time, but Thomas had received a special blessing to go on supply runs. If Adam made up everything about infection and corruption in the outside world and his ability to cure it and prevent it, wasn't he being a little lazy by not giving her a special purification for supply runs? Did he not expect her to question any of it?

"I'm glad I don't have to go. I would be scared to death," Rose said. "I hate that you two have to go, but I thank you from the bottom of my heart for doing it."

Thomas began to stand up. He lifted Rose's hair off her neck and let it fall. "One week from today. I will explain protocol—rules of behavior—on our way there."

"Okay. Thank you, Thomas." Twig couldn't wait for next week to come.

Thomas kissed Rose's head and left. Twig started to get up.

"Oh, wait, Twig. I have to talk to you about something, too."

"What's that?" Twig said, sitting back down and tucking her legs beneath her.

"Well, this is kind of weird, but Adam and Yasmine wanted me to tell you about the classes you'll be taking now."

"Different classes?"

"Yeah." Rose was hesitating. "Because you're getting married. All the betrothed girls take these…these 'how-to-be-a-wife' classes." Rose giggled nervously. Her fair skin was turning red. Twig sat in silence. She wasn't sure how to react.

"Who teaches them?" Twig finally asked, unsure of what to say.

"Well, I'll be there, but mostly Yasmine teaches." Rose stopped for a moment. "It's more like a conversation, really. Answering questions you might have, and some instruction."

This marriage was really in motion. "Are they like Meetings?"

"No, no, not at all."

The lights went off. Someone from the morning's kitchen crew must have shut them. No one would expect anyone to still be in the dining area. Both Rose and Twig looked up.

"It's weird, right?" Rose said conspiratorially. "*Love* classes."

"Yes," Twig answered. "Definitely." Although it seemed more terrifying than weird.

"Verdant Green classes will start in a few weeks. I'll let you know."

"Verdant Green? That's the name?" Twig thought about what Adam had said about keeping her pure.

"Isn't it the most beautiful name?"

Twig didn't say anything for a moment. She was at a loss for words.

"I know, Twig. It's kind of awkward." Rose leaned closer to Twig and whispered, "But you do get to learn all of these crazy things!" Rose put her hand over her mouth and started to giggle. Her red hair bounced around her tiny, pretty head.

Twig tried to smile and share in Rose's mirth, but she felt a pit in her stomach.

BOOK TWO

Extended Family

25

Twig's dreams became brutal. Something deep inside her was scratching at the surface. It had started with the painting at Gran's. Every night since, images would come to her in her dreams and reappear at random times throughout the following days. She might startle awake only to have the dream disintegrate when she tried to remember it. But pieces would pop back into her mind as she went through her daily motions. She might be in the shower, and suddenly she would remember the imposing brick house or young Avery with her platinum hair and haughty expression. Not the beaten, checked-out Avery of today.

The man with the smile and the prematurely graying hair was always there, holding toddler Twig and calling her Livvy. Eventually it became clear that this man was Avery's husband, Twig's father. At least in her dreams...in her visions.

She knew he couldn't be her real father. Avery had come to the Family pregnant. Twig's father had left them when he found out Avery was going to have a baby. Maybe she just wished she had a real father right now. Someone to protect her in a way that Avery couldn't.

But the last few weeks had shown Twig that secrets were all around her. Cellphones and money transfers and lies about the outside world. And her painting and her dreams told her that she was involved in them. How could she dream of these things, paint these things, if she had never seen them or anything like them? She was anxious and scared but mostly confused.

Was she going crazy? Had she damaged her brain in the accident, and the doctors had missed it? Was it something they would have picked up if she'd gone back for her scan?

What was the alternative? That she'd been lied to her whole life about who she was and where she came from? This kind of circular thinking was becoming unbearable.

Twig stared out at the concrete in front of her. It kept disappearing as the small white van lapped it up and pushed her and Thomas toward Turrialba for her first supply run. She wanted to be excited—she *should* be scared—but she was consumed by her thoughts.

"Is something wrong, Twig?"

Do you remember when my mom came to our Family? I mean, I know you were young, but do you have any memory of that? Twig wanted to ask. Thomas was two years older than Twig. He might have some memory that could help her.

Twig tried to imagine how she might to explain things to Thomas. *I've been having…memories? Visions? Delusions? I don't know.*

"You know, Rose really admires you," Thomas said suddenly.

"Me? What?" Twig was shaken from her thoughts.

"We both do."

"Wow. Thanks, Thomas."

"I don't mean to be too forward, but it seems like you've been through a lot with your mom, and, despite that, you are always so upbeat and nice. Always so helpful to everyone. We can both see why Adam chose you for his wife." Thomas paused for a moment. "You will be an amazing leader for us."

Twig felt a little stunned. "Thank you, Thomas," she said softly. "That is really nice of you to say." Of course she couldn't ask him her questions. She might as well go straight to Adam. Thomas would report on her immediately; he wouldn't think twice about it.

"So, there are some things we have to talk about," Thomas said, his tone more formal.

"Sure," Twig answered. She was glad to be taken outside of her thoughts.

"There are rules we have to follow once we get to Turrialba. It is very important that we follow these rules to the letter in order to prevent getting infected, getting lost, or worse."

"Worse?" Twig asked.

"You are a woman, and Turrialba is a dangerous city. A lot of terrible things can happen."

"Of course," Twig said, feigning a somber tone. It wasn't that she was mocking Thomas; she just didn't believe that the world outside of the compound was wholly evil and dangerous—not anymore. Between the hospital and Gran's, she'd seen otherwise.

"One: don't look anyone in the eye. That is important. Avert your gaze. You will be surrounded by citizens of the outside world, and they will try to charm you and engage you in conversation. You don't speak Spanish, so that helps. I'll give you a few words to get by, but other than that, avoid conversation. You will have to deal with people at the post office, the general store, and the food market. It can't be avoided. Just give them your money, get your change and merchandise, and go."

"Okay." Twig nodded and turned to look out the window. The vegetation glowed green on either side of her. Stray dogs trotted along the road looking for food and the next place to sleep. Small houses in various states of disrepair dotted the narrow road.

"Two: only go where we absolutely need to go for our supplies. I know you won't believe this, but I have to tell you or else you won't be prepared. You will be tempted to look around. You'll be tempted to go into other stores and watch the people. The temptation will be powerful, but it will only lead to pain. I'm sorry to bring this up, but you could be attacked or abducted."

Twig was only half-listening. She continued to stare out the window, grateful for the change of scenery. She was learning something new about herself. She liked adventure, and so far, she loved meeting new people from the outside world: Leo, Hazel, Dr. Young, Marianna, and Gran. She felt her heart and mind changing just like the scenery outside the van. Her mood lifted more and more by the minute.

They passed through the town of Tuis, which consisted of a large Catholic church and several bars housed in residential homes. Neon signs advertising different brands of beer blinked in their windows.

"We're going to go to the post office, general store, and then we'll get groceries. We can sit in the van and have our sandwiches at lunchtime."

"Sounds like a plan," Twig said with a quiet smile. She wondered about running into Leo at any of those places.

Thomas parked the car in front of the post office, only a block away from the main square of Turrialba. Twig gasped when she stepped out of the van. The plaza was teeming with life. Twig squeezed Thomas's arm. She couldn't believe what she was seeing—seeing, hearing, and smelling!

"It's okay." Thomas mistook Twig's amazement for fear. He held her shoulders awkwardly.

"I'm sorry," she said, recovering herself. "I'll be fine. I'm sorry." Thomas blushed as Twig untangled from his stiff half-embrace. "I'm okay now. Please, lead the way."

"I wish we could wear masks."

Twig thanked Adam silently for not making them wear masks. What if she ran into Leo with a mask on? He would probably run the other way.

"I'll give you a little tour. It's best if you get your bearings. I don't want you getting lost. And if we get separated, try not to panic, and we'll meet at the van. Okay?"

"Yes. Okay. Good idea," Twig agreed.

The plaza was like a small park, with green grass and little concrete paths winding throughout. People with big carts sold things like ice cream, candy, and drinks. Children played in the middle of the square. Old women with straw bags sat idly on benches watching them. Young women in tight clothes, happily showing off their bodies, orbited around the plaza with purpose, running their errands.

The colors. The textures! The hospital and Gran's house were fairly tame when compared to the life bubbling around her in Turrialba. There were so many different smells. Twig found herself delighting in the aroma of fresh baked bread from the *panaderías* one moment, only to have her nose filled with something repellant, urban and wet, the next. There was beauty, and there was ugliness. She loved it all. She had to feign fear and slow her steps as she walked beside Thomas. She wanted to run ahead.

A van with a megaphone attached to its roof was slowly making its way around the square. Noise blared from its speaker. At first Twig was taken aback, thinking it was Adam's voice. But there was more than one voice, and they were speaking Spanish.

"Festival de musica esta noche!"

"They are announcing a music festival that will happen tonight in the square," Thomas explained.

"A music festival?" How wonderful. She wished they could stay.

"A lot of bad people come to things like that. And they bring a lot of bad things with them."

"I understand," Twig lied, though her curiosity was piqued. Thomas was the perfect person for Adam to send on supply runs. He either had incredible self-control or—Twig hated to think it—no imagination or curiosity. Either way, he was loyal to the bone.

A clock decorated a bell tower in the plaza's center, reminding Twig of home, except this clock was so big you could see it from wherever you stood. For the first time, Twig could simply look at a clock to see the time. Twig thought of Adam. He was the clock in the center of the compound, and it was the opposite of Turrialba. More often than not you couldn't see Adam, but you always felt like he could see you. She even worried he could see her now. See inside her. See her thoughts.

At the post office, Thomas showed her what he called their "P.O. box." He opened it with a small gold key and shoved its contents into a bag. "For Adam's eyes only," he explained.

"Of course," she answered. She wondered what could possibly be in all of those envelopes.

"Mostly bills, I think," Thomas said, as if reading her thoughts. Twig was dying to ask Thomas if he had ever snooped, but she knew he hadn't. Thomas taught Twig about postage and how to use their money in exchange for goods. The women who worked at the post office didn't seem to notice Twig or Thomas. They sat quietly doing their work. Twig noticed they looked hot and bored but hardly threatening.

Next came *Libreria Fantasia*. Thomas said it was Turrialba's general store, but it felt like heaven to Twig. They had everything! Rolls and rolls of fabric, dishes, cleaning supplies, medical supplies, stuffed animals, candy, yarn, stickers, toys, puzzles, clothing. Twig could have spent hours there. There was so much to look at.

Thomas made a dash to the back of the store for something. Twig ran her hands over the fabrics and dripped a Slinky between her hands. She was wide-eyed and giddy. It was as if she had been living in black and white, and now she was seeing color for the first time. She had a new appreciation for the rainforest. What would life have been like without the only color and texture she had ever really known? And now she had Gran's house—her art studio and her treasure of art supplies.

Thomas returned with a shopping bag and dragged a stunned Twig out of the store. "I know—it's a lot to take in. It can be overwhelming the first few times, but you will get used to it."

Twig had so many questions, but she kept quiet. She didn't want to say the wrong thing and lose the privilege of coming into town.

"Let's eat our sandwiches now, and then we can go to the market and then head home." They walked back toward the van. Twig wracked her brain for a way to get a few minutes by herself. She was desperate to get away from Thomas and look around. She felt as if she was on a leash. When the van was within eyesight, Twig got an idea.

"Thomas, I desperately have to go to the bathroom. Can I meet you at the van? I can see it from here. I'll just go into one of these restaurants. They will have a bathroom, right?"

Thomas frowned, but nodded. "I hadn't thought of that. I will wait for you right here."

"It's my…woman's time," Twig whispered. "I need a few minutes."

Thomas blanched. "Go ahead. Take your time," he replied weakly. "I'll meet you at the van."

"Start eating without me."

The restaurant Twig chose had green linoleum floors that were specked with white-and-gray circles. The tables were covered in oilcloth. A stout Asian woman with black hair pulled into a ponytail and rosy red cheeks from the heat of the kitchen greeted her with a big smile.

"Welcome to Meng's. I'm Meng," she said, then raised her eyebrows. "One?"

Twig didn't know what she meant. *One?* She blushed, but she was happy this woman spoke English. "May I use your bathroom, ma'am?" Twig did have to go, and what was she going to do? Ask this woman if she could just look around her restaurant for a while? Did people do things like that?

"Of course, dear. It's in the back. Just promise to come back soon to try my noodles."

Twig paused. She didn't want to lie to the woman. The woman seemed to notice Twig's reluctance to answer, or maybe she felt bad for Twig, because she smiled warmly and pointed to the back of the restaurant. "I'm only joking with you, dear. The bathroom is that way."

Twig smiled and headed to the bathroom, giving a small bow of her head in thanks.

The bathroom was much cleaner than Twig had expected. It was painted a sage green, and a vase of white orchids sat on a small black table where a candle also burned. Twig washed her hands and looked in the bathroom's mirror. She wanted to stay and stare at herself, examine her face, her neck, her hair. You couldn't do that at home. She thought of Thomas and knew she had to get back to the van. He would only give her so much time before he came back to find her.

When she came out, she took one last look around. There were plates of steaming noodles coming from the kitchen, and most people had small glass bottles on their tables that said "Coca-Cola."

And then there he was.

Leo.

Red-and-blue plaid shirt, olive-green khakis, and leather flip-flops. Twig would know him anywhere. And right behind him, coming through the door and looking as gorgeous as Twig remembered, was Hazel. She was dressed in a yellow, cotton halter dress and her arms glittered with turquoise beaded bangles.

Oh! Twig's heart began to race in her chest. She was sure the people around her could hear it. She didn't know what to do.

"Hi, Meng!" Leo called out to the woman who owned the restaurant.

"Leo! Hazel!" The owner of the restaurant called back, waving them in. "Have you come to use the bathroom or eat my noodles?"

"Noodles!" Hazel smiled.

"And then ice cream at Hector's?" Meng asked them.

"You know us too well," Leo answered.

Meng began to lead the two of them to a table. They were walking in Twig's direction.

Leo spotted her. "Twig?"

"Hi," Twig said shyly. He remembered her!

"Uh, hi?" Leo said. "Come here, girl! I've been looking all over for you." Leo extended his arms toward Twig. Twig hesitated for a moment, remembering infection, Adam, Thomas. *No!* she chastised herself, shutting down those thoughts. She smiled in joy and amazement and fell into Leo's warm embrace.

And then she froze awkwardly. Her body felt on fire in his arms. She didn't trust herself to speak. She had been waiting for this moment, and now she suddenly felt so unprepared for it. So unprepared to talk to people like Leo and Hazel. Leo stood back and tilted her chin up to him.

"Hey! You okay?"

"Yes," Twig gasped. Embarrassed, she began to back away, but she ran into a set of chairs. She wriggled herself away awkwardly, not sure where to go. Meng's place wasn't very big. "I'm sorry," she began to stammer, covering her hands with her face.

"Hey! Get back here." Leo reached out and took Twig's hand.

She laughed a little. His warmth was putting her at ease. She felt her hand relax in his. "Hi," she said quietly.

"Hi," Leo said surely.

"It's really good to see you."

"I know."

They stood there staring at each other for a few moments while the world around them fell away. That's just how it felt. She didn't care if

Thomas or even Adam walked in at that moment. She bit her lip to keep from floating off the ground.

"I really have been looking for you everywhere." He pulled her closer to him and whispered into her ear. "Why do I have the feeling you're going to have to run off again in a minute?" Suddenly Twig was aware of her white dress, her hiking boots. She had been in a hospital gown when they met before. Would he think she was dressed strangely?

Twig laughed quietly and nodded her head. She needed to get back to Thomas. She'd been gone too long.

"Okay, listen. You escaped me once, mystery lady, but I'm on to you now. How can I see you again?" Leo stepped back and looked at Twig with an expression of mock admonishment.

"Meet me here at eleven o'clock one week from today," Twig blurted out.

"Okay. I'll be here," Leo said matter-of-factly.

"If I'm not here, please know that I wanted to be, but couldn't. That's the only reason. I can't."

"Then I'll be here *two* weeks from today at eleven." Leo's tone was serious now. Serious and sincere.

Twig smiled. "Okay. But I'm going to try to be here next week."

They couldn't tear their eyes away from one another. They both began to laugh.

"Hi, Twig," Hazel said in a warm, teasing voice.

"Hi, Hazel," Twig said, the flush reigniting.

"Whoa," said Meng to Hazel. "What's this all about?"

"Tell you later," Hazel answered. "I need a table, though. I'm starving. Move aside, you two. Who knew the best Chinese noodles I would ever eat would be in Costa Rica?"

"I'm so sorry. I'd better go." Twig began to gather her dress in her hands and run toward the door. She was suddenly frightened that

Thomas would come into the restaurant after her. "It was so good to see you," she said to Leo and Hazel. "Meng, thank you for letting me use your bathroom. I'll try to come back to eat."

"Twig—"

Twig turned around.

"Take this. We never got to listen together." Leo was holding out his iPod nano and earphones to her.

"Oh, no. I couldn't do that. That is so nice, but I couldn't."

"Please. I can get it next week."

"But what if—" Twig began.

"Please, I've got an iPod shuffle. I won't miss it. It's yours."

Twig looked at Hazel for help.

"Don't look at me, honey. This boy has a mind of his own. I'd take it if I were you."

Twig took the device and the headphones from Leo and cupped them carefully in her palm.

"They are all addicted to something... Technology..."

Twig could hear Adam in her head, but she pushed his voice away. She wasn't going to become addicted. She just wanted to hear the music, to get to know Leo through the music he listened to.

"Thank you," she said quietly. She was humbled by the generosity of the gesture.

"I want a full report when I see you next week. Loved it, hated it... The whole deal."

"You got it. Thank you again. I'm so sorry, but I have to go."

Twig thought she heard Leo say something like "Bye, Cinderella," but she wasn't sure, and she didn't know what he meant. She hoped she hadn't offended them by running off.

As she ran toward the van, she stuck the nano and headphones awkwardly into the side of her bra.

26

Twig lurched awake. Thomas was staring at her. The van was parked. They were back. She must have fallen asleep on the drive home.

"Twig? I think you had a bad dream. I wanted to let you sleep."

"What time is it?" Again, asking the time. She just didn't know how to judge the world around her any longer.

Thomas looked out the window. "Probably around four."

The dream was so vivid. She could still feel the adrenaline of it coursing through her body. Her mind was cloudy with sadness.

There had been a tennis court. She'd been a toddler again, tottering after fluorescent-yellow tennis balls. Her mother had been there, dressed in white, a thin diamond bracelet glittering from her wrist as she threw the ball up and hit it with her racket toward the smiling man from Twig's other visions—her father. He returned the ball and the game was set in motion. Twig sat on the sidelines chasing after balls.

Her mother and the man began to argue. There was tension in their voices.

Her mother lobbed the ball haphazardly and it sailed over the man's head. He cursed, running after it.

The balls were hit harder; the voices grew louder.

"Mommy?" Twig called out, sensing something was wrong.

"Livvy, it's okay," Avery reassured her.

They ended the game, and the two adults poured themselves lemonade from a pitcher. The ice in their glasses clinked with every sip. Avery's bracelet sparkled as she held her glass up to drink. Twig covered her eyes to protect them from the gleam coming off her mother's diamonds.

"Shiny!" Twig pointed toward the bracelet.

"That's right, Livvy," the man said.

Avery was angry. The man spoke in a soothing voice now instead of yelling, treating her as if she was a cornered animal.

"I'm sick of this," Avery said, looking into her lemonade as if it had suddenly gone bad, or as if she'd found a bug in it. But she wasn't talking about the lemonade.

"Mommy," Twig cried.

Avery ignored her.

The man—he'd *felt* like her father—scooped Twig up in his arms, but she scrambled away, trying to reach her mother.

Avery stormed off the court. Twig tried to chase after her, but Avery didn't look back. Twig was sobbing. Her father scooped her up again and gently stroked her hair.

"It's okay," he soothed. "It's okay."

"Twig?" Thomas said with alarm.

Tears rolled down Twig's cheeks. She could barely make out Thomas. Her chest heaved with grief. She was disoriented after such a deep sleep.

"I have to go, Thomas," Twig said. "I have to go see Doc."

"Can I walk you there? Was it our trip today? Was it too much? I should have been more careful with you. I knew—"

"No, Thomas. This is about something else. Really, I promise." Twig had opened the van's door and was already halfway out. She looked back at Thomas. "I'm okay. I'm going to be fine. Don't worry, all right? And thank you for today."

Twig ran toward Doc's cabin. She was nearly blinded by tears, but they didn't slow her down. It felt as if she was half asleep, one foot in the dream world and one foot in waking life. But that was how life felt these days.

She couldn't stand it. Doc was a psychiatrist. He could help her. She couldn't carry this burden anymore. She couldn't handle this juggling act. If she was brain damaged after all, then she needed help. If these were just dreams, she needed to make them stop. If this was the truth of who she was, she needed to know.

And if Doc and Adam couldn't be trusted, she needed to know that, too.

She knocked hard on Doc's door. He answered at once.

"Twig?" Doc looked confused.

"I need to talk to you."

"Okay. Come in, come in. Are you hurt?"

"Hurt?" The question stalled Twig for a moment. "No, no. I'm not hurt."

"Come have a seat." Doc led Twig into his office. Maya wasn't there. It was almost dinner call.

It occurred to Twig that this was a bad idea. She shouldn't talk to Doc—she should go to Avery—but she dismissed her doubt. She wouldn't get any straight answers from Avery, and there was no one else.

"I've been having…" Twig paused. She really didn't know what to call them. "I've been having visions, or dreams, or…" Twig's hands were shaking, "…delusions. I don't know. That's why I'm here. Maybe I have a serious head injury, and the doctor missed it."

Doc stared at Twig with concern in his eyes. "Would you like something to drink? Some tea? We're going to get through this. You did the right thing, coming to me."

"No, thank you. I just want to get this off my chest."

"Okay. I'm ready when you are."

"I don't know where to start, actually." Twig laughed nervously. She bit her lip to keep from sobbing. She was freezing despite the heat and humidity of the day. "Can I have a blanket?"

"Of course." Doc got up and grabbed a blanket from a loveseat beneath the window. He laid it over Twig's shoulders. She hugged herself to get warm.

"Why don't you begin by telling me when this all started."

"The night of the accident," she said. Nothing had been the same since that night. "I started having these dreams. I'm not sure when I had the first one, or what exactly happened in it. Now they are constant."

Twig went on to tell Doc every single vision and dream she could remember. The house, Avery, her father, the fighting. Doc listened patiently until she was finished.

"Twig," he said gently. "These are dreams, and they make perfect sense."

Twig hung on to his every word. The more he spoke, the more she was sure she had made the right decision by coming to him. When had she become so mistrustful? He'd been her doctor since childhood. How could she have come to doubt him so much? This is what Adam was always telling them! How seductive the outside world is. She'd been ready to turn her back on her Family!

"First of all, I delivered you myself. You have to remember that."

Twig nodded.

"Secondly, these dreams make perfect sense if we analyze them. Would you like to do that now? Are you up for that?"

"Yes!" Twig gasped. "Any kind of explanation."

"I believe this was all brought on by Adam's announcement that he is going to marry you. You were traumatized by the shock of it, in a way. That shock was further exacerbated by your head trauma."

That made sense.

"Let's start with the house."

"Okay." Twig nodded.

"It's a simple place to start, and I think it will reassure you." Doc cleared his throat. "The house represents family. You described the house in your dreams as big and imposing. That means you are overwhelmed by family life. In our case, by collective Family life. Does this make sense so far?"

"Yes."

"You said the house was brick. That means it is impenetrable. You have closed yourself off to others. You have shut yourself away in order to protect yourself."

Individualism.

Twig took a deep breath. That made so much sense. She had. She had kept her thoughts to herself. She had been sneaking out. She had attended the Meetings, but she hadn't participated in the group at all.

"More?" he asked.

"Please."

"Okay. The father character in your dreams is simple wish fulfillment. What would be better right now than to have a fantasy biological father to protect you during your times of trouble? The patriarch to keep the suitors at bay, if you will." Doc stopped. "Up until now, Adam has been that father for you. Now his role is shifting."

Twig felt morose. She had thought the same thing herself, but this meant she really didn't have a father. She had one somewhere, but he was not the loving man of her visions. Her father had abandoned her mother. Her father didn't care that she existed.

"I'm sorry, Twig. That was insensitive of me."

"It's all right, Doc. I had actually thought of that." She was going to have to grieve over that by herself.

"And the last part is really very simple."

"Mom."

"Yes. You are obviously very angry with your mother and feel abandoned by her. This is why she appears so angry and distant in your dreams."

Twig thought about this. She wasn't sure that was exactly how she felt about her mother. She would have to think about that more.

"Now, Twig." Doc was looking at her with concern. "What concerns me about this is the fact that reality blurred for you."

Twig's chest tightened.

"As you know, your mother has a history of mental illness."

Twig suddenly felt defensive and vulnerable. She shouldn't have done this. Now she was totally exposed.

"I've always been concerned that you might have to deal with some of those issues yourself at some point. These things tend to be genetic."

"Are you saying I'm sick, Doc?" Twig began to shake again. "I mean, if that is true, shouldn't we at least go back to the hospital for my brain scan?"

"No, no. I don't think you are sick. And I feel quite certain that the injury you sustained to your head has resolved itself." Twig wondered how he could be so sure. "What I do think is that you are under a tremendous amount of strain, and I think you are vulnerable to mental health issues because of your mother, not because of the physical trauma you suffered. That being said, it is important that you don't become over-wrought. You need to take it easy." Doc stood up and crossed the room.

"I am going to give you an antianxiety medication that I want you to take before bed and anytime you feel anxiety coming on."

"Is it safe?"

"Totally safe. I want you to come talk to me once a week as well. I don't want you to attend any Meetings right now. You're too fragile. And be sure not to mention any of this to anyone."

"Are you going to tell Adam?"

"Not for now. Let's just see where this goes. I'll tell him that I don't want you to attend Meetings, and that's all. That I think you need to take it easy in terms of what you take on emotionally. Deal?"

"Deal."

"Now listen to me, Twig. The next step would be to prescribe an antipsychotic medication. We don't want it to get to that."

"Am I close to that?" Twig asked, horrified. She wasn't even totally sure what that meant, but it didn't sound good.

"No. I don't think so. But let's not test it, okay?"

"Okay." Twig was fighting back tears.

"Do you want me to walk you to the dining hall? You should try to get something to eat." Doc had gotten up and was filling a small plastic bottle with little white pills.

"No, I'm okay. I need the air."

"Of course. I'll see you next week. Same time?"

"Yes."

Twig's head was spinning as she left Doc's office. She was trying to digest everything he had said when someone grabbed her hard by the elbow.

"Follow me."

27

"Sit."

It was Tina. She led Twig behind one of the cottages used for lectures and Meetings. Twig sat down. She was too exhausted to put up a fight. Too tired to be scared.

"You and I are going to make a deal," Tina whispered.

"What?" Twig asked.

"A deal. I'm going to do something for you, and then you are going to do something for me." Tina looked hard at Twig from beneath her heavy fringe of bangs.

"What are you talking about? I don't understand."

"Everything Doc just said in there was a lie."

"You heard all of that?"

"I was stopping by and heard voices from his waiting room. He left the door open."

"So you heard…?"

"Every word. Fiction. Lies. Pretty creative, off-the-cuff lies, but still lies." Tina brushed her bangs to the side.

Twig stared at her in shock. Was Doc lying, or was Tina lying, trying to cause her more confusion? Tina certainly had a reason to hate her, but did she want to drive her completely crazy?

"So, I'm going to tell you the truth, but then you're going to do something for me."

"What can I do for you, Tina?" Twig had no idea what she could offer Tina short of leaving and letting her be Adam's wife again.

"I am going to leave this place one day, and you are going to finance that move."

"What?"

"Well, you are going to get your *father* to finance that move."

"Please, Tina. What are you talking about?"

Tina sighed. "Where do I begin? One, Doc didn't deliver you. You came here when you were about three."

"What? That's crazy—"

"No, it's not, Twig. At first I thought Adam was marrying you because you're young and he's attracted to you. That's not so out of character for him. Wanting more children is only an excuse. But the more I thought about it and the disruption he's causing the Family, the more I realized he had another motivation." Tina drew in a deep breath.

Twig sat as still as she could. She was stunned. She didn't know who to trust.

"So then I decided he wanted your money. That's the only reason he ever wanted your mother in the first place. Her money practically built this place."

"Money?" Twig asked, bewildered.

"That big house—that's all real. And there's a lot of money that goes with it."

"My father, then. I have a father?"

"As far as I know. You're going to have to get the details from Avery."

"Please, Tina."

"Look, Twig. You're going to have to confront your mother. And one of these days, when I decide to leave, you're going to have to figure out how to get me that money."

Twig shook her head, stunned. "What if I can't?"

"Then I will make your and your mother's lives a living hell."

"But Tina, this is crazy. I didn't even know I had a father until two minutes ago. How am I supposed to—"

"Remember what Adam said, Twig. You're resourceful; you'll figure it out. It won't be tomorrow, but one day I will ask. And one more thing, Twig."

Twig looked up at Tina, waiting for another blow.

"Those pills? Don't take them. You don't need them. Do your knitting and sewing, talk to your mother, meditate. You can cope. I have no problem with medication when it's needed, but you don't need it."

Twig had forgotten about the pills. They were tucked into the pocket of her dress. Under Tina's sharp gaze, she was suddenly acutely aware of Leo's iPod nano stuffed in her bra, poking at her side.

"Tina, aren't you afraid I'm going to report you to Adam? Tell him that you want to leave?"

"You'll soon find out, Twig, that once you're married to Adam, there is nothing about you he won't know."

28

"Wait, why did they want to make you walk around the hospital?"

"Well, they didn't want to *make* me." Twig sighed. She was getting frustrated. She was trying to talk to Ryan and just wasn't getting through. "The doctor said it was healthy for me to get out of bed after my injury. It was time to move a little bit."

"But without your mom and Adam? Why did they make you do it without them?"

She tried again. "I think the doctor knew it would be my only time to…well, to see the world. He was really kind. It was like he wanted to give me a chance." Ryan raised his eyebrows with skepticism in response.

"A chance to what? That sounds pretty typical. Tempt you when no one's around to protect you."

She could see she wasn't getting anywhere. "Anyway, that part doesn't really matter. He told me things."

"What kind of things?" She hadn't expected Ryan to be so defensive. Twig bit her lower lip and took a deep breath, trying to figure out how to phrase what she was going to say.

"The outside world virus, for instance. It… Well, it's different than we've been taught."

"Says who? This doctor who wanted to separate you from your mom and get you alone to influence you?"

Twig ignored this and tried to continue. "You can't—I mean, he said you can't get infected the way we've been taught. A virus is a physical sickness, and there are only certain ways you can get one. Like if you touch someone who has a cold and then wipe your nose."

"That doesn't sound so different from what we've been taught."

"But that's the thing. Not everyone in the outside world is sick and contagious. Many, many people are healthy."

"And who told you that?"

"Well, the doctor, but I also saw it with my own eyes. I met this sister and brother, and they were so amazing, Ry. They were so friendly and full of life." Ryan was quiet, thinking over what she'd said.

"Twig, I'm sure they seemed nice, but why in the world would you trust those people? How could you possibly know if they were healthy? And trust them over Adam? That doesn't make any sense."

"Well, maybe Adam doesn't know. Maybe he has bad information or old information," Twig tried.

"He knows everything, Twig."

For a moment, Twig heard Tina's voice inside her head. "*Once you're married to Adam, there is nothing about you he won't know.*" She shivered slightly and shook her head.

"Okay, let's put all of that aside for now. I can't explain why I believed it. I just felt it. But I'm obviously doing a terrible job of explaining it. Anyway, there's something else that is much more personal to me."

"Go on."

"The day of the accident, I had this vision. And when I got home from the hospital, I started having more of them." She didn't mention Gran or her painting. She'd made a promise to Avery. "Detailed visions of having another life before our life. I saw all of these things that I don't think I could have dreamed up. My real father, my mother before she came here, this house—this huge brick house—"

"But were you asleep? Were you dreaming these things?"

"Sometimes."

"So you were probably just dreaming it all. The mind is really complicated. And you did hit your head pretty hard."

"That's what Doc said. That they were just dreams. And I believed him, but then Tina—"

"Tina? What does Tina have to do with this?" He was agitated, unwilling to even hear her out.

"Why are you being like this, Ry? I need to talk to you."

"Well, think of what you're telling me, Twig. This all sounds like madness." Twig looked down, hurt. "No, I don't think you're mad. I didn't mean that at all. I just meant you're asking me to swallow a lot."

"I know, I know. But I need to talk to someone I can trust, Ry. I can't trust anyone else right now!"

"It's okay. I'm sorry. I'm still the same person, even if…if this is going to take time for me. Go on. Tina. You were talking about Tina."

Twig looked at him. He nodded again for her to continue. "Well, I had just had this conversation with Doc today when we got back from the supply run. I went to see him because these visions have become so intense. I thought I was going crazy. He basically said what you said—that they're dreams. Only he told me I'm bordering on psychosis because I can't tell if they are dreams or reality." Ryan frowned with sympathy. Twig wasn't so sure he wasn't thinking she had gone crazy.

"So Tina happened to overhear our conversation, and she told me Doc was lying. That I do have a father, and that I wasn't born here. That I've been lied to my whole life. I lived somewhere else with my mom before I came here. Somewhere else with my father, Ryan! That means I have a father out there. One who may be missing me—"

"I don't mean to sound harsh or skeptical here, Twig. But why would Tina tell you that? That makes no sense."

"She said she wants to leave. She said she is going to leave one day and that I am going to give her the money to do it."

"What?" Ryan was shocked.

"I know." Twig had spent so much energy trying to explain things to Ryan over the last thirty minutes that her sense of urgency was dying off. Now she just felt tired. Utterly tired and still completely confused. "Apparently my father is very wealthy, and she said one day I have to get her money so that she can leave."

Ryan shook his head. "You have to report her. That's all there is to it."

"I think it's more complicated than that. I'll never find out who I really am if I bring Adam into this right now."

"But you know he's already involved. I'm sure of it. Doc tells him everything."

"You're probably right, but if I can talk to my mom before they get to her, I might be able to find out the truth. If I just pretend like I believe what they've told me, they'll let it be. I can't totally explain it, but if I report Tina, I know the truth will get buried. Plus, Tina already hates me. I don't need to make it worse."

Ryan was silent for a moment. Then he looked at Twig. "Can I ask you something?" he said abruptly.

"Of course."

"Did the doctor say anything about people like me? Or have you met people like me, when you've gone into the outside world?"

"People who are gay?" Twig asked gently, thinking she knew what he meant.

"Yes."

"I'm so sorry, Ry. I got caught up in my own stuff. I have been selfish, and to be honest, I really don't know. But I can find out! I will. I'll ask someone..." She paused, thinking of Leo. "I'll ask someone next week when I go into Turrialba."

"But they might lie," Ryan said, sounding defeated.

"Ry, I wish I could make you see. It's different out there than we've been told. From what I've seen, *we've* been lied to."

"We'd better go." It was after dinner. No one was really around. Most people had retired to their cottages for the evening.

"Okay, but will you think about what I've said?" Twig stood up and dusted off her dress. They were sitting in full sight of the compound. The light from the tower illuminated the ground in front of them. Twig hadn't had the energy to sneak off. Sometimes the best hiding places were in full view.

"I will, but Twig, listen: this is still your life." He remained sitting, looking up at her.

"What do you mean?"

"I mean, you can be mad, sad, and confused, but this is your life, and no one can take that away from you." He blinked at her. "I'm not sure if I'm saying this well, but do you know what I mean? Maybe you've been lied to, but your relationships with me, with Sophie, with your mom, even with Evelyn—those are all real."

Twig nodded. She extended her hand to help Ryan up, but he didn't take it. He smiled, pretending he didn't notice it, and hopped to his feet. Twig's heart sank. He didn't want to touch her. He didn't believe her.

"I love you," he whispered.

"Do you?" she asked, looking at him, searching his face.

"Of course I do. I know we aren't totally in sync here, but that doesn't change the fact that I am your best friend. Now go get some sleep. Things will always look a little better in the morning."

"I love you, too," Twig said. She meant it, but inside she felt deeply disappointed. Their conversation hadn't gone at all how she'd expected.

She had to talk to her mom.

When Twig got back to her cottage, Avery was asleep. She would have to wait until tomorrow to talk to her. Part of her felt relieved. She wanted answers, but she wasn't looking forward to having the conversation with Avery. Twig stretched out on her bed and put Leo's nano discreetly beneath her quilt. She put the bud in her ears and began to press buttons. A twangy guitar started to play, and a woman with a voice as clear as a bell began to sing with a pain that coiled itself around Twig's heart. So calm and so tightly wound with emotion at the same time.

Twig felt the music in every part of her body. She peeked under the covers, and the words "Lucinda Williams, 'Side of the Road'" glowed up at her. When the song ended and the quiet stillness of Twig's bedroom returned, still felt sad, but she felt lighter, too. Like she could breathe better. The song had cleansed her, in a way. She pressed the buttons on the nano again until she figured out how to turn it off. Then she carefully tucked it beneath her mattress. She was asleep in minutes.

29

Twig aimed the staple gun and pulled its trigger.

"You are really getting the hang of this!"

Twig looked up to see Gran's friend Daniel smiling at her. They were stretching canvas. Avery was taking a nap in Gran's house.

Twig neatly folded the canvas at the corners and stapled them into place. When she finished, she handed it to Daniel. He added it to the stack they'd created against the wall near Twig's easel. They'd been working for nearly an hour and had created a nice assortment of sizes. The activity took Twig out of her head. She was completely distracted by learning the new skill.

She hadn't been able to talk to Avery on their ride out to Gran's. Something was wrong. Avery was a stone of silence and sadness. Twig had wanted to question her anyway, but the heaviness of Avery's mood had been too intimidating for Twig. She'd decided she would wait until they got to Gran's. And maybe having Gran there when Twig confronted her mother wasn't such a bad idea. But as soon as they'd arrived, Avery had disappeared into the back of Gran's house, saying she was going to sleep for a while. Gran had encouraged Twig to let her go.

"Thank you so much for teaching me, Daniel," Twig said, pleased with their work.

"No problem. You are a fast study. Fast… Is that how you say it?"

"Sure," Twig said. "'Fast,' 'quick'—either one. Your English is so good. I wish I knew more Spanish."

"We studied a little bit of English in school, and being around Gran all these years helped."

Daniel lived in Turrialba with his mother. He did all kinds of odd jobs for Gran.

"How do you get here, Daniel?"

"To Gran's?"

"Yeah."

"I drive."

"But where do you enter?"

"You haven't been to the front of the property?" Daniel pushed his large black glasses up on his nose. His black hair was pulled into a low ponytail.

"No. We always ride in through the trees."

"Ah, the *entrada encantada*."

"Sí," Twig said, pleased that she understood.

"Come on, I'll show you."

Twig looked toward Gran's house. Still no sign of Avery. "It seems extra hot today, if that's possible. I actually wish it would rain." Twig redid the knot that was holding her heavy hair off of her back. She wiped a bit of sweat from her neck and followed Daniel.

"We've been working hard, too." Daniel laughed. There were dark rings of sweat beneath the arms of his blue T-shirt.

"What does your shirt mean?"

Daniel looked down at the front of his shirt as he led Twig toward a path that had emerged east of the main house and the studio. White letters in a simple font spelled out *LOS OJOS SE HAN*. The *O*'s made a pair of cartoonish eyes incased in a pair of reading glasses. They seemed to be peering over the words.

"Oh." Daniel blushed slightly. "The eyes have it. It is a... I am not sure how to say it in English. A play-with-words."

"A pun?" Twig offered.

"Yes! A pun. Thank you," Daniel said sweetly. "I am an optometrist."

"An eye doctor?"

"Sí. A doctor of optometry, not medicine."

"Wow. That's so cool. How do you find the time to help Gran out all the time and teach me how to stretch canvases? I had no idea."

"Well, I've had to close my practice," Daniel said sadly. "For now," he suddenly added.

Twig waited for him to explain.

"My shop was in San Jose. That is where I studied. When my father became ill—he was an artist like you—I had to close the shop to come home and help my family," Daniel said sadly. "But," he brightened, "it is because of him that I know how to stretch canvas and use turpentine and many, many other things.

"He passed last year," Daniel continued, his smile fading, "and now it is just my mother and me."

"I'm sorry about your father, Daniel," Twig said sincerely.

"It's okay. Well, it's not okay. It hurts very much. But we have a lot to be thankful for. We are very blessed."

Twig admired Daniel's sense of gratitude. She also couldn't help but notice that he had called her an artist. Was she an artist? According to Adam, artists were some of the most selfish people that existed. Maybe he just misunderstood them. Maybe he didn't understand art, or never really knew any artists. Art was a solitary thing for her, but maybe it didn't have to be. If art was a part of their lives, she was sure she would love to share it with others. Not just the work she created, but the act of creating itself. That was why she liked to teach knitting and sewing. She had never thought of it like that before. It had always served a need. They needed clothing, so they sewed. But all along it had given her a different sort of fulfillment.

"This is it."

They had come to a road. Twig couldn't believe it. Of course it had to be there, now that she thought about it, but she had never heard a car. The area around Gran's clearing was so wooded it had easily remained hidden.

How did Gran ever find this place?"

"You would have to ask her that."

"Thank you for showing me this, Daniel. I think I should head back to see if my mom is up."

"Of course. I will walk you back. I need to get my stuff before I go home."

When Twig entered Gran's kitchen, Avery still wasn't awake. Twig frowned.

Gran was sitting at her kitchen table amidst her piles of glossy magazines. She was cutting out pictures and placing them in a box.

"It's one of those days, darling. I'm sure she'll be up soon. Care to join me?"

Twig had more time than usual since she didn't have to go to Meetings. But she wondered about Avery. Twig wasn't sure where she was supposed to be right now.

"What are you doing?"

"Ooh, you'll like this. Collaging."

Gran fixed Twig a small pot of tea that she said was from Kenya. It smelled like vanilla. Gran poured it into one of the green-and-gold cups while Twig sat at the table and began looking through the magazines.

There were travel magazines, home decor magazines, and cooking magazines, but her favorites were the fashion magazines. They were called *Harper's Bazaar* and were from the 1950s and 60s.

"I'm like a little country mouse, and you're this formidable woman of the world," Twig said, laughing as she flipped through pages.

"You are pretty formidable yourself, young lady. And those," Gran waved her scissors in the direction of the *Harper's Bazaar*s, "don't get cut. Those are Gran's babies."

"She's gorgeous." Twig stared at a young woman on one of the covers. Her eyes were huge and brown, like Gran's, actually—and like Adam's. They popped out from under an oversize and very glamorous straw hat. Her hair and shoulders were covered in a cream wrap decorated with the most exquisite red, turquoise, and yellow flowers. Her skin was ivory and pale, her lips full and painted red. The eyes, heavily shadowed in black powder, remained so innocent.

"That's Audrey, photographed by Richard Avedon. You have good taste, Twig."

"Who is she?"

"She was an actress. Her looks and spirit turned ideas of beauty at the time upside down. Richard would conjure these lively shoots for *Harper's Bazaar*, and when the two of them came together—well, you can see for yourself."

"Her name is Audrey?"

"*Was* Audrey. Audrey Hepburn. She has since passed. You'll have to see a movie she made called *Breakfast at Tiffany's* one of these days."

"I'd like that." Twig looked toward the kitchen door. "I think I need to wake my mom up. We need to get back. I wanted to talk to her about something while we were here. I'm worried it's going to upset her, and now I don't think we have time."

Gran began to scoop up scraps of paper. "I'll go get her, darling."

"Thank you, Gran. Can I help clean up?"

"Don't be silly, darling. Just leave it. I'll get it later."

Twig noticed that being around Gran and Daniel was helping her get used to talking to people outside of the Family. Conversation was less formal, and Twig felt like she was becoming less awkward. She imagined it was kind of like learning a foreign language: the more you were around it, the more you picked up.

"If you're sure," Twig said. She tapped her foot anxiously. They really needed to go, and she hadn't talked to Avery yet.

"Can it wait until tomorrow? The thing you need to speak to your mother about?"

Twig thought about this for a moment. She'd waited this long already.

"I guess so," she answered. "I'm very angry at her, to be honest. But I worry about her so much."

"Well, try to wait and come tomorrow. Hang in there."

"Okay." Twig nodded.

"And Twig, darling, remember this: relationships are messy. People are messy. I wish I had accepted that earlier in life."

Gran left the kitchen to get Avery.

"You'll have to go back by yourself, Twig." Avery stood in the doorway of the kitchen. Her hair was disheveled, and her eyes were puffy with sleep.

"Are you sick, Mom?" Twig went to her. She took her hand, but Avery pulled it away.

"No, I'm not sick. I just can't deal today."

"But, Mom. We have to get back. I'll help you. It will be okay."

Avery turned away from Twig and headed back down the hallway. "Go, Twig. I'm not coming."

"Mom! What about me? I can't get caught riding alone; I'll be punished!"

"You'll be fine," Avery said indifferently before Twig heard a door slam. *Fine?* How was she going to be fine? On the off chance that no one was at the stables? What was she going to do? She didn't have much time to think. She had to start riding back. Gran came back into the kitchen.

"I think you'd better just go, dear."

"But you don't understand. We'll get in trouble. Both of us."

"She is in bad shape today, dear." Twig wanted to scream at Gran and Avery. What were they thinking? How could Avery be so selfish? Twig didn't know what to do. She looked from the dark hallway where Avery had disappeared to Gran's front door. Maybe Avery knew something she didn't. Maybe she had thought this through. If Twig left now, then maybe, just maybe, no one would notice her when she got back to the stables. No one had been there when they'd left. She felt herself shaking with fear and anger. She forced herself to utter a good-bye to Gran, even though she felt furious with her for letting Avery stay.

Twig rode home fast and deep in thought. She was trying to figure out what to say if she got caught riding alone. Her pulse raced with adrenaline. It was hot and very humid, and she was covered in sweat. She could feel the sun burning her shoulders where she'd rolled up the sleeves of her dress. Twig was so deep in thought that she didn't notice the two guards until it was too late. They looked like they were patrolling the rainforest. She was still a ways off from the stables. Were they looking for her?

"What are you doing out here by yourself?" one shouted at her. "Come over here."

"I—" Twig fumbled with her words, trying to figure out what to say. "I was trying to find the group, and I got confused. Doc will understand. I need to see Doc. I'm so glad you're here. I got disoriented."

"You need to come with us."

Twig's heart was pounding. The guards were allowed to dole out punishment without checking with Adam.

"Please, can you go get Doc or Adam? They know I haven't been well."

"Just come with me." One man pulled Twig roughly off Sapphire, and the other began to lead the horse in the direction of the stables.

"You'll ride with me back to the compound," the man said sternly. Twig looked longingly after Sapphire.

She didn't know either of the men, but they had the large build Adam chose for guards. Twig climbed reluctantly onto the guard's horse. She hated to touch him. He kicked his horse in the ribs, and the horse broke into a run in the direction of the compound. This was Avery's fault.

Avery. Her anger quickly turned to worry. What was going to happen to Avery? Twig prayed she would somehow get home safely.

"I am Adam's fiancée," Twig said suddenly. "I am his fiancée, and I haven't been well. Please take me to Adam. Now." She did her best to sound commanding. If she could just get to Adam or Doc, she could explain.

"I know who you are," the man barked back. Maybe he also knew where she'd been this afternoon. Maybe Adam had sent the guards to collect her. She decided not to say anything else. What were they going to do to her? What would they do to Avery? Twig thought about jumping off the horse and trying to run, but she knew she would just get hurt and look guilty if she did that.

"Can you tell me where you are taking me?" Twig finally asked when they entered the compound and she slid off the man's horse.

"Isolation."

"Isolation? But I—"

"That's enough."

"But—can you please go get Doc?" She could say she took too many pills and had gotten confused. Doc would understand that.

The man led her to an unused cottage and shoved her into an empty bedroom.

"Please, can I have some water?"

The guard didn't answer. He just shut the door, and Twig heard the lock turn. She was terribly thirsty and hot from her ride. She would need to use the bathroom soon, but there was no toilet.

She looked out the room's one small window into the forest. No one was around. She wondered if anyone would hear her if she screamed. The room was hot and stuffy. She tried to open the window, but it was painted shut. She looked around the room. Nothing. Just heat. Twig sat down, trying to breathe. She had to have her story straight. She got up again and began to pace.

She'd become confused. She thought she could ride out and find the group, but she got disoriented. Would he believe that? Should she say she took too many pills? Was there even a group ride today? She should have checked that. Doc could verify that she had been confused lately. But what would he do? Put her on antipsychotics? Tell Adam she was crazy?

Twig slid to the floor once again. Her bladder was full and becoming painful. How long could she hold it? Could she make it until someone came for her? She wasn't sure which she needed more: a drink or to pee.

* * *

When it got dark, Twig knew no one would be coming for her. She felt it in her gut. She had urinated in a corner of the room an hour before. She couldn't hold it anymore, and now the room smelled of urine. She felt ashamed and afraid.

They must know. They must know about Gran. Otherwise why wouldn't they come ask her for an explanation? Did they even know she was there? What if the guard had forgotten to report back? And her mother—where was she? Wouldn't she make them come for Twig? No, she wouldn't be able to do that, and Avery might be in isolation herself right now. Or worse. Twig was never even able to talk to her. She'd never heard any answers about their past.

Twig began to cry. She would be sleeping here. What was this world of secrets and punishment they lived in? This world where one man controlled everything: information, schedules, where they slept and whom they married, what they believed in. This world had seemed so great until so recently. It was so great when it was the only life she knew.

Thoughts buzzed through her brain. Letters, words, sentences. She was scared to stop thinking. She kept up the noise in her head to banish the lonely silence of the room. She wished she had Doc's pills now. She could feel herself panicking.

Control. It was all about control. The infection in the outside world. She was almost totally certain now that it was a lie. She had enough evidence from her trips outside of the compound. What did this lie accomplish for Adam? Control. Complete control. Did everyone follow him out of fear or out of awe? Maybe both. They worshipped him. He had taught them that he was their god. Twig thought of what Daniel had said earlier that day, that he and his mother were blessed. But blessed by whom? Certainly not Adam. Daniel didn't even know Adam existed.

Somehow, despite her thirst and her fear and her burning brain, Twig fell asleep. She fell in and out of dreams all night. Adam came to her and kissed her. Stroked her hair. Watched her. She tossed and turned. Her body hurt from the hard floor. She saw her father and Avery. Ryan digging ditches. When she woke up, the room was full of light, and the smell made Twig gag.

Still no one came. She had to urinate again in the corner.

She sat beneath the window and wondered anew how long she would be here. Her throat itched with hunger and thirst.

* * *

Hours later, the doorknob turned, and Adam stood in the doorway. He flinched at the smell. "Twig, come with me."

Twig was scared of him. She didn't move. She hated herself for feeling ashamed of the pools of urine in the corner. He came toward her. He took her hands in his and pulled her up to standing. He took his canteen from his belt and offered her water. She fumbled for it, so anxious for the drink.

"Come with me." He walked her outside. She opened her mouth and took the first deep breath she'd taken in hours. Her head hurt. "Have you learned your lesson?"

Twig wished desperately that she knew what he was talking about. Did he know about Gran's? She knew her best bet was to stay quiet. If she were lucky, he would tell her what lesson she was supposed to have learned.

"We do not ride out by ourselves. We don't try to catch up with the group." Adam frowned at her, repeating the words she had said to the guard.

Twig felt her stomach contract with relief. Was that all? The guard had told him her story, and he had believed her?

"Tell me your sin. Confess it now."

Control.

What better way to control his new bride than to show her his power over her with a night in isolation without food or water just for riding out alone. She wondered if Avery had been caught.

"Forgive me, Father. I am so very sorry, Father. I broke a rule. I rode out alone." She didn't say anything about getting confused or not feeling well. Keep it simple. Let him lead.

She looked at him and it occurred to her how very cruel he was. Before this, she had thought Avery and other rule-breaking Family members had done something wrong—that they deserved their punishments—because she believed in Adam. How wrong she'd been to ever judge the others.

"Doc said you have been fragile lately, Twig. But we both know Doc can be a big softie. He's indulging you." Twig didn't think there was anything soft about Doc. "I am not going to be soft on you because I know what's good for you. You two can have your little sessions, but I will always hold you accountable. Yesterday, for instance: if you had followed my rule, you wouldn't have become disoriented. You see where you went wrong? You do not ride out alone. That is why you needed to spend the night in isolation. To think about what you had done."

"Of course, I am so sorry. I was wrong, Father."

"Follow me." He began to lead her toward the stables. She followed obediently. She desperately wanted to know what had happened to her mother, but to say anything would give Avery away. She would have to wait.

When they arrived at the stables, Farriss was there. He looked solemn and sad.

Something was wrong. Twig could feel it. . . . *Sapphire*. Had the guards done something to her? Were too rough when they took her back to the stables yesterday?

"Farriss, what's wrong?" Twig asked quietly.

Farriss glowered at her, but he did not say a word. Adam led her back to Sapphire's stall. She was there. She was fine. She whinnied with delight at the sight of Twig. She pressed her head into Twig's neck and lovingly enveloped Twig's hand with her big, pink tongue and mouth. Twig let out a deep breath, her pain from last night dissipating as she nuzzled into the soft breadth of Sapphire's neck.

"You need to say good-bye to her, Twig," she heard Adam say behind her.

"What do you mean?" She must have misheard him.

He took her hand and pulled her gently away from the horse. Sapphire stuck her head out of her stall, moving her head from side to side to indicate she wanted more of Twig's affection. Adam held Twig's shoulder while Farris put a bridle on Sapphire's head and then led her out of the stall into a ring in front of the stables.

"I don't understand." Twig turned to look at Adam. He nodded, indicating for her to walk to the ring, but he stopped her from actually entering. Farriss disappeared into the stables and then came back with a large, black satchel. Twig watched him in horror. Something was very wrong. She felt bile rising in her throat.

"What are you doing?" She could only manage a whisper. Her eyes filled with tears, her throat closing. Farriss removed a case from the satchel and took out a syringe that had a very long, thin needle. He filled the syringe with liquid.

"Tell her what you are doing, Farriss," Adam said.

"I am administering a tranquilizer," Farriss said. His voice was a stone of anger and distance. He was obviously in pain. Twig saw black at her periphery—a liquid blackness seeping inside of her as Farriss stuck the needle into Sapphire's neck.

It couldn't have been more than a minute since Farriss administered the shot when Sapphire's limbs went sickeningly limp and folded beneath her. The horse dropped to the ground. Twig opened her mouth and vomited. Adam held her back from running to Sapphire's side. She began to shake violently. This was happening too fast; this couldn't be happening. She had to stop this.

Farriss took out another syringe. Twig grabbed onto Adam. "Please," she begged. "Please stop this," she could barely speak. "I'll do anything. Stop this now." She trembled and clawed at him. He put his arms around her. He nodded toward Farriss to continue.

Farriss took a deep breath. He wiped his brow with his sleeve. Wiped the tears that had begun to spill from his large, dark eyes. "Are you certain, Father?"

Adam nodded in response, tightening his grip on Twig.

"Please let me say good-bye," Twig managed to say. "Please, I beg you."

Adam released her. She tore away from him and ran to Sapphire, fell to her knees and put the horse's head in her lap. She stroked her, covered her in kisses. She let her fingers fly over the horse's muzzle, head, ears, and mane, trying to memorize every inch of her. Sapphire's eyes were open, blinking. Twig stared deeply into them. "I'm here, baby. I'm here. I'm so sorry." She was sobbing.

"Farriss, continue." Adam was standing over them now.

"Twig, put her head down," Farriss said. "Stay away from her mouth. She may bite." Twig looked at him, confused. His voice was so hoarse it came out as a whisper. He injected the horse once more.

"Keep talking, Farriss," Adam instructed.

Farriss didn't take his eyes off Sapphire. "I've administered a sodium pentobarbital barbiturate. It will depress her central nervous system to the point of respiratory and cardiac arrest. It will kill her."

Sapphire began to thrash about, suffocating from the inside.

Twig's own lungs felt as if they were shutting down on her. She was crouched next to Sapphire's head now. Almost as soon as it started, the thrashing stopped. Twig watched Sapphire's belly, which still moved up and down, but in the limpness of her head and sudden stillness, Twig knew she was gone. The only life left in her was the cruel workings of the body, something strange and mechanical still persisting when all else was gone. Sapphire was gone.

The horse's belly went still. Farriss waved his hand over Sapphire's eyes. They stayed motionless, her pupils dilated, still and infinitely black.

"She's gone," he announced.

Twig felt something collapse inside her. Waves of thick black tar covered her insides. She lay down next to her horse, pulled herself into a fetal position, and rocked to stop the pain. She pressed herself into Sapphire's neck until Adam picked her up.

"You are washed clean now, my darling," he whispered in her ear, carrying her away. "Your sins are washed away." He carried her out of the corral and back toward the compound, speaking to her calmly and evenly the whole way. "I know how painful that was for you, but I had to teach you. I had to get your attention, my dear, sweet love. You are going to be my wife. You are held to a different standard. You cannot waver. You are a leader now."

"Was it a trick?" Twig said, barely hearing what he was saying to her. "Please, Father, tell me you just wanted to scare me. Please. Tell me if we go back, she will be fine. She'll wake up. You just wanted to scare me..."

Adam sat down with Twig still in his arms. She was so weak with grief that she collapsed into him. She waited for him to tell her Sapphire was still alive. Twig would see her again, she would ride her again, care for her again, feed her, groom her. Her heart would beat beneath Twig's devoted embrace.

"It grieves me to hurt you like this, my little one." His face contorted with pain as he looked at her. "But it has to be. You will never forget now. You will recover from this, and you will find new strength. I promise. This pain will go away."

"No," she said, still shaking violently. "I will never be the same."

"No, you won't. But you'll find that, ultimately, that is a good thing. It was a bad attachment. An attachment like that is something that will only weaken you and draw away your focus. And your focus needs to be on your Family, on what I teach you."

"On you," she said.

"Yes, on me."

"I can stand now," she said. She had to get away from him. "Can I go to my cottage now, Father?"

He looked at her for a moment, searching her face for something. He took a deep breath. "You may hate me now, Twig, but this will bring us closer." He looked at her with sympathy. "Go home now. Go rest. You are excused from the day's activities, but I want to see you at dinner."

Avery was in the kitchen pacing when Twig walked in.

"We need to get our stories straight," she said as soon as she saw Twig. Her eyes were wild with anxiety. She was visibly shaken. She didn't notice the state Twig was in.

"He's forced me into a real corner." Avery was firing words out like bullets. Twig slumped into a chair, not listening to a word her mother was saying. Right now she didn't care about anything. She was so filled with pain and shock that she felt half dead.

Avery stopped talking when she finally noticed Twig wasn't listening. She squinted her eyes at Twig and asked quietly, "What happened?"

Twig closed her eyes. Fresh tears she didn't think she had left spilled down her cheeks. She felt utterly alone. Avery came to her side and kneeled down next to her, her brow furrowed with worry. She took Twig's hand gently and repeated her question. "What happened, Twig? Are you hurt? Did he hurt you?" Avery took Twig's face in her hands, and Twig broke into sobs, her slight back convulsing. Avery gasped. "Did he—" she paused. "Did he touch you?"

Twig opened her eyes and looked at her mother. "He killed Sapphire," she said. She gazed at her mother, her expression pleading for some sort of explanation, some sort of help.

"Oh, Twig," Avery sighed. She shook her head with sympathy but was obviously relieved. "I'm so sorry, Twig. Come here." Avery took Twig in her arms.

"She's gone, Mommy."

Avery just held her. "I'm so sorry, baby. So very sorry."

"It feels like he ripped my chest open. It hurts so bad." Twig started to feel like she was going to faint. The black was at her periphery again, and she was dizzy. She pushed Avery away and put her head between her knees to keep from passing out. "I need some water. I was in isolation all night."

Avery ran to the sink and got Twig a glass of water. She looked around the kitchen, but all they had were bananas. "Just take a small sip, and when you can manage it, take a small bite of this, just to get some potassium back into you." Twig took the water, but she shook her head at the banana. She was too nauseated.

She looked at Avery. Something in Twig began to harden. This was Avery's fault. This was the result of her selfishness. If Avery had come with her yesterday, none of this would have happened.

"What is wrong with you?" Twig said stonily. "Really, what is wrong with you? This is your fault."

"What do you mean?" Avery asked, confused, eyeing Twig warily.

"You couldn't just come with me yesterday? You were *tired*? A little *sad*? Just didn't *feel like it*? Did anything happen to you when you came back? Did you spend a night in isolation pissing on yourself?"

"Twig, calm down."

"I am sick of being calm! You are a selfish monster, and you have lied to me my whole life!"

"Twig, what are you talking about?"

"You know what I'm talking about."

"Do you want to have this conversation now?"

"Yes! Yes, I want to have it now! Do you? Are you going to run away from me like the coward that you are? Or are you actually going to talk to me?"

"I was planning on talking to you when you came in. I talked to Doc, and he gave me a pretty nice ultimatum."

Twig took a few more sips of water. It felt better to be angry than to feel the pain of Sapphire's loss.

"Are you sure you're okay, Twig? I know you are angry, but maybe we should try to get you some broth or something—"

"I'm okay. We need to talk about this. What did Doc say to you?"

"He told me you came to him, asking about your childhood, your father, and me. The thing I don't understand, Twig, is why you would go to him and not come to me."

Twig turned sharply toward her mother. Her anger was rising again.

"I was going to tell you yesterday at Gran's!" Twig said, completely exasperated.

The two women stared at each other in silence for a moment. Twig was nearly shaking, holding back her rage.

"It was all lies. I just want you to know that. Everything he told you. You are not crazy," Avery whispered, trying to appeal to Twig. "He told me to tell you that you were imagining things, but you're not."

"I know," Twig answered. She was calming down. She was too exhausted to hold this pitch of emotion much longer.

"You know?"

"I mean, I think I know. Tina said as much."

"Tina?" Avery looked confused.

"Yes, she overheard my talk with Doc," Twig said warily.

Had the last forty-eight hours been real? Now she began to wonder if she'd dreamt it all during her feverish sleep in isolation. Had she really had that conversation with Tina? It seemed so unreal now.

"And she told you Doc was lying? Why would she do that?"

Twig sucked her breath in. "She said I'd have to do her a favor one day."

"A favor?"

"Give her money. She said she's going to leave one day, and that I need to give her money to do it."

"Jesus." Avery was shaking her head. "She can't threaten you. You're the apple of Adam's eye right now. What is she thinking?"

"He has a really nice way of treating the apple of his eye," Twig said bitterly. She thought of Sapphire.

"May I?" Avery pulled out the chair next to Twig. Twig nodded but got up to refill her water glass.

"Keep sipping. You need to take it slow." Avery had experience with coming out of isolation. "So you didn't buy it when Doc said you were as crazy as your mother?" Avery looked at Twig. They were both calmer now.

"I bought it completely, actually. I mean, not that I think you're crazy, Mom. I just bought what he told me. Why wouldn't I? If it weren't for Tina, I would have taken the pills he gave me. I would have thought that I had lost my mind, or was close, anyway." She stopped talking for a moment, thinking. "Do they want to make me lose my mind? By killing my horse?"

"This is all my fault. All of it. You're right, Twig. I'm a terrible person and a terrible mother." Avery looked at the floor.

"It's true."

Avery looked at Twig, surprised.

Twig smiled—a strange, hopeless smile, but a smile. "You kind of are. But Doc and Adam make you look pretty good. And you're the only mother I have." Twig's voice turned serious again. "But don't ever do that to me again, Mom."

"I won't," Avery said quickly. "I promise, I won't." The two women were silent for a while.

"I thought he loved me," Avery said suddenly, her voice low and sad.

Twig looked at her mother. Was she talking about Twig's father? Her real father? "Go on," Twig said.

Avery smiled for a moment. "I had just started graduate school at NYU. We—your father, Cary, and I—lived in Connecticut, and I was commuting a few times a week to the city."

"You were in graduate school in New York City?"

Avery smiled again. Something flickered in her gray eyes. "I was going to be an anthropologist, if you can believe it."

"I can believe it, Mom," Twig said, coming out of her fog. She reached for the banana and began to peel it.

"I was certainly messed up then, but in a different way. I sort of had your energy and spunk without your wisdom to curb it all. You have this ability to contain your emotions that I've never had."

Twig thought about Leo and wondered how much wisdom she had. She had also been meditating daily since she was eight years old. It kind of made keeping your emotions in check easy. But she kept quiet and listened.

"I was really wild, always hard to control. I just always did whatever I wanted. The more people—my parents, your father his parents—tried to tell me what to do, the more I went the other way.

"It's ironic that I've ended up here. Caged in the lovely mountains of Costa Rica with the freedom of a parakeet." Avery gave a smirk and shook her head.

"Anyway, to make a really long story short, I met Adam at NYU. He wasn't a student, but he was holding these meetings on campus." Avery turned her attention to Twig. "Take another bite of banana." Twig did.

"You have to understand, Twig, I was really young. I married too young, I got pregnant too young, and I wasn't exactly working with a full deck to begin with."

"Mom."

Avery held up her hand. "It's okay. Back home I was diagnosed with something called bipolar disorder, which basically means I would dip into major episodes of depression and every now and then have some really intense, destructive highs. Your father really did try to help me. He took me to the best doctors, and I started taking medication." Avery looked wistful, her expression full of what could have been. "I mean, he wasn't perfect by any means. He was always away at work and completely under his parent's thrall, but he did genuinely care about me and tried to help. And he loved you, Twig."

"He did?" Twig asked quietly.

"Yes, like crazy. I can't imagine how deeply I've hurt him."

Twig felt a nauseating blend of feelings surge up in her stomach.

"So, along came Adam with his ideas and his charm. I was a perfect target."

"Target?"

"Yeah, target. He was collecting people for this." Avery gestured in the general direction of the compound. "The Family."

"Where's Evelyn?" Twig suddenly interjected, looking around her. She didn't want to stop talking, but they had to be vigilant. Adam would be watching.

"Evelyn will probably be at Rose and Thomas's house again tonight. I don't think she is going to take her eyes off Rose until that baby is safely in this world. We can talk more after dinner."

"Rose is pregnant?"

Avery nodded. Twig's eyes popped open. *Wow. That was fast.*

Twig looked down, suddenly feeling ashamed. "I have to bathe before dinner. We can't be late." She let her voice harden. "We *will* keep talking after." Avery looked back at her daughter with compassion.

"Yes. I'm so sorry, Twig." Avery took Twig's hand. "Let me help you. I'll run your bath while you undress. Give me your dress, too—I'll wash it." Twig followed her mother toward the bathroom. She dreaded going to dinner. What would everyone think of her? What did they know? What had been said about her? She had the strange realization that it didn't matter what they thought. She was Adam's fiancée. She would be their Mother before long.

And she would trade places with any one of them.

* * *

Avery and Twig were seated in the living room of their cottage, big glasses of icy lemonade in front of them on their coffee table. Avery hadn't taken a bite of her dinner, and Twig had managed what she could. Now she sat with her head on her mother's shoulder.

As Avery had predicted, Evelyn was with Rose and Thomas. She said she was going to spend the night at their cottage. It was a blessing having the place to themselves for the night. They could breathe more freely without Evelyn's craning presence.

"I already miss Sapph so much. I feel like this will never stop hurting. It was so senseless, such a waste of life. Such a good, sweet life."

"I know, sweetie." Avery held Twig's hand and just sat quietly with her, holding her pain.

"I wish we had a stereo. It would be nice to have music," Twig said quietly, suddenly remembering the nano. She'd have to show Avery after they talked.

"I've gotten so used to living without it that I don't really miss it anymore," Avery said.

Twig knew she should be spitting venom at Avery or giving her the silent treatment. She should be demanding answers and apologies. But everything in Twig's experience with her mother kept her from these reactions. She was so hungry for Avery's love, her companionship. It was such a balm after what she'd been through in the last twenty-four hours.

And they had never had an evening like this to themselves. Never. Maybe if they'd had years of sitting on the couch together like this, drinking lemonade and talking or reading or doing nothing. But there had always been people around, or Avery wasn't around—physically and mentally.

It was also such a relief to talk to Avery about what had been tormenting Twig for weeks.

"Okay, so continue. Distract me. Please."

Avery stared at Twig for a moment. "You've been through a lot lately."

Twig sighed. "So you were at NYU, studying anthropology…" Twig lifted her chin toward Avery to signal her to continue.

"It's very strange to talk this way about the man who is supposed to be your future husband, but here goes:

"I was at NYU, and Adam was more… Well, he was different. He has his whole leader-of-the-Family, Adam-with-a-capital-*A* persona now. But back then, he was…" Avery took a breath, searching for the word, "…unformed. Unformed and vulnerable.

"He was really romantic. He would pick me up from class with a picnic basket, and we'd find some grass and shade, eat cheese, drink wine from plastic cups, and talk and talk. Wow, could we talk to one another back in those days." Avery looked over at Twig. "Is this too weird?"

"No, it's fine. I'm getting to hear about this part of you that I've never known. I'm sort of pushing the Adam part aside for now."

"Well, brace yourself, because this story does not have a happy ending."

"Braced," Twig replied. The past was twisted and barbed, but this moment felt safe, and the whole evening stretched out before them. She was drained and deeply grieved, but this moment felt still. It was a break in the chaos surrounding her lately.

"He told me there was nothing wrong with me, that society's norms were too narrow, that they were suffocating me. He said society didn't have a place for me and made me feel crazy as a way of try to keep me under control. He said bipolar disorder was just a concept made up by the medical community—a label, a metaphor. It wasn't real. He said he had a place for me, and I would never feel like an outsider again." Avery let out a big, sad laugh.

"What a bunch of crap, but I bought every word of it. I was so young. You believe that kind of stuff when you're young." Avery shrugged. "As you know, Adam didn't turn out to be some purveyor of worldview expansion who made room for my quirks and ticks. He did the opposite."

"That's what I've been wrestling with lately," Twig answered thoughtfully. "I thought there were all these good things about our lives, our Family. But I keep finding out about all of these lies and secrets. What happened? Or was it always this way? Why would you come here if it was?"

"That's what I was trying to explain before. Adam *was* different. He had these out-there, friendly ideas, and he was more of a hippie." Avery shook her head. "Well, he became corrupted, and his vision for a utopia became perverted with power. This is so hard. I know you've been raised to admire him. And now you're supposed to *marry* him—"

"It's okay," Twig said. "I need to hear this. I need to hear all of it, and we haven't even started talking about my father or my grandparents."

Avery looked hard at Twig. She seemed to be taking a mental x-ray, trying to assess whether Twig was going to crack or unravel if she continued with her story.

"Mom, yesterday I thought I was crazy. Everything else is up from there." Twig tried to sound cavalier. "Just tell me. Stop worrying about me."

"It feels nice to worry about you for a change," Avery said humbly.

Twig grabbed Avery's hand.

"So, your father was in politics," Avery continued. "His whole family was in politics and pretty much always had been. Big politics—senators, governors, et cetera. I was kind of apolitical and more interested in the human aspect of things. At the time, Adam's way of looking at the world seemed more humane and enlightened than your father's. I was really attracted to that. Joke's on me, huh?" Avery said sourly.

"Add in his flattery, his attention when I was feeling both alienated from your father and as if I was falling off the map being a new mother, and ta-da…" Avery flung her long fingers in front of her as if the gesture were the final ingredient to a spell she was casting, "a Family member is born."

"I don't totally understand." Twig didn't. Why would her mother leave her father, her life, for Adam?

"I mean that I would have followed him anywhere. In my defense, I thought I was in love, and I thought the feelings were mutual."

Twig tried to keep herself from judging her mother. She wanted to ask Avery how she could betray her father, how she could leave him, and how she could take his daughter away from him because he was boring or had the wrong political views. She forced herself to keep those thoughts to herself. Avery was on a roll. Talking was obviously having a therapeutic effect on her. She had shed her usual skittish nature for the moment. Twig didn't want to ruin that.

"There's more to this story, but imagine a whirlwind romance and a lot of mind-blowing sex—"

"Ugh," Twig groaned. The thought of Adam and her mother having sex was not something she needed to imagine.

"I know." Avery cringed. "There is no justifying it. I just want you to have some idea of what I was going through at the time."

"What is he thinking, wanting to marry me? Does he want to torture you? Actually, never mind." Twig held her hand up and tried to wave away the images that were flying uninvited through her mind.

"Now, honey, this part is going to upset you." Avery squeezed Twig's knee.

"It gets worse?"

Avery sighed.

"Okay, go on," Twig said, holding her breath.

"I decided to leave your father and go with Adam. He wouldn't tell me where we were going, but he said he was starting a community. He said the only way I could show him that I really loved him—that I was truly committed to him—was to go with him. He said I was the woman he needed at his side to realize his vision for this group."

The very words Adam had said to Twig.

"All of this sounds so insane now, so stupid. But this is what happened: I was supposed to meet him at a bus station in New Jersey and bring all the money I could. For weeks I emptied accounts, stashing hoards of cash in my underwear drawer, shoeboxes, anywhere I could hide it." Avery began to cry quietly. "I've gone over this night so many times in my head. Wishing I had never gone. Thinking of ways I could have gotten away."

Twig listened. Her heart was pounding.

"I stole away in the middle of the night. You were fast asleep. So little and so sweet and so innocent. I just took you." Avery's tears dried up, and her voice became serrated, filled with self-hatred.

"I had this big suitcase full of cash, our clothes, and all of your sweet little toddler things, your sippy cup and your blankie." Avery stopped for a moment.

"Anyway, I got to the bus station. It was almost 2:00 a.m. and Adam was there with a bunch of other people. They had a bus, which was probably stolen. He was so dismissive of me, like he didn't know me. I don't even care about any of that now. It's thinking of you sleeping in your little car seat, so trusting. How could I have—"

"Mom, it's over. I'm here. That little girl is me. She's not there anymore." Twig had tears in her eyes. Especially after today, that little girl was gone.

"I know. I know you are. This is painful. I'm sorry."

"It's okay. Take your time."

"I had this little mallard-green BMW. I had renounced consumerism for Adam, but I loved that car. He took my suitcase and slammed it on the trunk. He removed the money and handed all our belongings to one of his cronies, who tossed it all like trash into a nearby dumpster." Twig gasped hearing this.

"And here is where I always get stuck. There was a split-second where I could have jumped in the car and taken us away. But I froze. I was so shocked and so scared… I froze. I just wanted to get you out of the car and in my arms, and then he demanded my keys and my phone. They went in the dumpster after the suitcase."

"Mom." Twig covered her mouth with her hand.

"I pleaded with him to take the money and leave us. And that's when he turned his charm back on. He said he was just stressed. He held me and kissed me and said everything was going to be just how we talked about." Avery shook her head bitterly. "That's another moment I replay. If I had persisted, would he have let us go?

"They led us to the bus. I was holding on to you for dear life. I already knew I'd made a mistake. Yasmine came and sat next to me. She took you, saying that you would be fine. I fought to hold you, but Doc came and stuck a needle in my arm.

"When I woke up, I was here. You were playing with Sophie and Ryan, and Adam showed up and introduced me to his wife, Tina, and their daughter."

"Did you try to get away?"

"I think you've heard enough horror stories for one day. In a nutshell, they kept me busy from the minute I woke up until I had to pour myself into bed every night—not that they let me or any of the newcomers sleep at all. Between exhaustion, the emotional violence of the Meetings, and being completely cut off from everyone I knew, I didn't have much energy to try to find a way off the compound. I couldn't even find a phone. And Doc was pretty trigger-happy with the syringe back in those days."

Avery's voice became serious. "I did try a few times, and it ended badly. And then I found Gran. It was early on. Every now and then, just when I thought I couldn't take anymore, Adam would let me ride out alone. There weren't so many people back then. The rules were different. It was on one of those rides, as I was half-trying to relax and half-looking for some kind of escape route, that I came upon Gran's place. I stopped trying to leave once I found Gran."

"So why don't we just leave now?" Twig knew it wouldn't be simple, but they could do it.

"How? We have no money and no resources, and if I step foot into the U.S., I'll be thrown in prison for kidnapping for the rest of my life. At least here, I can be with you."

"What if we call my father? I'm sure he would be so relieved that he would forgive you. You were taken against your will."

"I was, but I wasn't," Avery said.

"But you were."

"He will not see it that way. *I* barely see it that way. Trust me, your father has had more than a decade of sadness and worry and grief. There is no way he is just going to forgive me."

Avery took a deep breath, shaking her head. "It's getting late," Twig said, tapping Avery's knee, "but I want to show you something."

Avery raised her eyebrows and leaned back on the couch while Twig went to the bedroom and brought out the nano.

"It plays music."

"Who are you? Adam? Do you have a cellphone, too?" Avery joked.

"I wish," Twig said. If she did, it would be a lot easier to talk to Leo. "A friend gave it to me," she added.

"Hello! What friend?"

"The boy I met at the hospital. Do you remember him and his beautiful sister?"

Avery seemed to be trying to think back.

"Oh, Mom. His name is Leo, and he is amazing," Twig gushed, forgetting all of her sadness and worry for a moment. "His sister is named Hazel, and I ran into them when Thomas and I went to Turrialba!"

"Did Thomas see you talking to them?" Avery asked with concern.

"No!" Twig said proudly.

"And he gave you this?"

"Can you keep a secret?"

Avery just stared back at Twig.

"Okay, stupid question. We're supposed to meet again next time Thomas and I go to town."

Avery frowned. "That sounds dangerous. What if Adam sees you or has you followed?"

"I don't care," Twig blurted out. "I won't stay away out of fear. Leo and his family are only here for another month or so. Adam's already taken enough from me," she added with anger.

"Ah, so you do have some of me in you," Avery said, raising her eyebrows. "But I think we need to talk about the two of us being much more careful from now on."

Everything in Twig wanted to say, "You need to be more careful," but she knew Avery would take it as criticism and wouldn't be able to handle that.

Not wanting to ruin the moment, Twig hopped back up on the couch next to Avery, the nano in hand. She put one of the earbuds into Avery's ear and one into her own and then snuggled beside her to listen.

"Ooh, I used to love this song," Avery said.

"What's it called?" Twig asked excitedly.

"'They Say It's Spring,' by Blossom Dearie." Avery put her arm around Twig and stroked her hair. The truth had removed some barrier between them.

Avery sat up suddenly and pulled the earbud out of her ear. "Wait, how old is this Leo guy? He's either way too old for you, or he's got an old soul's taste in music."

"I think he's my age."

"Okay then." Avery sat back and replaced the earbud, the irony of her motherly concern not lost on either of them.

"Wait!" Twig stopped the music and sat up. "The virus in the outside world—it's a lie, right?" Twig had lowered her voice to a whisper.

Avery nodded. Then she put her hand up to stop Twig from saying anymore. Twig wondered how many people in the Family knew this, or knew it at one time and had buried that knowledge. She put their earbuds in and started the music again.

Twig was exhausted. She let the music drift over her and fell asleep with her head on Avery's shoulder.

30

They decided to eat at Meng's. Twig ordered soup but could barely touch it, she was so full of nerves. Slurping up an unruly plate of noodles was out of the question.

It was her first date with Leo.

She laid it on thick with Thomas in order to get away. She hoped she hadn't overdone it. She'd told him she was so disgusted with the outside world that it was better that they split up, divide the errands, and get home as quickly as possible. Why spend one minute more in this den of sin than they had to? Ever since she had spent the night in isolation, ever since Sapphire had died and she'd talked to Avery, Twig's loyalty to Adam had disappeared. She was still just as scared of him, but her ambivalence toward his actions had vanished. He might have his reasons for the things he did, but there was no justification for taking an innocent life. There was nothing he could say to explain away Sapphire's death.

Twig shook off her thoughts of Adam. She was very happy to be there having lunch with Leo. He didn't seem as nervous as she was. His energy was almost puppy-like as he dug into his noodles without reserve. Twig liked that; it put her more at ease.

"Is Twig your real name? I mean, is it a nickname?"

Leo didn't know how pointed a question this was. She decided to go with the simple answer.

"Apparently, when I was a kid, I loved to build these little structures with sticks—kind of elaborate things. So I guess the name just stuck."

"I like it. It suits you. What's your real name?"

"Next question," Twig said tentatively. She didn't want to be rude, but she had to throw him off this line of questioning. She was pretty sure her real name was Olivia. She had heard it enough times in her dreams. But she couldn't share that information right now. She hadn't even asked Avery yet.

"Ah, touchy subject. Enough said."

"No, it's just Twig. I've always just been known as Twig for as long as I can remember." Twig put her hand on Leo's reassuringly but removed it quickly. He smiled at her.

"You're a mysterious one."

"Much more mysterious than I'd like to be."

"Should we get the awkward stuff out of the way?"

"Yes. How do we do that?" Twig leaned forward with interest. She would love to be able to speak to Leo without feeling as if she was navigating a maze of self-consciousness. It was almost as if they were from separate planets.

"Well, can I ask you a question and have you know that my motivation is purely wanting to get to know you? I'm a bit worried I might offend you."

"Don't worry about that. Go ahead."

"Well, can you tell me about… Ahh, how do I put this?"

"Just say it. Really, it's okay," Twig said reassuringly.

"Okay." Leo took a deep breath. "I am just curious about your clothes and why all of your posse seems to wear white."

"Yeah. That." Twig leaned back in her chair. Leo dug into his noodles while waiting for Twig to answer.

"Now *you* just say it," he laughed when she hesitated.

"Okay." Twig took a deep breath. "I live in a community called the

Family. Oh, does that sound really weird? I've never said that to anyone before. It sounded really weird when I said it out loud."

"I sensed some weirdness when I met you, but I'm still here," Leo said warmly. "I mean, I'm not judging, I just mean it's okay. I'm sure I've got all sorts of weirdness for you to uncover. So, a kibbutz type of community? What are we talking?"

"Well, we're a collective. We believe in the needs of the group over the needs of the individual."

"Whoa." Leo stopped eating. He knitted his eyebrows in thought and sat back in his chair. His energy definitely became more serious. Despite being unnerved by this, Twig continued. She might as well tell him about her life and her Family. If he didn't like her, she would be disappointed, but what else could she do? Even if she wanted to leave the Family, she couldn't exactly pretend that she was just a girl from the outside world.

"We live communally on a compound in the mountains near here. As you know, we all dress the same. And basically everything we do is to help our community thrive. Cooking, gardening, classes, et cetera." Twig waited for Leo to respond again before she continued. She didn't mention Adam on purpose.

"Honest response?" Leo took a sip of his water. His plate of noodles still stood untouched since Twig had started talking about the Family.

"Please."

"It either sounds like some sort of Huxley utopia or a communist cult."

"What's a cult?"

"What's a cult?" Leo sat back, surprised. He cupped his chin while thinking her question over. "Hard to say, exactly. What you described sounds kind of cool—people going off and doing their thing. It's just that all of the stories you hear about cults are really bad. Jonestown and Waco, just to name a few."

Twig looked at Leo blankly.

"Never heard of those?"

Twig shook her head.

"That makes sense. I'm sure whoever started your group wouldn't want those stories handed down. They would scare you to death."

"Try me."

Leo studied Twig with his big, warm eyes. "Next question?" he acquiesced.

Twig laughed. "That bad, huh?"

Leo nodded soberly.

Twig wanted to tell him that she was questioning her place in the Family, but she didn't want to ruin their first date. It seemed too heavy for first-date talk. "Does it matter? I mean, if I'm part of an ideal society or a cult? I mean, of course it does, but for you and me, right now, does it matter? I would 100 percent understand if it does."

Leo took Twig's hand in his. "Nah, it doesn't. Just don't try to recruit me." Leo laughed, but Twig went red with embarrassment.

"Oh, I would never, I—"

"Hey," he said gently. "I was totally kidding. Really. Bad joke. Let's just get to know each other. And when we travel too far down a road—"

"Next question?" they both said in unison.

"Exactly!"

They laughed.

"I'm really happy to see you," Leo said. "To sit and talk with you."

"Me, too," Twig said, her laughter subsiding. "I will say this. I live with a lot of rules and a lot of…" she paused, thinking of the right word, "…control. I'm sorry our time together has to be so short."

"I'm sorry, too, but I'll take what I can get."

Twig smiled. She really liked him. She knew they lived in completely different worlds, but over lunch like this, they seemed just like two people getting to know each other. He seemed unusual, too. Twig got the sense that your average American surfer boy wouldn't take the time to see past her clothes and, as Leo said, her "posse" and get to know her.

The rest of their time together was spent talking about music. Leo scratched out some of the song names and artists from the iPod. He also gave her a charger, saying the nano would run out of juice before long.

Twig told him how she'd found Lucinda Williams, Jeff Tweedy, Blossom Dearie, the Rolling Stones, and Kanye West so far. She told him how Lucinda Williams' "Side of the Road" and Jeff Tweedy's "Remember the Mountain Bed" had touched her most.

Leo was excited to tell her that "Remember the Mountain Bed" was Jeff Tweedy singing a poem by Woody Guthrie.

"Epic romance, that song," Leo enthused. They both blushed a little bit.

Eventually they had to cut their conversation short. Twig had to race to do her errands.

Twig was still giddy when she and Thomas pulled back into the compound. She used her extra energy to talk Thomas's ear off about all the disgusting things she saw in Turrialba. Thomas was easy. She was afraid she wouldn't be able to hide her happiness from Doc as she knocked on his door for their new weekly sessions. She had to stop, take a deep breath, and clear her face of all emotion. She steadied her breathing and got ready to lie through her teeth.

At first, Doc's questions were direct and easy to answer. Yes, she was taking her medication. No, she hadn't had any more of the disturbing dreams. Yes, she was feeling better. No, not well enough to resume participation in Meetings. But then he asked her about the isolation incident, about Sapphire. Twig had to fight not to let her anger with Adam surface. It had only been a week. She was still traumatized. Lunch with Leo had been a welcome and lovely distraction from her pain and guilt. If only she had done something different, then Sapphire would still be alive. She knew it wasn't her fault, but she couldn't help blaming herself somewhat.

"I was told you described being disoriented."

"Yes," Twig said.

"What happened?"

"I took two pills instead of one. I was feeling very anxious."

"Ah," Doc seemed satisfied. "That was not very smart, but it explains things. I've never known you to break a rule."

Or at least I've never been caught *breaking any rules,* Twig thought in response.

"I'm embarrassed about it, Doc. I didn't even tell Adam because I was so embarrassed."

"Of course. Didn't want to look bad to your betrothed. He was awfully hard on you, wasn't he, Twig?"

This was a test. "It hurt, but I understand why he did it."

"Do you?"

"Yes," Twig nodded. "I am going to be his wife. People will look to me as a model of behavior."

"Okay. It couldn't have been easy for you, though."

"No," Twig said.

"One pill, Twig. At bedtime or in an emergency."

"Yes, of course. I learned my lesson the hard way."

"Same time next week?"

"See you then."

* * *

In anticipation of her second date with Leo, Twig put her head down and worked. She didn't want to garner any suspicion. She knew she was walking a very thin line.

She got into her yoga practice in a way she never had. She immersed herself in the burning of her muscles, the tightening of her core, the tiny, varied worlds that lived within each pose. She didn't have any problems with her wrist. In those moments, she experienced freedom.

Evelyn stayed with Thomas and Rose. It might not have gone through official channels, which was unusual, but no one said anything about Evelyn's new living situation. Everyone was happy with how it was working out. Perhaps Evelyn had asked Adam, but no one had said anything to Twig or Avery.

During the day, Avery and Twig ignored each other. Twig was scared Adam would be threatened by their newfound closeness. At night, if they were both free, they knitted or baked or did some girly activity previously unknown to them as mother and daughter. For a while she stayed away from Gran's, but when she couldn't stand it any longer, Twig began to sneak back out to paint at dawn. But now she always dragged Avery out of bed to come with her. Avery owed her at least that much. They doubled up on Bill Evans and made the journey together. Twig knew she shouldn't be going, but she couldn't stop herself. Painting was like a fever she'd caught. The desire to do it burned through her.

And, finally, she began to attend Verdant Green classes. They felt more like rituals than classes. First there was a rather medical discussion about sex and reproduction. Then Yasmine would read different passages about marriage and love from varied sources: some poetry (which Twig loved and had never heard before), or a big, satin-covered book that Yasmine called her book of romance. There were drawings in it that made Rose and Twig blush and giggle nervously. Rose would sweetly tell stories about Thomas and her. Twig would mostly listen, taking it all in. She thought about Leo even though she knew she was supposed to be learning how to please Adam. What was she going to do? The thought of having sex with Adam clawed at the back of her brain. Would it hurt? Could she get out of it? Thinking of it reminded her of swimming in one of the rivers on the compound, her legs dangling deep in the blackness, never really knowing what was underneath the surface of the water.

And Adam was there waiting for her after class. Every time. They would exchange a few words as he linked his arm in hers and walked her to her next activity. She found a way to be around him. She let the fight seep out of her. She smiled. She laughed. She let him look deep into her eyes. And she watched it all from above.

* * *

The next time Twig met Leo, they explored Turrialba. Popping in and out of stores, buying cups of coffee and cookies, Twig began to feel less inhibited, less awkward. Knowing there was no virus, she ate and drank with abandon. She spoke to shop keepers with the few Spanish words she knew. She was emboldened by the adventure of it all. Her heart soared. Feeling more comfortable, she turned the questions on Leo.

He grew up in Santa Monica and had just graduated high school. He was going to Yale to study architecture. Maya Lin was one of his heroes. Music was his life. Surfing was his other life. He talked about being half black and half white, living in two worlds. His mom was African American and from what he described as an evangelical, Protestant family. "Church folk," he smiled. His dad was white, Jewish, and from Los Angeles. Living in two worlds. Lately, Twig could relate.

They got in an argument about politics. Leo said his politics were liberal, and that he was a patriot through and through. He dug his country. This rubbed at Twig a little bit. She couldn't help it after everything she'd been taught about the United States over the years.

"Remember when we said we could just say it if we had something awkward that we needed to say?"

"Shoot."

"Well, doesn't the rich elite in your country own over 40 percent of the wealth? Aren't people starving in your country while other people wear five-hundred dollar shoes and drive cars that cost enough to educate an illiterate person and send them to college?" She felt a little accusatory, but she was still very skeptical about America, regardless of how she felt about Adam.

"That's a pretty simplistic view." Leo was obviously annoyed by what she had said.

"What do you mean?"

"What you said is true, but there's inequality everywhere. I'm willing to bet that, pound for pound, America has probably given more people the opportunity for a better life than any other country in the world. We're not perfect and we have our problems, but, by and large, Americans are decent people who care about their neighbors and their kids. There are parts of our country that I hate and people who are hateful and wrong, but you can't have the kind of freedom our system affords us without giving them a voice along with everyone else."

"But children starve in your country," Twig rejoined.

"Twig, there are children starving in every country on earth. It's a sad and terrible thing, but whoever is telling you that America is the only place where that happens is wrong. It's certainly happening here in Costa Rica."

"It doesn't happen where I live."

"And where do you live, Twig? How many people are in this Family of yours? You haven't said, but no matter what the number, you are living in a bubble."

Twig went quiet. He was right. She felt humbled and stupid. All her boldness disappeared.

"I don't mean to be harsh, but what you said—"

"That's how I've been taught to think," Twig said honestly.

"I'm sorry," Leo said. He moved closer to her. They were sitting on the large stone steps of a cathedral, and Leo took Twig's hand.

"I must seem so boring, so ignorant to you," Twig said. She was sure her novelty had just worn off.

"There's nothing boring about you, Twig." She squeezed Leo's hand in response.

"I don't want to be like this," Twig said quietly. "My education has just been very…" she paused, searching for the right word, "limited."

Leo shrugged. "Everyone's is, in a way," he admitted. "Hey," he added, knocking his knees against hers playfully. "Would you object to me changing the subject?"

Twig smiled. "Please!" She felt stupid and was grateful to move on. "But before you do, can I ask you something?"

"Of course."

"I have this friend at home. He…" She treaded lightly, not knowing what response she would get. "He is homosexual."

"Okay. I'm with you."

"How do people in America feel about people who are gay?"

"How do people in America feel about gay people? That's a loaded question. I'll do my best to answer that as a straight person, but I think you would have to ask someone who is gay to get the most legitimate answer." Twig looked at him.

"Right, you don't know any gay people who live in America. Like I said, I'll do my best." Leo raised his eyebrows. "I think I should first say that regardless of how heterosexual people feel about gay people—because some are very accepting and some are very vocal about hating them—there are places where I think gay people feel safe and don't feel like they have to hide. In some places, they are free to get married, and a lot of them fight for our country in the military. If you walk down the street in the

Castro district of San Francisco, you will see many gay couples living out in the open. And yet, many states continue to ban same-sex marriage, so…" Leo frowned. "I'm not really answering your question, am I?"

"So there are *some* places where someone who is gay could live freely? A man could be with another man?"

"Or a woman with another woman. Yes. I just don't want to give the impression that it isn't complicated, or that's there's not still a lot of homophobia and hatred out there."

"How do you feel?" Twig squinted her eyes at Leo. "About two men or two women being able to marry?"

"I'm all for it."

"Good," she said sweetly. He had such an open, loving nature. "So what were you going to say before? When you were going to change the subject?"

"I have this thing I like to do. I haven't really talked to anyone about it, but since we're having a sort of put-it-all-out-on-the-table kind of day…"

"Ooh, tell me." Twig's eyes lit up.

"God, you're beautiful," Leo said, looking suddenly a bit dazed. "Really. It almost hurts to look at you sometimes."

"Thank you," Twig said modestly. "That's funny, that's how I think of my mom's beauty. I would never describe myself that way, but thank you."

"I mean it."

Twig blushed. Their eyes locked. There was too much energy surging between them for Twig to let shyness pull her away.

"You are, too," she said softly. She meant it. Their knees were touching, swaying together lightly to some unheard music.

"Come here." He cupped her face gently with his hands. She put her nose to his and imagined she heard the sweep of their eyelashes touching.

"Is it okay if we kiss? I mean, because of your Family?"

The ramifications burned across Twig's brain like a quick and powerful flame. But this was the first kiss she had always wanted. A do-over. She could pretend the kiss with Adam never happened.

"It's okay with me," she said.

He touched his lips to hers. Softness. His lips swept across hers like feathers. He paused, their lips held together by the slightest pressure coming from both of them, soft and radiating a million trails of tiny sensations. It wasn't until the tail end of the kiss that they truly pressed their lips together.

They pulled away and laughed lightly.

"What were you going to tell me?"

"Tell you?" Leo looked at her with a puzzled expression on his face.

"The thing you like to do that you haven't told anyone about? And that was my first real kiss." To her, it was.

"Come here!" Leo gave Twig one of his bear hugs and kissed the top of her head with honey-dripping affection. "Don't try to just throw that in there, girl."

"Well, it's kind of embarrassing!" Twig giggled.

"It's not, and I'm honored. And the thing I was going to tell you about was my life soundtracks."

"Life soundtracks?"

"Yeah. The perfect song for the moment."

"Ooh, I like that. I do something like that. Well, sort of like that."

"What is it?"

"Colors. I give people colors." A flashback of telling Adam this crossed Twig's mind. She wished she hadn't shared it with him. She didn't want Adam to know anything about who she really was, and now she understood why she couldn't find a color for Adam. The truth of him was hidden beneath layers of lies.

The memory threatened to cheat on this moment with Leo. "But I want to hear about your songs," she added. "You first."

"Like before, sitting here with you on these steps and the rightness between us…the ease. Sometimes only a song can describe a moment like that."

"The ease? I think you were pretty mad at me a few minutes ago."

"That's part of it. That's real."

Twig looked up at him. "Really?"

"We're going to disagree sometimes. That's cool."

Twig felt very moved.

"Not what you've been taught?"

Twig giggled. "Ah, no." Twig laid the side of her head on Leo's shoulder and watched a family walk up the stairs toward the church. There was a distinguished-looking father, a kind-looking mother, and two young children. They seemed peaceful as they meandered up the stairs.

A normal family, Twig thought. How simple their little group appeared.

"What's your song for right now?" Twig asked.

"'Mellow Mood' by Bob Marley. It's on the nano—maybe you'll hear it tonight."

"I hope so. I have to go soon," Twig said, but she didn't move her head from Leo's shoulder.

"I know. Tomorrow is Thanksgiving at home. I'm bummed to miss it. It's my favorite holiday. You guys don't celebrate Thanksgiving, do you?"

"No. I don't know that much about it."

"Ah. It's by far the best meal of the year—at least the way my mom cooks it."

"What do you have?" Twig had to get to Thomas's and her meeting spot, but this was obviously important to Leo. She wanted to stay and listen.

"The basics—turkey, stuffing, yams—but my mom has this way of making everything just a little different."

An idea was forming in Twig's head. It was an outlandish idea, but maybe she could make it happen.

"I have this friend. She lives near where I do. I'd have to ask her, but maybe we could have a Thanksgiving dinner at her house next week."

"That'd be amazing." Leo became thoughtful. "You don't have to do that, though, Twig. I don't want you to go through all that trouble."

He probably meant cooking. He had no idea. But she wanted to do it. A million little things would have to come together, but she wanted this.

"Let me see if I can pull it together first. I'll give you the details when we meet next week."

"Okay, girl." Leo clapped his long, beautiful hands together. "You're on. But no pressure?"

"No pressure. But, Leo?"

"Yes?"

"You really eat turkeys?"

"Have you ever had any meat, Twig?"

Twig shook her head and shuddered. They both laughed, and Leo grabbed her. "I'm going to get you to eat some meat!" Twig squealed in mock protest.

"Never!" she screamed, laughing harder than ever before.

When Twig and Thomas pulled back into the compound, everyone was gathering. The stage had been set up, but no one was on it. It was beginning to rain.

"What do you think is going on?" Twig asked Thomas.

"I don't know, but there's our gang. Let's go ask."

Ryan, Sophie, Rose, and Kamela were standing together, waiting in the rain. Thomas walked up to Rose and put his hand on her stomach.

"What's going on here?"

Rose smiled back at him. They were so in love. Twig couldn't help thinking of Leo and their kiss today.

"My dad has some kind of announcement," Kamela said.

Twig looked at Ryan. He gave her a "search-me" look in response. "*I have to talk to you,*" she mouthed. He nodded in response.

And then Adam was behind them. He put his arms around Ryan's shoulders. "How's my guy?"

"I am well, Father," was Ryan's response.

"How are all of my dear children?" Adam put his chin on Ryan's head.

"Good, Father. Thank you, Father," they all mumbled, feeling slightly awkward. They were getting drenched by the rain.

"My dear, dear children." Adam gave Ryan a final squeeze, smiled at the rest of the group, and leapt onto the stage.

When he cleared his throat, everyone became quiet despite the rain. Twig marveled at how he managed to corral such a large group with a cough.

Adam stood on the stage and clapped his hands together. "Wet!" he said, pushing his hair off his face and wiping water from his eyes. Everyone laughed.

"Family, I'm going to make this short. I know you have things to do before dinner."

The crowd listened in silence.

"I'm going away for bit. It's time for me to embark on a pilgrimage. Time to spread the word." Everyone clapped. Twig clapped along with everyone else, but for different reasons. She never really thought about it when Adam left before, but this time she felt a great sense of relief.

"If you want to talk to me before I go, come see me after this. Doc's in charge if you need anything in my absence. I leave on Monday. I will miss all of you and will be thinking of you. Of course, there is no place I'd rather be, and I will return as soon as possible." He finished speaking and led them in prayer.

When he finished and no one approached with questions, Adam

dismissed them. "Doc, Farriss, and Twig, come see me. Everyone else, see you at dinner."

They were soaked at this point, but Twig waited patiently for Adam to finish talking to Doc and Farriss. Farriss gave her a nod. They hadn't spoken since Adam had made him put Sapphire down.

"How are you?" Adam had his warm hands on her shoulders. Everyone else had dispersed.

"I'm good," Twig said cheerfully, trying to channel her emotions about his announcement into her answer.

Adam squinted his eyes and looked at her for a moment.

"Really?"

Twig wondered what he was thinking as he scrutinized her. "Yeah, I'm good. Just keeping my head down and doing my thing."

"Doing your thing? That's cute. I don't think I've heard you say that before."

Twig didn't respond to this. Had she picked that up from Leo? She'd better be more careful.

"Walk with me." Adam slipped his arm through hers.

"Okay," Twig said, assuming he was just going to walk her to dinner. But he led her away from the dining area.

Instead, he took her to his cottage.

Twig had never been to Adam's cottage before. He had always lived by himself while Tina and Kamela shared a cottage next door. She wondered where she would live once they were married. Twig was surprised to see that he kept his front door locked and used a key to get in. The cottage was spotless and just as sparse as her own living quarters but much bigger. Several doors were shut. Twig wondered what was behind them.

"I'll be right back." Adam came back with towels and a dress. "You can change in here." Adam led her to a bathroom, which was obviously a spare, as there wasn't a thing in it. No bars of soap, no towels. Twig was drenched and, despite feeling terribly uncomfortable, was happy to change. Why had he brought her here? He wouldn't try to have sex with her before they were married, would he? She noticed you couldn't hear the intercom in here. The quiet rose around her.

When Twig came out, Adam was sitting on the couch with two glasses of wine in front of him on the coffee table. He was running a small towel through his thick hair.

"Hi," he said, beaming.

"Hi," she said back a little hesitantly.

"Come. Come sit."

Twig sat next to Adam. Her heart was pounding.

"I brought you here because I want to show you something."

"Okay," Twig said quietly. She felt so tentative around him, so quiet compared to how she felt with Leo. She was scared of him, terrified that she would say the wrong thing and upset him.

Adam handed her a glass of wine. "To us."

"To us," Twig repeated, trying to smile. She had to be convincing. The surer he was of her, the more he would leave her alone until they got married. Or at least, that's what she hoped.

"Go ahead." He nodded for her to sip her wine.

"Is it okay?"

He nodded again.

She took a small sip. It crossed her mind that it might have something in it—something to make her sleepy or drunk, like the pills she took in the hospital. But there wasn't anything she could do except drink. It tasted like velvet on her tongue.

"It's a very old wine. Perfect to honor our union." He realized what that sounded like to Twig. "Our union in marriage, Twig." He patted her knee and laughed. "Stay here."

Twig noticed Adam didn't touch his wine. He got up from the couch and disappeared behind one of the closed doors. Twig's brain buzzed wondering what was behind those doors. She took another sip of wine.

When he returned, he was carrying a leather-bound book about two inches thick.

"Open it."

Her hands were shaking, but she managed to take the book and open it to the first page.

Photos. Photos of her when she was a little girl. She turned the pages slowly. More photographs. It was like watching herself grow up—playing, gardening, eating, and even making her secret nature paintings. An entire photo album devoted to her. On the last page, there was a recent photo of her, asleep in her bed. Twig had no idea when it was taken. She felt sick.

"I've always known you were special, Twig. And I always knew we would be together one day."

Adam wants you. He's not going to let you go.

He had been planning this. This marriage. Longer than she or Avery could have ever imagined. It had nothing to do with growing the Family, or wanting more children. The thought sickened Twig. How many other girls had he been photographing? Or was it just her? Avery was right. He wasn't ever going to let her go. He had just been waiting for her to grow up.

"They're beautiful," she whispered. "But you've known. About my… um, my paintings." The word "painting" felt wrong now, compared to what Twig could create with real paint and canvas at Gran's cottage.

"It's okay that you are nervous, darling." Adam took the book from Twig's hands. He put his arm around her and moved next to her so that there wasn't any space between them.

"Look at me."

Twig took a deep breath and looked at him.

"You were just a girl. I needed to know the ins and outs of you. I've been watching you for a very long time, as you can see."

"But why wasn't I punished?"

"You were. When I was ready to put a stop to it, you were," he said. "That's all in our past, now. I think we understand each other?" He brought his head close to hers, and his lips touched hers. She felt the pressure of his mouth and knew that she would never feel for Adam what she felt with Leo. Shame and anger surged up in her as he prodded her lips with his tongue. Tears began to well in her eyes.

She shot up. "It's the wine. I'm so sorry." Twig covered her mouth and ran to the bathroom, slamming the door behind her. She vomited in the toilet. Adam was at the door asking if she was okay. She had to pull it together. He couldn't know he repulsed her. If he felt rejected or threatened, there was no telling what he might do.

"I'm okay," she called back. "I'll be right there." She splashed cold water on her face. She opened the door and buried her head in his neck. "Forgive me, Fath—" she stopped herself. "…Darling," she said instead, mimicking his endearment for her. "I'm not used to the wine. Please, just give me a little time. This is all so new for me."

"Of course." Adam squeezed her and stroked her hair. "I love you. I love you, I love you, I love you!" Adam lifted Twig's head so he could see her face.

"I love you, too," she said and put on what she hoped was the most winning smile of her life.

31

It rained all night. Twig couldn't sleep. It was an unfriendly rain that pounded at the windows and clawed at the roof relentlessly. She considered taking one of Doc's pills. Adam's photo album had frightened her to the core. Sickened her. Unnerved her. He had been watching her. Documenting her year after year. The last photo especially had scared her. Was he still watching her that way? Did he know about Gran and Leo and was just playing with her? Did he photograph her in town, eating at Meng's and kissing Leo on the steps of the cathedral? Would he set a trap for her to walk into?

No. If he knew, he would make it known immediately. He would think she was making a fool of him, and he would never put up with that. And yet that hardly comforted her. It was as if she now realized how fine a line she'd been walking. She'd always felt watched on a more general level, but he had been specifically watching her. And his hypocrisy knew no bounds. He had a camera. The thing she had wished for time and again and knew she could never have. He railed against technology, but she had seen him use the very things he deemed so evil.

But none of that mattered. He lived by different rules because he could. He was their leader, and that was that. He could do whatever he wanted.

But should she stop breaking the rules? *Could* she? For the first time, she could sense the ticking clock counting down. Her newfound freedoms, so beloved, were limited and would soon have to come to an end.

But she would squeeze the marrow out of every moment she had left.

32

Twig held a piece of bread between her teeth to keep from crying. She was chopping onions.

Leo was coming over for dinner.

Twig and Gran had spent an afternoon looking through Gran's numerous cookbooks. They decided on a simple turkey, stuffing made with cornbread and crispy bits of what Gran called Facon, a sweet potato casserole, biscuits, cranberry sauce with ginger and orange, and a green salad. The kitchen smelled divine. How and where Gran had procured the materials was a complete mystery. Gran's generosity seemed boundless. Avery was out walking while Gran and Twig cooked.

"What is this music?" Twig asked, removing the bread from her mouth and scooping the onions into a bowl with the edge of her knife.

"Cesaria Evora," Gran answered. "She's from Cape Verde, an archipelago off the coast of West Africa."

"She's wonderful. Have you been there?"

"Cape Verde?"

"Yes, or Africa in general?"

"Many times." Gran was whipping the sweet potatoes into a fluff. "I have many lovely memories of Africa." Gran put down the bowl of sweet potatoes for a moment. "But Cape Verde was a Portuguese colony and is very different from Africa in general."

"Maybe someday I'll go there," Twig said wistfully. "I never really considered travel until recently."

"Until meeting Leo?"

"That, and finding out I'm from somewhere else to begin with," Twig laughed awkwardly, knitting her brows and shaking her head.

"Of course. So you and Leo are really fond of each other?" Gran asked.

"Yes. I mean, I haven't known him very long, but…" Twig finished her sentence with a sigh.

"Ah, to be young," Gran said warmly.

"Were you ever married, Gran?"

"Oh, yes. But is that the question you really want to ask?" Gran raised one of her pretty eyebrows. Her black eyes glittered. Twig had that gossamer feeling again of being reminded of something unnamable and vague when she looked at the drama of Gran's eyes. Twig didn't know much about movie stars, but she imagined they looked something like Gran.

"Go on," Gran prodded in the same way she had prodded Avery the first day Twig came to her house.

"Have you ever been in love? Do you remember the first time you felt it?"

"I have been in love many times, my dear, and I remember all of my first times. My marriage, however—that was a different feeling. A much more dutiful type of feeling."

"I know what you mean," Twig said glumly.

"How are you doing with all of that? If I may ask?" Gran had a crisp and direct way of speaking. She didn't waste her words or gestures.

"I feel like I shouldn't really talk about it, but maybe that's habit." Twig thought of Adam's photo album. Without thinking about it, her eyes glanced outside the window. *He's away,* she told herself. *He's away right now.*

"That's why I came here," Gran said suddenly. "To get away from duty. When my husband died, I felt…well, I felt released, to be honest. So I packed it all up and came here."

"Wow." Twig was stunned. Gran didn't usually talk about herself.

"Come on, dear. Let's get started on the pie while we talk." Gran gave Twig an empathetic nod. "Then we'll go get dressed. We'll be in a good place to let everything take care of itself while we get dolled up."

"Oh," Twig said quietly. "I only have this to wear." She held out her white skirt in her hands.

"Not if you'll let me play your fairy grandmother for the evening."

"I don't know what that means, but it sounds good to me!" Twig laughed.

"You don't know the story of Cinderella?"

Twig shook her head. But… Cinderella… Wasn't that what Leo called her when they met that day in Meng's?

"We could talk for hours, couldn't we?" Gran laughed lightly. "We can't cover one new item before another one comes rolling off the press."

"Hmph," Twig muttered. "Story of my life."

"Yes, I imagine it would be." Gran looked thoughtful for a moment. "Listen, I'll get the dough from the fridge, and you can roll it out and pinch it onto the plate while I skin the apples. I want to hear more, and maybe I can tell you the story of Cinderella."

Gran knew a lot about the Family from Avery. She also knew about Twig's engagement. Perhaps that added to the sense of ease Twig felt between them. Twig could also tell there probably wasn't much Gran hadn't seen or heard. She didn't shock easily. Twig could see why Avery had chosen Gran as her confidante. She listened and she cared, but she didn't pity.

Gran set down a big ceramic bowl filled with apples on the kitchen table. Twig sprinkled flour on the table and began to roll out the dough with a large wooden rolling pin. Gran told Twig the story of Cinderella while they worked. Twig couldn't help but think how much the toddlers back at the compound would love a story like the one Gran was spinning.

Of course, she would never be able to repeat the story to them.

When they finished making the pie, Gran loaded Twig up with a pile of fluffy yellow towels and told her to shower. She was going to finish a surprise she was working on.

Twig showered beneath the lemony foam of Gran's shampoo and then pulled on the bathrobe Gran had left for her and wrapped her hair up in a towel.

Like everything else, Gran's bedroom was exquisite. It was small and the walls were painted a pomegranate red. The bed was covered in a white quilt, and a thin blanket woven through with threads of yellow and turquoise was folded on the end of the bed.

A black-and-white photograph, neatly matted and framed, hung above the bed. It was blurry but looked like a woman running on the beach with two young children.

"Are those your children?" Twig asked, looking around the room. A candle burned next to a vase full of flowers on a dark, wood dresser.

"Yes," Gran said quietly. She was standing near the window wearing a simple but well-cut black cotton dress. Handfuls of glittering pink beads hung around her long neck.

"Where are they?" Twig pressed.

"My relationship with my children is very strained." Gran paused. "That would be a very diplomatic way of putting it. We don't talk."

"Really?" Twig was surprised. Gran seemed so easygoing.

"Listen, those are stories for another day. I will say that being a woman, as you are finding out, is a complicated thing, and being a mother is an even more complicated thing." Gran looked thoughtfully at Twig for a moment. "But alas, let's get you dressed!"

Gran's closet was as big as her bedroom and was like something out of a fantasy for any girl, but especially for Twig, who had been relegated to a life of white eyelet dresses and brown, worse-for-wear hiking boots.

"Behold, Gran's vice." Gran swept her hand around the small room where she kept her clothes, shoes, bags, and jewelry.

Twig gasped.

Things shimmered and sparkled, begging to be touched, sifted through. Twig ran her hand across the many different kinds of fabrics. Everything was hung by color. Cashmere sweaters, silk dresses, satin skirts, high heels, flats, scarves, jackets... You name it.

"I can't wear a third of it in this climate. But I've collected it from across the whole world, and the wardrobe goes with me wherever I go."

Twig thought about Leo calling her a mystery. Gran was the real mystery.

"Daniel will be picking Leo and Hazel up at the hotel any minute now, and we have lots to do to get you ready. I'm thinking something Audrey-like. Something simple but gorgeous."

The guest list for the dinner party was small and almost perfect. Leo and Hazel were meeting Daniel in the lobby of their hotel in Turrialba, and he would drive them to Gran's and then back to the hotel after dinner. Avery—Twig couldn't wait for her to meet Leo and Hazel—Gran, Daniel, and his mother Magdalena would all be there. Only Ryan was missing. Even if she could have convinced him to come, there was just no way they could manage it. Twig couldn't even think of a way to sneak him out, and even if she could, it would be too great a risk for all of them. It was disgusting what Avery and Twig had done to get out of dinner, but there was no other way. It had involved a duo of public vomiting at lunch. Everyone had shooed Avery and Twig to their cottage. The two women knew no one would want to see them until the morning.

Twig fingered a steel-gray silk dress that had enormous foamy green flowers embroidered into the fabric. The flowers looked as if they were glowing.

"Ah, good taste. Yves Saint Laurent for Christian Dior, 1959."

"Oh," Twig said, none of those names meaning anything to her. "It's marvelous."

Gran used a hairdryer—Twig was appalled that she'd gone her entire life without one—to make Twig's hair stick straight and then pulled it back into a severe ponytail. She twisted the tail into a thick donut bun on at the base of Twig's neck. She put a little mascara on Twig's already long lashes and added some light-pink lipgloss to her lips. Simple, elegant, and understated.

"Ah, very Hitchcock. I like it. More Grace Kelly than Audrey, but Audrey would approve."

Twig looked in the mirror. She barely recognized herself. She looked so glamorous, so put together. So unapproachable.

"The dress will soften it," Gran said, as if reading her mind.

Twig stepped into the dress. The silk rustled, making a delicious sound. Gran zipped up the back. It fit perfectly despite Gran's height.

"You are vintage size, darling. Things always came up short for me—not that it stopped me."

The neckline of the dress scooped wonderfully low without showing a thing. The bodice was fitted, showing off Twig's small waist, and a full skirt bloomed beneath. The sleeves ran three quarters of the way down Twig's arms. She felt slightly embarrassed and slightly exhilarated by how sexy her body looked and felt in the dress. She hoped Leo would like it.

Gran laid some beautiful yellow-and-gold glass beads across Twig's neck.

"I like the contrast with the gray. Do you?" Gran steered Twig to the mirror.

"Yes!" Twig smiled. "I feel like I've stepped into one of your magazines."

"It's very 1950s housewife glamour. And these to match." Gran held up a satiny pair of gray ballerina flats. Suddenly she frowned. "What size are you?"

"An eight and a half, I think." Twig only had one pair of shoes to compare.

"Well, I'm a nine. Should work."

Twig looked at herself in the mirror again.

"Let's go get the food out, darling. You're perfect."

Twig gasped when she walked outside. She nearly dropped the big bowl of salad she was carrying.

Gran had outdone herself.

A long table was set beneath an overhang of trees. It was covered in a turquoise fabric that had a slight sheen to it and carefully set with an eclectic mix of dishes and glasses. Pink ceramic, red glass, Twig's favorite green-and-gold dishes, small bowls of white orchids, and a runner made from a piece of mirror lined with small white candles.

Twig put her bowl down and did a twirl, letting her voluminous skirt billow around her.

"Gran! It's beautiful!"

Gran clasped her hands to her chest. "Oh, I'm so glad you like it, dear. I know this is a very special evening for you."

Twig heard the crunching of leaves beneath feet before she saw Daniel, a petite woman who must have been his mother, Hazel, and Leo come through the wood.

"Holy vintage goddess!" Hazel shrieked. She came running over to Twig, pawing her dress. "What is this? You look amazing, Twig!" The two girls hugged, giggling.

"Thank you! It's all Gran." Twig gestured toward Gran.

Introductions were made. Hazel and Leo brought cookies and coffee as a hostess gift. Daniel's mother baked something that smelled delicious in a covered orange pot. Gran graciously accepted the gifts, obviously touched.

"Magdalena, Hazel, Daniel, would the three of you be so kind as to help me in the kitchen for a moment?"

"Of course!" The three of them followed Gran into the house, leaving Twig and Leo alone.

"Do you want to see my studio?" Twig was nervous all over again.

"Your studio?" Leo beamed.

Twig started to lead Leo toward the small cottage when he grabbed her hand.

"Come here for a minute first." Leo held Twig in an embrace. They stood there for a minute, hearts pounding, getting physically reacquainted after their recent time away from one another.

"I'm so glad you're here," Twig whispered. "I don't think I've ever felt so happy." As soon as the words were out, she wished she could take them back. What would he think of her? He'd probably had a million moments like these. "I'm sorry," Twig said, shaking her head shyly. "Come on." Twig broke away and grabbed Leo's hand to lead him toward her studio.

"Okay, I'm coming," Leo said quietly. "But let it be known: you're adorable, and Jesus, I don't have words for how you look tonight."

"It's pretty awesome, isn't it?" Twig twirled again. She knew she had definitely picked that word up from Leo.

Leo smiled. "Pretty awesome."

Showing Leo her work, Twig realized how much she had accomplished in the last month. She didn't have the exact language to describe them, but Daniel had been introducing her to different styles of art. Along with what she secretly called her vision paintings, there were abstracts, landscapes, and expressionist works. The latter were the most interesting. Women with long faces and a wonderful combination of muted colors and high contrasts.

Leo pointed to one of the women. "I like these the most. They are amazing. I mean, they are all amazing, but I really dig these."

"Really?" Twig asked. She hadn't shown anyone her work before. She'd been kind of secretive about it. She hadn't even shown Daniel or Avery or Gran, who had told Twig she wouldn't look until Twig was ready.

"You should be showing these."

"What do you mean?"

"I mean in a gallery. People would buy these for sure, Twig. I'm not a huge art expert, but my mom is an art history professor, so I know a bit."

"Hmm." Twig imagined herself briefly in some big city selling her artwork.

"What is going on in here?" Hazel burst through the door. "Twig!" she exclaimed. Her eyes scanned the room, taking everything in. "Oh my God! Lee, Mom has to see these."

Daniel came to the studio, followed by his mother, Gran and Avery. The studio could barely contain the group. Twig noticed Avery looked beautiful dressed in a plain taupe shift and matching sandals, both Gran's.

So much for secrecy, Twig thought. She was lavished with praise and peppered with questions. Finally she held up her hands.

"This dinner is for you guys. Let's go eat!" Twig shooed them out the door, and she and Leo exchanging a meaningful look as they walked back out into the yard.

"I really am impressed," he whispered as he helped her into a chair at the table before he took one next to her. Avery, who was within earshot, nodded at Twig and mouthed, "*So am I.*"

Twig put her hands to her face to cover the hot blush in her cheeks. She loved the attention and found it almost unbearably embarrassing at the same time.

Gran brought out a bottle of champagne. She splashed a little into everyone's glasses and then raised her own.

"To a table of bandits!"

Everyone cheered.

Conversation was easy and fluid. Gran and Hazel discussed fashion.

Gran complimented Hazel on her plaid capris and gold sandals. Daniel's mother was seventy and saucy. Twig loved her spirit. Leo did a wonderful job of engaging Avery. It was a warm evening lit by stars and candlelight, budding friendships, and a freedom Twig had never known. It was heady.

During dessert and coffee, Gran brought out speakers, and Daniel and Hazel began to dance. Gran and Magdalena joined them, swaying gracefully to the music.

Leo and Twig took a walk. They sat down at a small clearing lit by moonlight.

"What a night!" Leo said, laying back.

Twig lay down next to him, and they looked up at the moon and the pinpricks of stars. He took her hand.

"Thank you for tonight."

"You're welcome," she said sincerely.

"You never see the stars like this in LA," Leo said. "Too many lights from the city."

"I think I take them for granted sometimes," Twig replied. "Well, sometimes I look up and they stun me, but so often I'm looking down, caught up in my thoughts."

"I know what you mean. That's what I love about surfing. Being out there in the ocean, it's so vast, so much bigger than me. It sort of sweeps my thoughts away. And there's no looking down and not noticing it, or you're gonna get whopped."

"I've never been to the ocean," Twig said wistfully.

"Listen, that kind of gives me the perfect opening for something I want to ask you."

"Okay," Twig said, raising her eyebrows with curiosity.

"Well, I know this is probably impossible for you, but I have to ask." Leo sat up on one elbow and looked down at Twig. Her heart caught in her chest. She loved his face so much. She could barely breathe anticipating his kiss. He smelled so good.

"My family is going on a surf trip to a spot near Nosara. I want you to come. I asked my parents and they're totally cool with it. They want to meet you."

"I—"

"Before you say no... We're leaving when we come back. It would be a way for us to have some real time together before I go home. Plus, it's a short trip—only one night."

Twig thought about the fact that Adam was gone. If there was any time she could possibly make this work, it would be now. And even though there were a million other eyes on her at all times, she seemed to be getting away with a lot lately. But this would be different. This would be all day, overnight. Missing every meal, every class.

She looked up at Leo. He traced her eyebrows with his fingertip, ran down the bridge of her nose, and finally put his finger to her lips.

"When?" she asked.

"A week from Friday." He seemed to be following her thoughts. "You don't have to answer now. You can tell me on Wednesday. If the answer is yes, we can work out the details then."

Before she could respond, he leaned down and kissed her. She cupped his head in her hands and pulled him to her.

After a while, the music from the party floated back into their awareness. They sat up, and Twig touched her nose to Leo's.

"Yes," she said in a strong, clear voice.

"You'll go?"

"Yes."

She didn't know how she would manage it, but she was going.

She had been lied to and betrayed, unjustly and cruelly punished. She was about to enter into a marriage with a man she detested. Leo was leaving. This would be her last chance to spend time with him. She was going.

She would deal with the repercussions when she got back.

33

"Are you sure about this, darling?"

Gran and Twig were packing a small suitcase for the trip.

"You sound like my mom."

"I'm sure I do."

Gran had opened up her closet to Twig. Twig was trying on a
black-and-white twist bikini that sat low on Twig's hips. Gran said
it was pure 60s Bond girl—Domino from *Thunderball* specifically.
Twig couldn't believe how sexy she looked. She was discovering how
powerful and expressive clothing could be. No wonder Gran took
her wardrobe everywhere she went. Twig wanted to take a really
long look at herself in the mirror—study her stomach, the curve of
her breasts—but she was a little embarrassed. Something like shame
hovered at the surface, too, but she didn't want to feel ashamed, so
she fought it. She admired Gran so much. If Gran said this was
acceptable, then it must be. She had to be brave. Otherwise, she
might as well just go put her white dress back on and forget all of
it. She wasn't going to do that. Everything she'd seen so far about
the outside world, she liked. She had to know more. This might be
her only chance.

"We really need to have a movie night," Twig finally said. Twig
reached for a small notebook and dashed down *Thunderball*. She was
keeping a list of the movies she wanted to see one day. "And I love it,"
Twig said, gesturing to the suit. "I don't look like a tramp, do I?"

Gran frowned at her. "Hardly—the suit is perfect. But really, darling, are you sure about the trip?"

"Of course not!" Twig said. "But I'm going anyway. You know when you just have to do something crazy and break free?"

"All too well," Gran murmured, deciding between a pair of oversize Aviator sunglasses and big, black Jackie-O-style ones. In the end she wrapped them both in a white silk scarf and placed them carefully in the soft apple-green leather purse that Twig would take with her.

Gran sighed. "I remember what it's like to be seventeen. You don't have to explain. Sometimes you feel as if you would go to the ends of the earth for that special person."

Twig blushed at Gran's insight. How far would she go for Leo?

"She said I didn't have to come back," Twig mumbled.

"Who did?"

"My mom. She said if I could get away and stay away, I should."

"And what do you think?"

"I told her I would never leave her here."

"She is a grown woman; she can take care of herself."

"That's exactly what she said, but that's not true. She's defenseless against Adam. We all are."

And it was more than just that. Yes, she was worried about her mother. But Twig couldn't wrap her head around just *leaving*. She would be totally dependent on Leo and his family, and totally ignorant of life in the outside world. She couldn't ask his family to be responsible for her.

"I see," Gran said sadly. "Well, it seems decisions have been made," she cleared her throat. "For now, anyway. Daniel will be here soon." Gran gave her a final once-over. "Wear the scarf in your hair, darling." Twig got the impression that Gran was forcing herself to sound more casual than she felt.

Twig and Leo had worked out the details for the trip on their weekly meeting. It had been brief because Twig wanted to finish her errands and get back to Thomas early. She hadn't wanted to risk getting caught so close to the trip. She also knew that she'd be with Leo on Saturday—an entire twenty-four hours together.

Daniel would drive her to the Cohen's hotel.

"I will take care of you," he'd promised. Twig knew he would while she was with him—while he could. It was the thought of later—after the trip—that scared her. But for now, she felt safe inside the cocoon of feelings that had grown around her. It felt as if nothing could touch her.

Avery would have to spend the night alone. She would be at risk while Twig was gone. That was the one part of the plan Twig didn't like. Avery tried to be a sport by saying it was her dream night—the place all to herself—but Twig could tell she was nervous.

"One more thing before Daniel arrives." Gran put a thin gold chain around Twig's neck. Hanging on the chain was a delicate *T* that dangled between Twig's collarbones.

"It's beautiful. But where…" Twig trailed off. "I don't know your first name, Gran. I feel sort of ashamed."

"Don't be. I never said it. It's Clare."

"Clare," Twig said, gently holding the charm between her thumb and forefinger. "So this…?"

"That, my dear, is a gift."

"It's too much," Twig said softly.

"One thing I have learned in all of my travels, darling, is that when someone offers you a gift, you accept it."

Twig smiled up at her. "I love it. I won't take it off."

When Daniel arrived, Twig and Gran were waiting in the kitchen. Twig's white dress, plain white bra, underwear, and hiking boots were folded on a chair in Gran's bedroom. Twig was transformed in tight jeans, an olive-green button-down shirt in heavy fabric that was cinched at the waist with a thick, black leather belt, and espadrilles. Around her neck, doubled up and hanging below her golden *T* were some of Gran's glittering black beads. The clothes felt heavy and so good in contrast to the wispiness of her dress.

Gran gave Twig a piece of paper with a telephone number on it and a wallet filled with money.

"If you need anything, even just to talk, call me. If you need us to come get you, call me."

"I'll be at the Harmony Hotel in Nosara." Twig had a sudden fear. What if that's where Adam was?

Impossible. She was just being paranoid. Extra paranoid.

"Yes, got it." The two women embraced.

"I'm nervous!" Twig giggled. "Let's go before I lose my nerve."

When Daniel walked Twig into the hotel lobby, Leo was sitting on a bench, his feet tapping with excitement. He rushed to them when he saw them, embracing Twig and then shaking Daniel's hand. Twig looked around the lobby. Glimmering tiles, indoor waterfalls, and an assaulting smell of ammonia. Twig would have wanted to stop and examine everything, but the smell made her head and throat hurt.

"Thanks so much for getting her here safe, man. It's good to see you. How's your mother?"

"She's good, thank you, Leo. See you back here tomorrow at two?"

"Yes. On the nose."

"Thank you, Daniel. I don't know how to repay you," Twig said.

"It's my pleasure. Have fun. I'll be here tomorrow."

When Daniel left, Leo looked down at Twig, his expression serious.

"Are you okay with this?"

"Yes," she reassured him.

"You're sure? If at any time you become unsure, you'll tell me?"

"I promise."

Leo didn't know that their meeting at the hospital was the first time Twig had been off the compound. She thought it would freak him out if she told him. He was already being so sweet and protective.

"Okay! Let's do this! My mom and dad and Hazel went to town for some breakfast. We'll go get them. Are you hungry?" Twig shook her head no as they walked out into the hotel's small parking lot.

Leo clicked a small, black box and big, silver car that said RANGE ROVER on the back let out a beeping sound. The door locks clicked open. Twig frowned.

"What's wrong?" Leo asked.

"There's just so much I don't know about."

"It's okay. You're like my little time traveler."

"Don't you think your parents are going to think I'm odd or out of place?"

"Nah. They are really open-minded people, but I also gave them a little heads up on the whole kibbutz situation."

"Did you call it that?"

"No, I didn't. I hope that's all right. I sort of discussed it with them the way you and I discussed it."

"I think that's better, actually."

"Okay, good. You are going to love them, and I know they're going to love you."

Twig sat beside Leo as he started the car.

"I'm good. I'm okay," she said, more to herself than to Leo. She opened the window and let the breeze blow on her face, leaning back and gently taking Leo's hand. He squeezed hers in response.

Leo's mother was beautiful. She had the same cocoa-amber skin as Leo and Hazel—perfect skin that looked as if it had been mixed with cream and poured onto her body. She had a wide, friendly face and a sprinkling of freckles across her pretty nose. Her name was Alicia, and she taught art history at the University of Southern California. She took both of Twig's hands in hers and told her that it was lovely to meet her, finally, and that she'd heard so much about her. Leo stood by watching with pride as the two women interacted for the first time. Twig was instantly put at ease by Alicia's quiet warmth.

Jeff, Leo's father, was powder-pale with a big shock of red hair and watery blue eyes. He was a force, gregarious and kind.

"It's so nice to meet you, Jeff." Twig extended her hand.

"I would prefer if you would call me Mr. Cohen."

Twig reddened for a moment at her mistake.

A big grin, reminding Twig instantly of Leo, spread across Jeff's face. "I'm just kidding. If it's okay, we like to hug around here."

Twig laughed with relief as she fell into Jeff's bear-like embrace.

"Dad, you're awful." Hazel laughed as she chastised her father. It was obvious she adored him.

They piled into the Range Rover with Leo at the wheel and Twig shyly taking the front seat at everyone's insistence.

A game called Covers instantly ensued. The Cohens were all about music. Leo and Hazel had loaded up their iPods for the game. Leo would play a song and then play its cover. Everyone voted on which one was the best. Twig liked the game because it didn't matter that she'd never heard most of the songs. Jeff and Alicia hadn't heard half the covers Leo and Hazel had discovered. The first song was "Goodbye Girl" by Squeeze, and then a cover by a band called The Shins. Twig voted for The Shins because their version was more lighthearted. The original version was haunting. Both were good, but she was on the first vacation of her life, and so she chose jaunty over haunting.

Halfway through the trip, they stopped for gas, and Jeff took the wheel with Alicia by his side in the passenger seat.

"No cuddling, you two," Hazel warned Twig and Leo as they piled back into the car. Again, Twig's cheeks reddened with embarrassment. Hazel took her hand. "Not that I don't understand, I have many a man at home—"

"Now that's enough, Hazel," Alicia scolded from the front seat.

"I'm just saying. I don't want Twig to think I'm some kind of prude."

"Hazel has to beat them off with a stick back home," Jeff called from the front seat.

"Oh, I'm sure you do," Twig said sincerely. Hazel was ridiculously, powerfully beautiful. Her looks were one thing, but they were coupled with her grace and confidence.

"That's right. Dad. Did you remember to pack my stick?"

"I did, darling," Jeff answered without missing a beat.

* * *

"We're here!" boomed Jeff.

Twig startled awake. She had fallen asleep against Leo's shoulder. He was looking down at her.

"Hi there."

"Hi," she said sleepily.

"You are very cute when you're sleeping," Leo whispered.

Twig squeezed his hand in response, not wanting to annoy Hazel.

"I heard that, Romeo. But this place is so awesome that I don't even care," Hazel said, sitting up to look out her window as Jeff pulled into the round driveway of the hotel.

The rooms were simple with red terracotta tiles, big beds covered with white comforters, and white linen curtains on the windows. Leo, Hazel, and Twig had two rooms connected by a door and a large shared patio with a hammock and an outdoor shower.

One of the rooms had two twin beds and the other, a queen-size bed.

Twig wondered where she would sleep and assumed it would be on one of the twins with Hazel. On the one hand, she wanted to sleep in the same bed as Leo. The thought made her dizzy with longing, but along with her desire came a swarm of anxious butterflies in her stomach. What would he expect of her? But when she thought of being in his arms all night, she wanted nothing more—no matter how terrifying it seemed. She thought of her Verdant Green classes. She wanted that with Leo, not with Adam.

"I'm going to change, and then let's get lunch and hit the beach. Sound good?" Hazel asked, disappearing into the bathroom and shaking Twig from her thoughts.

Twig, feeling slightly embarrassed about what she had just been thinking, pulled Leo out onto the patio.

"Okay, quick check-in."

"Sure. Talk to me."

"I'm a little overwhelmed," Twig said breathlessly. Leo put his hands on her shoulders. "Can we have a 'firsts' list? For example, that was my first road trip, this is my first stay at a hotel, and here's a big one: this will be my first time seeing the ocean. Maybe we can have a code word so I don't feel like a misfit every time."

"Of course. First, I am honored to be able to experience these things with you. But one question: do you know how to swim?"

"Yes!" Twig was happy to report. They swam in the river at home. Not in bikinis, though. At home they wore one-piece bathing suits that had swim skirts attached to cover their upper thighs. Twig shuddered at the thought of Leo and Hazel seeing her in one.

"Okay, we're set. What should our code word be?" Leo asked.

"Hmm..."

"I know: dope."

"Dope?" Twig repeated, raising her eyebrows.

"Yeah. Every time it's a first, you just say, 'That sounds dope.'"

Twig put her hand over her mouth to cover her laugh.

"What?" Leo said, feigning hurt by putting his hand to his heart.

"I've never heard that before…"

"Another first!" Leo turned her back toward the room and patted her on the butt. "Now go get in your bathing suit. I'm starving."

Twig hopped at the feeling of Leo's hand on her butt and laughed, running away toward her suitcase.

The restaurant sat right on the beach. Lunch was phenomenal: tacos with black beans served on plantain leaves and covered with lime juice. The Cohens all ate white fish tacos that even tempted Twig for a moment, but she could barely eat—she was too taken with the expanse of glittering blue ocean in front of her. She sipped at her lime soda and felt herself begin to relax in a way she had never experienced. She had never seen anything as beautiful and as exciting as the ocean. There was still an underlying anxiety about Avery by herself back at the compound, but Twig did her best to ignore it.

After plying Leo, Hazel, and Twig with sunscreen and warnings to watch one another, Alicia and Jeff headed to their room to take a nap. The plan was to meet at seven o'clock for dinner. Seven! Twig wondered what they would do between now and then. There was so much time to do whatever they wanted.

Leo and Hazel spent some time discussing the best way to introduce Twig to the ocean. They decided to go with the way they were taught when they were children.

With Leo on one side of Twig and Hazel on the other, they each held one of her hands, and the trio ran screaming toward the waves. A strong swimmer to begin with, Twig was a natural. Before long, they swam out past the break and floated beneath the sun, letting the gentle current roll beneath their bodies. Twig was mesmerized by the breadth of green water. She lay on her back, letting her hair spread out like sunrays around her.

"Do you two mind if I go out for a bit?"

Twig looked at Leo questioningly.

"He means surfing," Hazel said. "Go ahead. Twig, you want to get some sun with me, read, and just chill on the beach?"

Nothing sounded better.

When Leo and Twig got back to the room, Hazel was curled up on one of the twin beds, fast asleep. Leo gently shut the door and put his fingers to his lips to signal for Twig to be quiet and not wake her.

While Leo rinsed his board and took a shower on their patio, Twig sat on the bed, luxuriating in this new feeling of freedom.

She had never experienced this kind of freedom before. Even her forays into the woods to make art or her later experiences at Gran's were rushed and cloaked in a sense of danger. Being here with Leo's family, she once again wondered what kind of world she'd been living in. How had she stood it for so long? How had she believed she was happy?

Every time she thought about home, a sharp pang, quick and black, would clench her stomach. If someone found out she wasn't there, what would they do to Avery? Taking this risk was worth whatever punishment she herself incurred, but she had put her mother at great risk. Twig pushed her thoughts away. She wouldn't be away that long. She'd be back there tomorrow. She was determined not to let the darkness of home ruin her one opportunity for joy before she entered into the prison of being Adam's wife.

Twig went to shower while Leo was outside, following Hazel's lead and rinsing her bathing suit before hanging it up to dry. Dipping back into her suitcase, she found a pair of cutoff jeans that she quickly fell in love with and a thin, long-sleeve T-shirt.

Leo was sleeping on the bed when she came out of the bathroom. She quietly propped herself on pillows next to him and picked up Hazel's novel. Before she opened it, she looked at Leo. He looked sweet when he was sleeping—masculine but peaceful. He must have felt her staring. His eyes, heavy with sleep, opened for a moment.

"You okay?" he asked her.

"Absolutely. You go on and sleep."

"Do you want to watch a movie or something? On my computer?" He kissed her shoulder.

"Um, that would be dope," she said, knitting her eyebrows and wrinkling her nose, waiting for his response.

"Really?" he said, waking up in surprise.

"Really." She shook her head.

Leo popped out of bed. "Oh my God! Okay." He unzipped a bag and produced something silver and metal and sleek, the size of a piece of paper. Twig marveled at it, not knowing what to expect.

"Is that your computer?" Twig asked as he plopped on the bed next to her and popped open what looked to Twig like a metal envelope.

"Sweet, right? I got it for graduation. Okay, this is a huge responsibility. I wish Haze was awake; we need consultation." Twig was thankful Hazel was sleeping. She would have been embarrassed for Hazel to know the extent of her ignorance.

"Hmm," Leo hummed. "Interesting. Not too violent. Kind of lame and kind of awesome… This could be just the thing."

"What is it?" Twig asked, curious.

"It's a movie called *Dirty Dancing*."

Twig laughed.

"We could pick something else."

"No, no. I have no idea. It's probably perfect. The name just made me laugh."

"We'll watch the first ten minutes, and if you don't like it, we'll watch something else. That's what my family does if we can't decide on a movie. Oh! That reminds me—we need to get ready for Lip-Synch Night."

"What's that?" Twig asked.

"You'll see! A little Cohen family tradition that will take place tonight after dinner. Maybe we should take a nap... You think you'll be able to make it through all of this without some sleep?" Twig laughed out loud in response. He had no idea what her daily life was like.

"I think I can make it." She smiled and put her arm through his.

Leo sat behind Twig, and she leaned into him as the movie started. He put his chin on her shoulder. Twig could both feel their desire for one another buzzing between them like a current. She was torn between wanting to watch her first movie or turn around and kiss him.

But what a distraction the movie provided.

The story, the visuals, the music, the dancing, and the characters. Things she could relate to and things she had never even imagined. She felt like she had been cut open, the experience affected her so much. She had never felt such a whirl of disparate emotions in such a short period of time.

She had to hold herself still through half the scenes. She had never felt so much arousal. It was like being on fire. The way the characters danced. The way they made love. She worried for a minute that Leo could see inside her thoughts. She was glad he was behind her and couldn't see the flush spreading over her face. Was he experiencing the same sorts of feelings, or was she just naïve? She was inspired, excited, and a little frightened by the movie all at the same time. It was a much more raw depiction of sex and sexuality than she had learned about in her Verdant Green classes. She couldn't help but wonder if Leo was used to women like the ones in the movie. Was it okay that she liked the feelings the movie inspired—and was completely afraid of them and maybe a little ashamed of them, too?

"Hey," Leo whispered. "If this is too intense, we can stop it. Go walk on the beach for a bit." Twig turned to him. His eyebrows were raised in question. "Watching it through your eyes, I can see it might be a little overwhelming."

"Thank you," she whispered back, "but I'm okay."

When the credits rolled, Twig took a deep breath. What a powerful experience.

"I've never seen anything like that." She laughed nervously. "I can't wait to see another one!"

"So, you liked it?" Leo asked quietly, enjoying her wonder.

"I did. I mean, it kind of freaked me out, too, but I feel transported," Twig said thoughtfully. "A little shaken, but mainly just transported."

"Are you tired now?" Leo asked sweetly.

"I am, actually."

"Rest for a few minutes. I'm going to start getting things ready for tonight."

Too excited to sleep, Twig read out on the patio while Leo prepared for Cohen Lip-Synch Night. She left him inside playing around with his iPod and computer. Apparently everyone had "submitted" the song they would be performing before they'd even left for Nosara. The whole idea completely terrified Twig, but she thought she might get away with being an innocent bystander.

"Do you know your song for tonight, babe?" Leo called from the room.

"No, no, I'll just watch," she called back, hoping he would let it go at that.

"Not gonna happen. Song?"

"Would you do a duet with me? Maybe one of the songs from the movie? Is that too corny?"

"It's mad corny, but that's what Cohen Lip-Synch Night is all about! We can do 'Love is Strange.'"

"Can you play it so I can memorize the lyrics before tonight? I've never done anything like this before. I might be awful," Twig confessed.

"I'm sure I'll be awful!" she added, glad he couldn't see her face and tell just how anxious she was.

"You may surprise yourself."

34

"That's a woman!" Hazel screamed. They had gathered back in Jeff's and Alicia's room after dinner.

Alicia and Jeff were belting out "Ain't No Mountain High Enough" with everything they had. They serenaded one another on the patio outside of the room, which had been transformed into a small stage. Hazel, Leo, and Twig were sitting on pillows, laughing and clapping with joy.

Twig had chills all over her body watching the couple look into each other's eyes and sing the love song. Alicia moved her body in a slow and powerful way. Jeff was transformed for the number, his normal effervescence channeled into a silky smoothness.

Hazel went next. She swayed in the candlelight, performing a number by Erykah Badu called "Appletree." It was perfect—so Hazel.

As she sang, Hazel's natural rhythm flowed through her. Her audience swayed along with her. Twig was captivated by Hazel's innate power and sensuality. It was obvious that she was used to performing. She controlled the space.

When she finished, Leo put his hand to his heart and said nobly, "I am humbled, sister."

"Of course you are," Hazel said seriously, and then broke into a big laugh.

"I can*not* follow that!" Twig said, pretending to run back into the room.

"Go get her, Lee!" Jeff said teasingly. "I have a sneaking suspicion there's not much that girl can't do."

Leo cued up the music before Twig had time to think. Hazel gave her a loving push toward the stage.

The music started, and Twig faltered.

She froze.

"If at first you don't succeed, try, try again!" Jeff shouted through cupped hands.

"Don't think, just do!" Leo smiled.

"And take a sip of this." Jeff gave Twig a sip of his beer.

Leo started the song again. Twig jumped into the role this time, remembering Baby from *Dirty Dancing* and her journey from reticence to confidence.

How many chances would Twig have to do something like this?

She let go. The chemistry between Leo and her took over completely.

"They're having a moment!" Hazel screamed. Everyone was laughing and clapping.

Leo fell at Twig's feet when the song ended, pretending to worship her. Alicia, Jeff, and Hazel stood up and cheered. As they all fell in a heap of laughter and happiness, Twig looked at the Cohens.

This was the family she wanted.

35

When they got back to their rooms, Hazel held up a hand, saying, "I don't even want to hear it. I'm sleeping in the other room. You don't have to thank me, just have mercy and keep it down so a woman can get her rest."

"'Night, Haze," Leo replied.

"'Night, bro. Good night, Twig."

"Good night, Hazel," Twig said, embracing her.

"What's all this?" Hazel said, sounding like Alicia and patting Twig on the back as she returned the hug.

"Thanks, Hazel, for today. It was a really special day for me."

"Well, there's more fun to be had tomorrow, so get some sleep," Hazel said in a maternal tone.

When Hazel disappeared into her room and closed the door, Leo looked at Twig.

"Are you okay with this? If not, I can totally go sleep in there."

Twig went to him and put her arms around his neck, cupping his head in her long fingers.

"Of course I am," she whispered. She didn't know what would happen tonight, but she knew whatever it was, she wanted it to happen with Leo first, not Adam.

They began to kiss and Leo lost his balance, falling back on the bed and taking Twig with him. They laughed and then shushed one another, which made them laugh harder for a moment.

Leo pressed his lips against hers, slowly, unrushed. Their lips locked, and they both gasped almost noiselessly with desire and happiness.

Twig took Leo's earlobe in her teeth gently and then whispered in his ear—something she'd learned in her Verdant Green class. Leo moaned and then took a deep breath. He rolled on top of her and looked down at her.

She might not be able to help what happened with Adam in the future, but she could have what she wanted now. She would have to endure Adam for the rest of her life.

Twig moved her hips beneath Leo and smiled teasingly.

Leo squeezed his eyes shut for a moment.

"What's wrong?" Twig asked.

"Trust me, I want you more than anything. I just don't want to rush it."

"Oh, okay," Twig said, feeling hurt and suddenly embarrassed for being so forward. She started to roll out from under him. She was mortified. What had she been thinking? Had she misjudged everything? She didn't know how anything worked.

"Wait." Leo pushed her back down playfully.

"I feel stupid," she said quietly.

"Please. Please don't. It's because of what we have that I want to take it slow. No need to skip ahead. Right?"

Twig didn't answer. She wanted to say she was worried she'd never see him again after this trip—that there wasn't time to take it slow—but that would sound so intense.

He seemed to read her thoughts.

"I'm going to come back."

"What do you mean?"

Leo rolled away and lay next to her. They turned to face one another.

"I'm going to come back during Yale's spring break. I've already planned it out in my head. That's not much time apart. Four months, tops."

Twig was silent, thinking it through. She would be married by then.

"You know what, I was going to wait until tomorrow, but let's do it now." Leo popped out of bed and grabbed his laptop from the desk. Twig sat up and watched him, perplexed. Leo came back to the bed and sat next to her.

"Do what?"

"I want to make you an email account," Leo said, starting to type while she looked over his shoulder.

A feeling of sadness caught Twig. "But I—"

Leo held up his hand. "I know, I know—you can't use it. But I just need to do this in case you *are* ever able to get to a computer. Maybe when you're in town on your errand run you can get to an internet café. I just would never forgive myself if I didn't do this."

"Okay," she said quietly. "Of course." Maybe Gran had a computer.

"Behold: Google. Your world will never be the same."

Leo showed Twig how a search engine worked. He asked her to name any topic and showed her the world of information the computer beamed back. She chose Audrey Hepburn and loved looking at the images that came up. An idea like a flashbulb popped into her brain. She could do a search for the names Avery and Olivia and the words "missing persons" But what would Leo think? He didn't know about any of that. Like he said, maybe she could find an internet café when she got back. Her desire to preserve the joy of the trip overrode her curiosity for the moment.

"Now I'm going to set up your account. I'll use all of my info and just give you the name and password."

Twig was touched and deeply relieved that he seemed so intent on finding a way for them to communicate when he went home. The thought of being without him after tomorrow was like a knife in her gut.

"Did we make a mistake?" she asked suddenly. "Getting involved?"

"What?" Leo turned to her, hearing the seriousness in her tone. He stopped typing for a moment and set the laptop aside. He took her in his arms. "No, no."

"Well, you're leaving tomorrow, and—"

"Twig," Leo whispered, stroking her hair.

"But you're going to be just starting college. I don't want to take you away from that. I want you to be happy there."

"Ah, I'll be *fine*. Don't worry about me. I know what I'm doing. Okay?"

"Okay," Twig said halfheartedly.

"Come on, let's finish this." Leo grabbed his laptop again. "How about the username 'leosgirl'? Is that too Leo-centric?"

"It's perfect." Twig couldn't help smiling at the sweetness of it.

"Password? Or do you want to keep that to yourself?"

"Sapphire. That's the name...*was* the name of my favorite horse."

"Nice." Leo punched away at the keyboard.

"Okay, so I'm sending you an email from my account. All you have to do is hit REPLY, write your email, and then hit SEND. I'll give you Hazel's, too." Twig leaned in to see what he was talking about.

It was late. They brushed their teeth and climbed back into bed together, holding one another tightly.

"I know we're taking it slow," Twig said as she drifted off to sleep, "but it would have been dope. Just wanted to say that."

She heard Leo chuckle as he snuggled up behind her. "You undo me, girl."

They both passed out moments later.

36

Twig woke up with a start. It was still dark outside and raining lightly. She looked at the clock. Five in the morning. Worry about Avery. Thoughts of Adam. She couldn't get back to sleep.

She changed into her cutoffs and pulled on one of Leo's big, zip-up sweatshirts. It was cooler by the coast in the mornings than it was at home. She wanted to make a sculpture on the beach and then let the tide come in and take it back.

The sky was gray and cloudy, and the water looked silver. She was struck by how much the sea changed with the weather and time of day. The restaurant stood empty and still above her, save the rare clinking of dishes as the employees set up for breakfast.

She worked steadily with her hands to sculpt the torso of a female. The tide grew more powerful as the sky became lighter and lighter. She worked faster, small waves beginning to lap at the woman's round, softy belly.

"I'd hate to see a wave come up and destroy that."

Twig looked up. Leo was watching her, his voice still hoarse from sleep.

"It's okay," Twig said. "That's part of it."

"What happened, Twig?"

"What do you mean?" Twig asked, wiping her eyes with her sleeve. Something about seeing him had made her start to cry softly.

"Come here," he murmured.

Twig went to him, and he wrapped his arms around her. "What's wrong?" he whispered. "You can talk to me."

Twig buried her face in his shoulder for a moment. They sat down in the sand. "Are you warm enough?" she asked him.

He nodded. "I'm fine."

"I have to tell you something."

"Okay," Leo said as if he had been waiting for this.

"I have to marry him." Twig swallowed hard to get the words out. It felt like swallowing something cold and steel.

"Who?" Leo asked quietly.

"Adam. You met him at the hospital. He's our…" Twig faltered. It sounded so strange outside the context of the Family. "…our leader," she said. "He chose me. I don't have any say in it." She paused. "He chose me a long, long time ago."

Leo was quiet.

"You have to understand—I don't love him. I hate him." Twig paused. It was true. She had come to hate him. "He's a liar. I don't know exactly what he's capable of, but I think he could be dangerous." Twig stifled a sob.

"When?"

"When what?" Twig asked.

"When are you supposed to marry him?" Anger was growing in Leo's voice.

"I'm so sorry, Leo. I didn't mean to betray you, I never thought—"

"I'm not angry at you, Twig. I know you can't help this. It's him."

"I don't know when exactly. February, maybe." Twig looked at the ocean. "And there's more… I think I might have a father in the States. He might be looking for me."

"You can't go back there," Leo said, somber.

"What?"

"You'll come home with us."

Twig looked at him, confused.

"You'll come back to the States with us, and we'll find your father, or we won't. It doesn't matter."

Twig tried to process what he was saying. The tide came in, and the woman toppled over into the sand.

"These guys are crazy, Twig. You don't know that because you don't have the context, but trust me. Koresh, Manson, all of them. They are psychopaths, and they *are* dangerous. I won't let you go back there."

"But everyone I love is there." Twig paused. "Except you. Even if I could get my head around imposing on you and your family like that—"

"Twig, I love you." He paused briefly, letting the words settle. "I love you," he repeated. "You're not an imposition. You've become a part of me."

"I love you, too," Twig answered simply.

"I know," Leo said, his voice softening. Twig started to cry harder, her body heaving on his chest. He squeezed her, rubbing her back.

The sea took the last of her sculpture.

Twig sat up, watching the waves recede. When she spoke, her voice was still shaking, but she had stopped crying.

"I can't go yet. I have to go back one more time. I have to talk to my mom. I have to make sure Ryan is okay. I would miss Sophie, but I know she'll be fine. I have to figure out what my responsibility is. I mean, can I just leave with the people I love, or do I have a responsibility to free everyone? I know it's hard to understand, but most of the people are happy there."

"It makes sense," Leo said. "From what I understand about cults, that's pretty typical. They're all brainwashed."

That word. Cult.

To Leo it was simple. She belonged to a cult. For her, it was her world, the only world she had ever really known. What would the outside world think of her? How would they treat her? Like a brainwashed freak?

"We are on vacation right now, Leo. Imagine being with me in the real world. I don't know anything, and you know everything. People will think I am a complete freak. I mean, it's one thing if I don't know a band or a song, but think of the basic things I don't know."

"I can teach you whatever you need to know," Leo said protectively.

"I would be a burden to you, but maybe if we could find my father... that would be different. Either way, I have to go back to the Family. I can't leave my mother and Ryan there."

"We can go back for them later. We can find your father and then go back."

"I can't. I can't imagine what Adam would do to her. He killed my horse for nothing—just to hurt me. I would go crazy wondering what was happening to both of them." That was true, but something else was scratching at Twig's brain. Leo was really on vacation. She wanted to give him a chance to get back to his real life, his new life at Yale, and see if he still wanted her then. She had to let him go. If he started school, got adjusted, and then still wanted her to come, she could go to him.

"But you will leave?"

Twig paused. "When the time is right, I will leave," she said finally.

Leo let out a big breath.

"Olivia."

"What?" Leo looked at her, puzzled.

"Once you asked me my real name. It's Olivia."

Leo looked at her with such sadness in his eyes, Twig thought her heart would break.

"It's a beautiful name," he said. "I just don't know how someone could do this to you." He held her face in his hands. "It is unimaginable to me. You hear about things like this and feel bad, but they seem so distant and far away."

"It's okay. I'm okay."

"We could go back together. We can bring the FBI. You were kid-napped, right? They could come with us, and we could get your mom and whoever you want. My dad's a lawyer; he'll know what to do."

Twig thought about this possibility. What if they arrested Avery as she had always feared? Even if they didn't, if they could work something out, what would that do to the people who loved their Family? Who was she to dismantle their life? She had to talk to her mother and Ryan and maybe even Gran before she made any decisions.

"Let me just go back this one time," she whispered.

37

The mood at breakfast was somber.

Everyone picked at a copy of the *New York Times* Sunday paper, which sat in a big heap in the middle of the table. Each section seemed to offer the Cohens some preview of what they would be returning to in the States. Alicia was ensconced in the Arts and Leisure section, and Jeff was hidden behind the Business section. Twig didn't know where to look. She wanted to take the entire paper home to study later.

Twig made Leo promise he wouldn't tell his parents her story until after they said good-bye. They might not understand and try to take things into their own hands. Leo said this was exactly what he wanted to happen, but out of respect for her wishes, he would wait.

Leo was quiet at breakfast. Twig wasn't sure who was more anxious about their parting in a few hours. She felt the package beneath her chair, waiting for the right moment. Everyone was so distracted that now seemed as good a time as any.

She cleared her throat. "I have thank-you things," she said shyly.

Jeff bent a corner of his paper down and peered at her for a moment. "Gifts?"

"Yes, gifts," she said.

Everyone folded up their papers and tossed them back into a heap on the table.

"I can't thank you enough for bringing me here and sharing so much with me. I know this was the last part of your vacation, and I just can't tell you how much this weekend has meant to me. So, these are small tokens, and if you don't like them you can throw them away or give them away. Here goes…" Twig handed each person a smallish rolled canvas tied with ribbon.

Intrigued, they began to unroll their paintings.

For Jeff and Alicia, she had chosen landscapes. For Hazel, a small, detailed painting of Sapphire. For Leo, one of the women he had admired in her studio. His was the largest.

"Twig, these are amazing. Thank you so much." Hazel got up from her chair and came over to hug Twig.

"Dear, you are truly gifted," Alicia said thoughtfully, studying her painting closely.

"This is going in my office!" Jeff said happily. "You did all of these? These are fantastic."

Leo came behind Twig's chair and put his arms around her. "I love it, and I love you," he whispered in her ear. A vision of him delicately putting an earbud in her ear at the hospital flashed into her head. So much had grown between them since then.

She tilted her head back to let him kiss her lips lightly.

The Cohens looked at the two of them, concern gently coursing beneath the tenderness of their gaze.

38

Daniel stood by quietly in the lobby of the hotel in Turrialba while Twig said her good-byes.

Jeff and Alicia gave her powerful, stoic hugs that said everything.

"You are welcome in our home anytime," Alicia said, holding on to Twig for an extra moment, strong and fiercely maternal.

"I'm going to be practicing my lip-synching in the mirror," Jeff joked with Twig. Then he grew more serious and looked her in the eye. "I am at your disposal if you ever need me, Twig. I mean it." He handed her his business card. "Just hang onto that. Call anytime, day or night."

"You'd better get going, Twig. They're going to scoop you up and take you home with them any minute now."

Hazel.

"Thank you for everything, Hazel." The two girls hugged.

"We'll meet you out in the parking lot, Lee," Jeff said as he, Alicia, and Hazel walked out of the lobby. "Good-bye, Daniel. Nice to meet you."

Twig turned toward Leo to say good-bye. "I feel like my heart is being ripped out of my chest," she said, looking up at him.

"I know, but I've been thinking. It's not that long, and we can talk every week when you come into town. You can find an internet café, and we can write once a week, too. Right? Not so bad?"

Twig felt lighter. "No, not so bad."

"I know it won't be the same, but it will keep us going."

"And you know if you ever don't hear from me, it's because I couldn't write or email, right? You will know that?"

"Yes. Of course."

"And if you get to Yale or get home and want to say good-bye, you will, right? You won't be embarrassed? You'll just tell me?"

"That's not going to happen, but yes, I promise. I won't just disappear."

Their plan made Twig feel better, more hopeful. Things seemed less final. She took a deep breath. She had to get a grip or she would never be able to walk out of that hotel lobby. She was saying good-bye to a lot, but she didn't want Leo to think he was leaving her in a hopeless pile of grief. She didn't want to put that burden on him.

She leaned into his chest, inhaled deeply to memorize his smell, touched his cheek to imprint the feel of him on her skin.

They pulled apart, eyes full of tears. Twig bit her lower lip to keep from crying harder.

Leo tried hard to smile. His big brown eyes were wet with tears. "You'd better go first. There's no way I can walk away."

"Okay," Twig nodded, tears spilling down her cheeks.

"We'll talk Wednesday—not so far away. When you check your email's inbox, it will be full, Leo's girl."

Twig and Daniel began to walk out of the lobby, but Twig stopped suddenly, motioning to Daniel that she needed one more moment alone with Leo. He nodded, making his way outside.

Twig dashed back for one more hug. She ran into Leo's arms, and he squeezed her tightly with relief.

"You don't have just one color, you know. You're a rainbow of colors to me," she said.

"I love you, Twig."

"I love you, too."

A few long moments later, Twig walked outside to meet Daniel.

When she arrived in the bright sunshine and warm air, Daniel asked, "Are you okay?" His eyes brimmed with kindness and understanding.

"Yes," Twig said. "Thank you for waiting, Daniel. Thank you for coming."

"Of course."

They drove back through the winding roads that lead from Turrialba to Gran's place in silence. Despite feeling wrenched away from Leo, Twig was looking forward to seeing Avery. She needed to know Avery was okay. She had been selfish to leave her. She needed the quiet safety of their cottage, too. A place to deal with all of these feelings. She was tired. She had woken up so early, and after the packing, the drive home, and most of all the good-byes, her emotions were spent.

They pulled up to Gran's house and stepped out of the car.

"I can get that, Daniel," Twig said as he reached for her suitcase in the backseat.

Then they both smelled it at the same time.

Smoke.

39

Without a word, Twig and Daniel started to run.

The suitcase bobbed heavily on Twig's thigh. She didn't even think to drop it.

As they came through the clearing, it took her a moment to make sense of what was happening. Both the house and the studio were intact, but the smell of smoke was thick and strong.

Daniel realized what happened first. "*Ay dios mío*," he muttered sadly.

A split-second later, Twig understood.

Her artwork. It was burning in a big pile outside the studio. She put her hands to her mouth and gasped.

Adam.

He came out of the studio and dropped another canvas on the pile without noticing her. Gran was following him. Her eyes were rimmed with red; she was crying. Her arms were crossed protectively over her body. They were arguing, and it was escalating. Twig put her hand out to stop Daniel. She wanted to hear what they were saying.

"We had a deal. You do not interfere. You were to have no contact with my people," Adam seethed.

"Your people?" Gran muttered, incredulous. "I said you could come live on my land with your family. With your wife and my granddaughter."

"And you've just been hanging in the shadows ever since, hoping I would forgive you someday."

"Of course I've always hoped that, Adam," Gran said. Twig gasped.

What did this mean? How did they know each other? Her granddaughter? That would mean…

"Well, it is never going to happen," Adam said, his voice steely. "You sealed the fate of our relationship when you decided to marry my prince of a stepfather, may he rest in peace."

"After all these years, Adam? Can't you let go of the hatred? I was a different person then. I was wrong, I've apologized, I—"

"I was just a boy. It was your responsibility to protect me."

Gran walked closer to Adam, sensing some sort of opportunity. "I am so sorry, my dear, dear Adam. Can you forgive me?" Adam stared at her as if, for just one moment, he was considering what she was asking of him.

Twig watched them. Why hadn't she seen it before? Their eyes. Those big, black eyes.

He was her son.

Twig watched Adam swallow hard, his throat moving up and down with the force of it. Whatever opportunity had opened, even for just a moment, was now shut again. "You're going to need to leave."

"Leave?" Gran laughed. "This is *my* land. You can't tell me to leave. I came here for peace. To live out my days. I'm not leaving, dear."

"No. You will leave. You'll see. I'll make your life a living hell until you—" He stopped. He'd noticed Twig. She took a step backward, bumping into Daniel.

"You're back," Adam said coolly.

"Adam," she answered, confused. She was trying to make sense of seeing him here with Gran. She was trying to make sense of what she'd just heard.

"Oh, honey," Gran said, holding her arms out to Twig. Twig paused, just staring at Gran in response.

"What happened?" Twig asked. She was beginning to shake. She felt disoriented.

"I'll tell you what happened, Twig." Adam's voice resounded with anger. "You betrayed me."

What does he know? Does he know about Leo? Did Gran tell him? Did she set me up?

"Daniel, you had better go home," Gran said.

"I can't leave her like—"

"GO!" Adam thundered at Daniel.

Twig flinched at Adam's tone, wanting to protect Daniel. She shot Daniel a look of apology. Daniel looked at her, waiting to go until she said it was okay. Adam seemed in such a state that she worried for Daniel's safety. Twig nodded softly. Daniel walked away slowly, his posture heavy with hesitation and worry.

"Twig, get over here." Adam motioned to the pile of burning canvas. The smoke was starting to sting her eyes.

Twig looked at Gran.

"Don't look to her for help," Adam ordered.

"You two know each other?" Twig asked, needing to hear it from one of them.

"We do!" Adam said jovially, feigning lightness. "Why don't you tell Twig how we *know each other?*"

"Take it easy, Adam," Gran said quietly.

"I've *been* taking it easy, and look what's happened here," Adam shouted.

"What exactly has happened?" Gran asked, anger brimming in her voice. "You decided you're God? That you can do whatever you want? Including marrying underage girls? Listen to me, Adam. You need a reality check."

Adam rushed toward Gran, pointing his finger at her like a gun. Twig ran between them, instinctually wanting to protect Gran.

"How dare you tell me what I need? Here's your reality check. We had an agreement, *Clare*, and you've broken it. Any hopes you had of having a relationship with your granddaughter just vanished."

"You're his mother," Twig confirmed quietly.

"I'm his mother," Gran said more to Adam than to Twig.

"Did you tell him I was away?" Twig asked, feeling more and more disoriented.

"No, no. Of course not."

"Then how...?"

"*How?*" Adam asked cruelly. "I came back from my trip and wanted to see you. I wanted to see my fiancée."

Twig couldn't help but cringe.

"Imagine my surprise when I went to your cottage and you weren't under the weather like everyone seemed to think you were. Quite the vulnerable position you left you mother in."

"Mom."

"Yes, your *mom*. You need to realize that you are part of a Family and that your actions affect everyone in it."

"Adam, she's a child," Gran objected.

"And as we have established, you know a lot about what's good for children, right, Clare?"

"Adam, please. We can work out what's between us—"

"Like I said, it's a little late for that." Adam grabbed Twig by the hand and pulled her along roughly. "Come on, Twig. We are going home."

"Tell me where my mom is," Twig said, planting her feet firmly where she stood.

"The more you resist, the worse it's going to get for the people you love," he said, ignoring her question. "Now come on, you can change when we get back. You look like a whore."

"Jesus," Twig heard Gran say quietly.

"Your clothes..." Twig started to say to Gran.

Gran waved her hand, indicating she didn't care about them.

"Does my mom know who you are?" Twig asked Gran, looking over her shoulder as she began to follow Adam.

Gran simply nodded, her arms still crossed, shaking her head bitterly. "If I had ever thought—I'll call the local authorities, Adam. You are out of control."

"Call them," Adam called back over his shoulder. "Be my guest."

Twig looked back at Gran as Adam pulled her along. She remembered Gran saying there were two sides to every story. That being a mother—being a woman—was a complicated thing. She hoped one day she would have a chance to hear Gran's story.

Gran started to say something but thought better of it. She put her hand to her heart and looked pleadingly at Twig. Twig nodded and put her own hand on her heart.

Twig turned and stumbled after Adam as he dragged her toward the road. She didn't feel like she had any other choice. A thought flickered through her mind as she glanced back at the pile of ash that was once her work.

The painting behind the studio. The one she'd hidden before she knew the truth of her life before the Family.

He probably hadn't found that.

And he hadn't destroyed the gifts she'd given the Cohen family.

It wasn't much, but it was a small piece of resistance.

40

The van was somewhat hidden.

Twig could see why she and Daniel hadn't seen it when they'd pulled up. They weren't meant to.

"When the time comes, you will account for every minute of your absence," Adam spat, dragging her toward the van.

Twig didn't respond. She saw that Thomas and Doc were both waiting in the van. Thomas looked horrible. His eyes were dark with fear.

"What's going on here?" Twig looked at Adam. "Thomas, what's wrong?"

"Did I tell you it was okay to speak? Get in," Adam ordered.

Doc sat in the driver's seat. Twig stepped into the back of the van and sat beside Thomas, who seemed to be trembling. Twig looked at Adam, who stood outside the car door.

"Whatever's going on, Thomas had nothing to do with my absence." Twig tried to keep her voice calm.

"I wouldn't say that," Adam said grimly. "I'd say he's been plenty complicit."

Twig began to protest again, but Adam held up his hand to stop her.

"See that blindfold beside you? You're going to use it on Thomas. Tie it really tight. Make sure he can't see anything."

"Adam, please," Twig started to plead. "Please, I am sorry. Thomas did nothing. I will make it up to you. I—"

"Tie it. Now!" he barked.

Twig looked at Thomas. "You'd better do it, Twig," he whispered. "I don't want them hurting Rose."

"What are you going to do?" Twig asked Adam while she tied the blindfold around Thomas's head. She was so scared, she was shaking. Her mother. What had he done to Avery?

"Twig," Adam held up a hand, his voice suddenly gentle. "Don't be afraid. Yes, I am angry. You betrayed me, but I am still your Adam. We are going to go work this out—just the four of us." Adam came into the van, sitting between her and Thomas. "I want both of you blindfolded. It pains me that you both have seen more sin than you ever should have. That is my fault. I should never have sent either of you into town." Adam smiled that fake, angry smile of his, the one he had used with the doctor at the hospital.

He blindfolded Twig and then held her hand, caressing her and running his fingers up and down her arm. "My beautiful bride," he whispered. "We're going to work this out, my children," he soothed.

"Please, Father. Please just tell me where my mother is."

"You're really worried about her, aren't you?"

"Yes, Father," Twig said, trying to sound humble.

"She's at your cottage, waiting for your return." Twig wanted to ask more, but Adam's voice sounded final. She knew asking more would be pushing it. Twig wondered what he was up to now. He had been furious at Gran's. Now he was trying to hide that fury, but Twig could feel it in his touch, hear it in his voice.

How stupid she had been. How stupid to think she could have gotten away with the trip. Gotten away with her time with Leo. She'd even gone as far as picturing herself and her mother having a completely different life. She had let herself hope.

Twig searched her mind for some way to stop this…some lie about where she was. She came up empty. She was so terrified, she couldn't even think straight. She wondered if she could seduce him in some way, charm her way out of this.

She heard Adam laugh. "Just stop it, Twig. I feel your little brain working. You really underestimate me. Don't even waste your time."

It was exactly what Avery had warned her not to do: underestimate him.

Adam addressed Doc. "Drive." Doc started the engine and shoved the gear into drive.

Doc. She went away on his watch, and in doing so, had made a fool of him. Twig knew he would never forget that.

Twig sat quietly while they drove, hoping that if she was silent, Adam would stop. Maybe he just wanted to scare her. They drove for a while. Twig tried to count seconds in her mind, tracking the minutes. Suddenly she heard rocks and branches crunch beneath the van's tires. She made a note to herself. They had pulled off of the main road.

"This is it," Doc said simply, cutting the engine. How Twig hated him. From the sound of his voice, he seemed to be enjoying this.

"Come on, my dear ones." Adam took off their blindfolds and led them out of the van. They were in the middle of the rainforest. The foliage was so thick that they were surrounded in darkness. Twig heard the eerie sound of howler monkeys in the trees above them.

"Let's start with a hug."

The four of them embraced awkwardly, obediently.

"Twig, can you admit your sins and ask for my forgiveness?"

Twig looked at him. She was skeptical. Was he really going to forgive her after all this?

"Of course," she answered. "Father, I have sinned. I am a sinner. I have been corrupted by the evil of the outside world, but I come to you now for forgiveness. I come to you to wash away my sins."

"You know you are dirty now."

"Yes."

"Say it." Some of the edge he seemed to be trying to hide came out in Adam's voice.

"I am dirty," Twig said through gritted teeth.

"Good. Yes. You are."

"Thomas."

Thomas fell to his knees at Adam's feet. He was weeping. "Forgive me, Father. I should have been more careful. Smarter. I was lazy. I was so, so very wrong. I am full of sin. I am nothing without you. Please, Father. Find it in your heart to have mercy on me. I am so, so sorry." Thomas sobbed, grabbing Adam's knees.

How Twig wished she could stop this.

"It's okay." Adam picked Thomas up and embraced him. "It is okay, my dear, dear son. I forgive you. Twig, come here." Twig approached them. "Both of you kneel. I will wash your sins away. I will wash you and make you as clean as the day you were born." He laid his hands on the tops of their heads. "I grant you forgiveness. You are washed clean of sin and evil. You have strayed, but I have brought you back. Now, Thomas, remove your clothing."

Twig and Thomas looked up in surprise. "I'm sorry, Father?" Thomas looked at Adam as if he hadn't heard him correctly.

"Remove your clothes. Twig seems to like clothes. Hand them to her."

Thomas began to unbutton his shirt.

Twig looked to Adam. What was he doing?

When Thomas had stripped down to his underwear, he folded his clothes into a rough pile and handed them to Twig. Twig accepted them, her eyes desperate to convey to him how sorry she was for causing him this humiliation.

"Ah-ah. Underwear, too."

Twig winced. "Adam, please."

"You shut up!" he shouted, his pretense of calm completely dropped. Thomas removed his underwear. "Let's go."

"I don't understand. Are we going home?"

"Yes. Yes we are."

Twig and Thomas began to follow Doc and Adam back to the van. Adam turned around. "We are going home. He"—Adam pointed to Thomas—"is staying here."

"Here? He can't stay here. He could starve! What are you—"

"I swear to God, Twig, if you utter another word... I can't stand the sound of your whore voice right now." Adam gritted his teeth and covered his ears.

"I'm not leaving him, Adam," Twig said resolutely.

Adam rushed at her and picked her up, carrying her toward the van. She kicked at him. "He's having a baby, Adam!" Twig screamed.

"Well, you should have thought of that before you decided to you go on your little vacation. Was it worth it?"

"I'm not leaving him," Twig screamed, continuing to struggle.

"Just go, Twig. You've done enough." Twig stopped at the sound of Thomas's voice.

"Thomas," Twig said.

"Just go. Make sure Rose is okay. Let her know that I love her. That no matter what, I will always love her. Tell her to stay calm for the baby. She has to."

"Thomas, I—"

"Twig, just go." Thomas turned his back on her. "You disgust me."

Twig started to tear up.

"Better listen to the man, Twig," Adam said smugly, extending his arm toward the back of the van. As she began to crawl in reluctantly, he gave her a little shove.

"Father," Thomas whispered. "Father, please. I thought you forgave me."

"I did forgive you, Thomas. Now I want nothing to do with you."

"But, Father. My family, Rose and the baby."

"See, Thomas. Your priorities are all screwed up. Your family isn't Rose and the baby. Your Family is the collective. But I am glad to know what's important to you."

"But, Father, I—"

"My decision is made, Thomas. Good-bye."

"He could *die* out here. How can you do this?" Twig said as quietly as she could when Adam entered the van and took the seat beside her. She didn't want Thomas to hear her.

"You did this, Twig. I didn't do this."

"Please, Adam. Leave *me*. Leave me instead." Adam ignored her, slamming the van's door shut.

Twig slumped back, utterly defeated. She would just have to get Adam alone and convince him to go back. That's all there was to it. She would do whatever it took. She would get them to come back for Thomas.

She tried to catch Thomas's eye as she stared at him through the van's window, but he wouldn't look at her. She felt as if she wanted to die as they drove away, leaving him there naked and exposed.

The image of Thomas standing there, his hands covering his genitals, burned into Twig's brain as they drove. Did this mean she'd been right to not leave with Leo? Or had she been wrong? Could they really have come back with the FBI? But what might have transpired while she was gone?

They pulled into the compound, and Doc parked the van.

"What are you going to do now?" Twig asked quietly.

Adam turned to face her. "I think your homecoming will be punishment enough. You should go get some rest. We're getting married tomorrow." He moved closer to her.

Twig was too stunned to speak. At the feel of his thigh alongside hers, she had to keep from being sick. She would never be able to rescue Thomas if Adam sensed her revulsion.

"You have to learn how to be a member of this Family again, but you will." Adam began to stroke Twig's hair. He took a handful of the beads around her neck and held them.

"I trusted you, Twig. You made a fool of me. I don't take that lightly, but I also understand." He dropped the beads and fingered the little *T* charm. "Twig, I lived out there. You forget that. I grew up out there. I know the highs of the outside world. The freedom that feels so good… at first. The delights—the food, the drink, the adventure of it."

Twig looked at him.

"Many of your brothers and sisters came from that world. They chose to come here, Twig. Doesn't that tell you something?"

"You tricked them," she said before she knew what she was saying.

"No. No, you see, I didn't. Look at your brothers and sisters. These aren't feeble-minded people or blind sheep. That freedom you are so in love with right now is a trap. Before you know it, you'd be living a life that has no meaning, no purpose. But right now you're having fun. Fun. Trust me, it wears off. It becomes meaningless. Meaningless…if you're lucky."

Twig found herself listening to him. Really listening to him for the first time in a long time.

"If you're not lucky, you'll find yourself whoring yourself out for another high. Prostituting yourself for whatever seemed so *fun*. Next, you'll become enslaved to it."

Twig didn't believe him—she would never believe anything he said again—but as she listened to him, she understood something for the first time. *He* believed what he was saying. It wasn't a matter of truth or lies. He probably didn't know where the truth left off and the lies began.

"Right now you are wrapped up in yourself. Your needs. Your desires and your wants. And that's what it is to be a teenager, really. But you'll grow out of it. You'll see. That sort of thinking comes to naught. It is, as I have always taught you, about the good of the whole."

Twig had heard enough.

"Once we channel this energy, it will work to our advantage. You'll see." He stroked her cheek gently.

"Okay," she whispered. "Okay." She wanted to spit at him, push him away, get his hands off her, but she forced herself to sit totally still. He was so erratic. She worried he might decide to strike her at any moment. He sensed her fear.

"You're scared of me," Adam said, rearing back.

Twig just continued to stare at him.

A smile played on Adam's lips. "Good. That's a start."

"Can I go now?" Twig whispered hoarsely.

"It won't always be like this, Twig. You'll see. We're going to be very happy together."

Twig nodded.

"Go." Adam swept his hand across his body, gesturing for her to leave.

Twig crawled out of the car. She tried to walk away slowly, but soon she broke into a run.

41

She had to find Rose. She had to get to Avery.

As she walked through the compound in her tight jeans and black boatneck sweater, the beads and little gold *T* glittering at her neck, she might as well have had blood on her hands.

Everyone stared at her accusingly. A toddler began to run toward her on her little legs, but her mother pulled her back. Rose stood in a cluster of people near the dining hall. Her small face was stained with tears.

"Just like your mother," Evelyn spat at Twig. "This is your fault, and don't you think otherwise for a minute."

Twig tried to ignore her.

"Rose," she said tentatively, "Can I talk to you?"

"No," Evelyn interjected. "You have done plenty. Just leave her alone. The two of you need to stay in that cottage, or better yet, just go away and leave us in peace. I, for one, wish you had never come back from your little trip. You're just—"

"Evelyn, just stop!" Twig snapped.

"Don't you yell at me." Evelyn began to puff herself up, ready for a fight.

"Mom," Rose finally spoke. Her voice was brittle with pain. "Twig, please go away. I don't want to see you."

"I know this is all my fault. I understand that, Rose. I am so, so sorry, but Thomas wanted me to tell you something." Twig pleaded with Rose to let her speak.

Rose looked at her, and what Twig saw in her expression threw her off guard for a minute: hatred. It was apparent that Rose could barely tolerate the sight of her.

"He just wanted me to tell you that he loves you, that he will always love you no matter what. To stay calm no matter how hard that is, for the baby. Rose, I'm so sorry." Twig's hands were pressed together, prayer-like, her fingertips covering her mouth.

Rose began to weep into her sleeve.

"Enough!" shrieked Evelyn. "Rose, come and sit down. This is insane. Leave!" she yelled at Twig, shooing her away.

"I—" Twig started to protest.

"Please, just go," Rose said.

Twig backed away slowly. She realized Sophie was in the group. She looked at her for some sort of help. Sophie shook her head.

Twig looked toward her cottage. She needed her mother.

Gran had once told them to remember who the real enemy was. But to the group, the enemy was Twig. They would never see Adam as anything but their leader. Twig was ready to do anything to get Thomas back, including accepting full responsibility for what was happening to him. But couldn't anyone see that leaving Thomas defenseless out in the middle of nowhere was the action of a deranged person?

She felt an arm on her elbow pushing her forward.

"I can walk on my own," Twig said defensively, pulling her arm away.

"You never have to walk on your own as long as I'm around," Ryan said, keeping his hand firmly on her elbow.

Twig nearly sank into him with relief.

"Before you go," Yasmine and Farriss called, walking quickly to catch up with Twig and Ryan as they headed toward Twig's cottage.

Twig turned around slowly, bracing herself for whatever blows they might throw. Yasmine put her hand on Twig's arm. "We'll work all of this out in Meetings soon. You'll see." Her tone was gentle. "What you did was wrong, but we will work it out. That's what this Family is about. Not one of us is perfect. We will all grow from this."

Someone could die. Someone they all loved. And this is what she had to say? They would work it out in Meetings?

Every second Twig was more and more sure that she did not belong here anymore. They all believed in Adam. He could do no wrong in their eyes. They didn't care about right or wrong or the truth. They had blind faith. And if anyone had any doubt, they were too scared to act. Adam controlled them with fear.

Along with her growing certainty came a black feeling of dread. She was trapped.

Maybe she had always been trapped, but now she knew it.

Twig nodded stoically at Yasmine and Farriss. Farriss looked back at her with what looked like genuine compassion.

"Are you going to be okay, Twig?" Farriss asked.

Twig felt as if she might collapse. She had to get back to her cottage. She needed Avery. She turned away and broke into a run. Ryan bolted after her. She heard them calling her name but kept going. She couldn't stand a minute more. Suddenly her Family seemed like a bunch of strangers.

Avery was waiting for them when they got to the cottage. She seemed fine, unharmed. She took Twig in her arms. How much their relationship had changed over the last few months. All the chaos and lies had thrown them together.

Twig whispered into Avery's neck. "How could he do this to Thomas?"

Avery started to say something and then thought better of it.

"He's moved the wedding up to tomorrow."

"I know."

"Does everyone know?"

"Yes. He made one of his little speeches before this unfolded."

"I have no sense of what time it is anymore. What did he say about Thomas?" Twig asked, collapsing on the couch. Ryan brought her a glass of water and sat next to her.

"He said he had to make a lesson out of him," Ryan said sadly. "It's almost dinner," he said as an afterthought. "I know that's a stupid thing to say right now, but I don't want you to get into any more trouble."

"Do they want me to go? Am I supposed to go?" Twig asked incredulously.

"I don't think so," Avery said. "I think we are the unofficial wedding party—in for the night."

Twig groaned and sat up. She pressed her palms to her eyes. "He could die out there. I have to find a way to help him. He could die, and it's my fault."

"There's nothing you can do." Avery looked at Twig.

Leo.

He would be getting on a plane tonight.

Could she somehow sneak over to Gran's and use her telephone? Use the number on Jeff's card and just… Just what? Have them come get her and then help her find Thomas?

What if they actually came?

No. She couldn't involve them in this. Adam was dangerous. Twig didn't know what he was capable of.

But she had to communicate with Leo somehow. Once she knew he was safely on the plane, she had to write to him. The thought of him waiting for her email on Wednesday was unbearable. After the wedding, that email would never come. She knew it. Adam would never let her out of his sight again.

Maybe she could sneak away to Gran's just one last time before the morning, before the wedding. Just send one email. It would make all the difference.

"Ryan, I have to talk to you."

"Okay."

"This is probably terrible timing, but I don't know when I'll have the chance again, and I feel like it's my responsibility."

Avery went into the kitchen to let them speak.

"I asked. I asked my friend your questions."

"Oh," Ryan said. "It's okay, it doesn't matter."

"It does matter. Please."

Ryan started to say something in response but then went quiet, waiting for Twig to speak.

"There are gay people out there who live safely and openly." She wanted to say this the right way. The outside world wasn't flawless, but it was better than life here. Ryan looked at her. "It's not perfect. There are some who do hate gay people."

"So what Adam says is true?"

"Partially true. Half truths. There are places where gay people can marry. You could find a partner who feels the same way you do."

"And there are places where people are beaten for being gay?"

"Yes. But, Ryan, people are beaten here for nothing!" Twig whispered, trying to get through to him.

"Twig, it's okay."

"But you don't understand."

"No, I do. I do. I am safe here. I am going to volunteer to marry Rose. To raise her baby with her."

Twig felt like she'd had the wind knocked out of her. "But... Why? Why would you do that? Ryan, please believe me—"

"Twig, I do, honey. I believe you. I believe everything you just told me. But this is my choice. I have a purpose here. Rose needs me. Please, just stop. Really. I am okay."

Twig looked at him with tears in her eyes. If she could ever get out, he wouldn't want to come with her. He was staying. Until he saw things with his own eyes and experienced them for himself, he would not be convinced.

There was a knock at the door.

Avery went to answer it. Doc followed her back into the living room.

"Looks as if we're having a little slumber party this evening, ladies," Doc said in his crooked way. He looked at Ryan. "You can go home now."

Ryan clutched Twig's hand. She looked down at their entwined fingers.

"We'll get through this," he whispered. He stood up from the couch and walked out of the cottage.

Twig went into her room, and Avery followed her. They left Doc sitting in the living room.

A little later, Maya came with dinner for the three of them. She greeted Twig coolly, her usual kindness gone. Twig noticed she was careful not to touch her. She wondered how Adam planned to undo all of this hatred. He was marrying an outcast.

Avery and Twig ate in their bedroom. Doc sat guard at the kitchen table, reading a book, brewing pot after pot of coffee. No one said a word after Maya left.

The desperation and fear on Thomas's face kept haunting Twig. Maybe he could get back to the main road and hitch a ride to Turrialba. Maybe someone would take pity on him and help him, if he let them. He didn't even have shoes. If he could just find his way back to the main road…

Twig signaled for Avery to follow her back to the bedroom. She stuck her arm beneath her mattress where she kept the nano. She had to bend down to reach back far enough.

Twig produced the little, orange plastic bottle of pills Doc had given her. "For Doc…"

Avery frowned.

They walked into the bathroom together, and Twig started to run a bath.

"I'm going back to Gran's," Twig whispered as the water poured into the tub.

"Honey—" Avery started.

"I have a plan. I'm going to get Daniel to find Thomas and take him to Turrialba, and I have to write to Leo."

Avery seemed to turn Twig's words over in her head for a moment.

"I think Thomas is a trap, Twig," Avery's voice was barely audible.

"What do you mean?" Twig whispered back.

"I think they are watching you and watching him. If you interfere, it will give Adam an excuse to unleash even more of his madness on you. On *us*." Avery took the bottle of pills in her hand and turned them around. She squinted to read Doc's small handwriting.

"This part of the plan, I like," Avery said thoughtfully. "Giving that old bastard a taste of his own medicine." Avery paused, thinking. "If we put a few in that coffee of his, it should give you enough time. He'll have a clean enough wakeup. This stuff isn't that strong. He shouldn't feel like he was drugged. You'll have to ride out in the dark by yourself. Do you think you can do that? I'll stay here and watch to make sure he doesn't wake up before you're back."

"Yes, I can do it." Twig was determined.

"You promise you'll just contact Leo. No Thomas?"

Twig frowned.

"I've known Adam a long time, Twig."

Twig nodded. She would figure something out.

"Why don't you take that bath? Try to relax a little bit."

Twig nodded and began to unbutton her jeans. She slipped them off and lovingly folded them into a neat pile beside the tub. She'd have to wear her dress—now her wedding dress—when she rode out. She might not have time to change when she got back.

42

Timing was everything. Avery said they needed to wait until later in the night when Doc would naturally begin to struggle to stay awake. Twig would need to be back by 4:00 a.m. at the latest. Any later and things might start to stir in the compound.

There was a wedding happening, after all.

Avery and Twig nearly laughed out loud as they used the heel of Avery's boot to crush the pills into a powder to slip into Doc's coffee. Avery said she would pretend she was going for a cup of water and then offer him a fresh cup of coffee. She would watch him drink it before returning to their room.

Twig sat under her covers in the dark with her eyes plastered open. Adrenaline was coursing through her veins. She kept checking the clock on the nano. The time seemed to be crawling by.

Finally.

Avery had fallen asleep. Twig nudged her lightly, and she woke up instantly. Avery hopped out of bed and walked out of the room. Twig's boots were at Gran's. She'd have to wear one of her old pairs. She'd put them on when she got outside.

Twig felt nauseated from the combination of nerves and the lack of sleep. She heard Avery and Doc's voices erupt into the silence of the night. Quiet, but there. Doc laughed quietly. Twig heard him say, "Thank you."

Avery walked back into the room and nodded at Twig.

Twig let out a sigh of relief. He had taken the coffee.

She was supposed to wait twenty minutes to make sure the drugs had taken their effect and then go. She waited thirty to be sure and then gave Avery a hug. She tiptoed into the living room in her socks.

Doc was out like a light, his head cradled in his arms on the kitchen table. As she left the cottage, she wondered what sort of conversations about her had passed between Doc and Adam.

Twig ducked through the compound, sure to avoid exposure from the front porch lights of the cottages. She wouldn't have a problem getting to the stables without light, and she was pretty sure she could get to Gran's in the dark.

Pretty sure. If she had Sapphire, it would be a sure thing.

Bill Evans was glad to see her when she arrived. She chose him because she knew he knew the way. He shoved his muzzle at Twig, which she gladly embraced. She saddled him and climbed on in the dark. She had done it so many times, the movements were a part of her.

They started out slowly. Carefully. For a moment, Twig thought she heard someone following them. She stopped and pulled the horse behind a tight cluster of trees. They waited for a moment.

Nothing.

The moon was benevolently bright, and soon they established a steady pace.

It felt good to be in motion, even if it was a fleeting feeling.

They reached Gran's before long. The smell of smoke was still strong in the air. Twig felt a twinge of pain thinking of her paintings, but on the list of things to worry about, they were nothing. They were merely an insult.

Twig put Bill Evans in the pen and ran to Gran's door. She knocked as hard as she could and rapped on the window, but no one came. She worried for a second that Gran had left, had gone back to the States.

She grabbed a shovel from the garden and pounded on the door.

"Who is it?" Gran's voice finally came. It was laced with apprehension.

"It's Twig."

Gran opened the door immediately.

"Come in, dear." Gran beckoned Twig inside and then stuck her head outside the door to make sure no one had followed her.

"Do you have a computer?" Twig asked immediately.

"Of course, dear, but—"

"I just need a computer."

"Can we talk for a moment?" Gran pressed.

"He's moved the wedding up to the morning."

Gran put her hand to her mouth. "I'm so sorry, darling. I never thought—"

Twig put her hand on Gran's arm. "I don't know why you didn't tell me you were his mother, but right now, none of that matters. I owe a lot to you. I'm so sorry, but I really don't have much time."

"Of course," Gran pulled her bathrobe closer to her body. "It's in here."

Gran lead Twig to an alcove in the back of the house that served as Gran's office. A thin, silver computer sat on the desk with a picture of a big apple on it. Gran popped it open.

"Do you have the internet here?"

"We have to dial up because we are so far out. It will just take a moment to get online," Gran explained. "Can I get you a cup of tea while you wait? Do you want to be alone?"

"No, no tea. Alone would be good. I'll be fast. Thank you."

"I'll be in the kitchen if you need me."

Twig didn't answer—she was staring too intently at the screen. Gran slipped away quietly.

Twig pecked at the keys, finally spelling out the webmail address.

She typed in "Leosgirl" for the username and "Sapphire" when it asked for the password.

Four messages. One from the email host, welcoming her to the site. Three from Leo.

The first email said "I Miss You Already" in the subject heading. He had written it right after they'd said good-bye and sent it from his iPhone. The subject heading pretty much said it all.

He'd written the second one from the airport. It was longer. He said he was going to find her dad for her. He had thought about it, and it was the right thing to do. He was sorry if he was putting his nose where he shouldn't, but he would get her the information, and together they could decide what to do with it.

Twig smiled.

She opened the last email.

He couldn't possibly wait until spring break and would have to come back much, much sooner. He loved her. Hang tight. He couldn't wait to see her again. They'd talk Wednesday. P.S. She looked really hot in her bathing suit. Had he mentioned that?

The last part made Twig laugh. She sat in the blue light of the screen, tears making their way down her cheeks.

She looked at the time stamp on Gran's computer. She had to hurry. If only she could have used all of the time she'd spent waiting for Doc to pass out.

Her typing was slow, but she managed. She told Leo about Thomas, the wedding, and mostly about Adam's threats. She thought about leaving all of that out, just saying good-bye, but he would never buy that. He would know something had happened and would be tortured with worry if she didn't tell him the truth. She told him she worried about finding her father because Avery would be prosecuted. She told him she didn't have any answers right now. She did know she loved him, and she needed to keep him and everyone else she knew safe. Right now, that was the most important thing.

For now, the only way to do that was to go through with the wedding.

She started to write more, but stopped. Her feelings for him ran deeper than she could ever manage to type in a rushed email.

It was hard to press SEND. Her fingers hovered over the keyboard. She didn't know if she'd ever speak to him again.

Feeling paralyzed, she just sat there like that, frozen for a moment. And then she heard voices drifting in from Gran's kitchen. She left the email on the screen, unsent, and began to creep quietly toward the kitchen.

It was Avery.

"Mom?" Twig was confused. "Did he wake up? What happened?"

It took Twig a minute to see what was going on. Avery was talking on Gran's phone. She was crying.

"Mom, what happened? Are you okay?" Twig ran to her. She looked at Gran for answers.

"She's here," Avery said into the phone.

Avery handed Twig the phone. Twig looked at it and then at her mother. She was completely confused.

"Is it Leo?" she asked. She put the phone to her ear awkwardly. She had never spoken on a phone before.

"Hello?" she said into it.

"Livvy."

Her body went rigid. She froze as chills ran up and down her spine and crawled over her skull.

"Daddy." She knew him. The recognition was visceral; it ran through her bones and winding neural pathways.

"Oh my God," her father said. He drew in a long breath on the other end of the line.

"*Daddy.*" Twig looked at Avery. Avery was smiling through her tears.

"Listen to me, darling, I've prayed for this moment for the last fourteen years, but your mother has explained everything to me. I know you are in danger there and don't have much time. You listen to me now, okay?"

"Yes, yes, of course." Twig had begun to cry.

"I'm coming for you, baby."

"But, Daddy, he's crazy. What if he finds out? There are guards—he could hurt you, he—" Twig needed him to understand. She could barely think of all the possible repercussions.

There was silence on the other end of the line for a second. She heard her father take another deep breath. She imagined his anger, his feelings of helplessness.

"That's what he wants you to think, Olivia. That's what these people do. They scare you into thinking there is no way you can get away. I'm coming, Livvy. I will handle him."

"But what about Mom?"

"All I care about is getting you both home safe. Nothing is going to happen to her."

"She won't go to prison?"

"No. Honey, I don't want you to worry like that. Please."

"He's making me marry him. In the morning. He's making me marry him this morning."

Silence again. Twig could feel her father's rage.

"I'm getting on a plane, but I'll send a private security team ahead of me. They can get there faster, and we don't have time to deal with the local authorities. I'm sorry to ask this, Livvy, but it will help. Do you know if there are guns there?"

"I think so," Twig said. "I think the guards have guns. I've never seen them, but I've heard them."

"Do you know how many men he has?"

"There are almost two hundred people here, but I don't know how many have guns or—I mean, many of those are women and children. I'm sorry, I don't—"

"It's okay, honey. That's fine. That's very helpful. Listen, there will be a helicopter and armed men coming. Do not be afraid of them. They will get you and your mother. They will bring you somewhere safe, and I'll be there as fast as I can."

Avery signaled to Twig that she needed to say good-bye.

"I have to go," Twig said breathlessly. "But I'm scared to get off. I don't want to lose you again."

"You won't. You will never lose me again. You just keep yourself safe, baby. I'll be there as fast as I can." His voice cracked. "And Livvy—it's not a real marriage. You're still a citizen of the United States, and you're not of age to be married without parental consent." Her father paused, getting control of his emotions. "Just do what you need to do to stay safe for the next twelve hours. This will all be over soon. You're getting out. Promise me you'll stay safe?"

"I promise you."

"I love you more than life itself."

Twig's heart leapt. She couldn't believe this was happening. "I love you, too, Daddy." Her chest heaved. "Daddy, one more thing." Twig thought of her unsent email.

"Anything."

"A friend of mine on the outside was going to try to find you for me. Will you find him? Tell him what's going on? Keep him safe?"

"What's his name?"

"Leo Cohen."

"It's done. I love you, Olivia."

"Good-bye, Daddy."

"See you soon, my precious girl."

Twig handed the phone to Avery. She stood there for a moment, too stunned to speak. Avery stepped toward her and put her hands tentatively on Twig's shoulders. They stared at one another, eyes filled with tears. After a few moments, Avery took Twig into a protective embrace.

"Why didn't you come with me?" Twig managed to whisper into Avery's ear. "Why follow me?"

"I realized as soon as you left." Avery stroked Twig's hair and continued to hold her close. "I knew it was the right thing to do—the *only* thing to do, after everything that's happened."

Twig finally pulled away. "Thank you." Avery wiped the tears from Twig's face.

"We've got to go," Avery urged her. "It's crucial we get back before anyone wakes up."

43

Twig woke to Maya's plump face glaring down at her.

"Twig, it's time to wake up."

Twig bolted upright. She looked over at Avery. She was just stirring as well. Avery looked back at her and raised her eyebrows.

"Where's Doc?" Twig ventured.

"He went back to his place to take a shower before the wedding," Maya answered. "I'm supposed to help you get ready."

"Me, too."

It was Anna. Twig hadn't seen her since the night she was beaten. Twig felt a rush of sadness for her. Had Adam seduced her away from her life? Away from college, her friends and family?

Twig shook off her sleep, wondering why Maya had brought Anna. It was obvious to Twig now that Adam and Anna had been in some kind of relationship before he brought her here—just like he had with Avery. Was he just torturing Anna by having her help prepare his new bride for his wedding? How many women had been through this with him?

Twig got up and looked around the room. No one seemed to know about their midnight excursion.

Her conversation with her father came back to her. Twig looked at Avery when Maya and Anna walked into the bathroom to draw a bath for her.

"Did I dream him?" she asked.

Avery shook her head and then put her finger to her lips to keep Twig from saying any more.

Twig tried to ignore the meaning of the rose petals Maya sprinkled into her bath. She submerged herself, letting her ears fill up with the charged silence beneath the water.

Later, she sat stone still while Anna combed out her hair. Maya had gone.

"Do you want to wear flowers in your hair?" Anna asked shyly. Twig only shrugged in response. Anna paused and then handed Twig a large, white orchid. Twig thought of the day she prepared Rose for her wedding. The day she found out Adam had chosen her for his wife.

"I think he'll expect it," Anna said quietly.

Twig's father's words came back to her. "*Just do what you need to do to keep yourself safe for the next twelve hours.*"

"You're right." Twig took the flower from Anna. She twisted her hair into a bun and pinned the big white flower into her hair near the nape of her neck.

"That looks beautiful," Anna smiled. "I miss girly things," she whispered.

Twig craned her neck around to look at Anna. "I'm sorry he made you come help me today."

Anna shrugged her shoulders. "He didn't," she said. "I volunteered. No one else wanted to come." She wrinkled her nose. "Can I ask you something?" Anna said.

"Sure," Twig said reassuringly. She had nothing to lose at this point.

"Why did you come back? If you had the chance to get away, why would you ever come back here?"

"My mom," Twig said simply. "Can I ask you something now?"
Anna nodded.

"Why did you come here? From the outside world? Why did you come here in the first place?"

"Well, I didn't really know what I was coming to," Anna said. "And by the time I got here, it was too late. But I probably would have come no matter what. I was too in love, too hooked to let Adam go." She paused. "I figure you're not going to report me?"

Twig laughed. "Ah, no."

"I was in school, and I thought I was having this very sexy affair with an older businessman from out of town. We'd go on normal dates to bars, to movies, to restaurants—"

"What?" Twig gasped and covered her mouth. She couldn't believe his hypocrisy.

"He even has normal friends out there. Or at least he has it set up to look like he does. I went to a dinner party at his friend's house. And I was attracted to his ideas—to his friend's ideas. After awhile, I couldn't relate to my own friends. They started to seem so shallow. So I became a bit isolated. I just had Adam. I would wait and wait for him to come back into town. I stopped going out with my friends at night so I could go home and wait for his call."

"I'm sorry. I'm sorry this happened to you."

Anna smiled sadly. "We'll probably never get to talk like this again." Twig thought of her father.

"No, probably not." Twig paused. Maybe they could take Anna with them. But she didn't want to mention it now. The conversation they'd just had was risky enough. "We should probably get going," she said.

"Twig." Anna grabbed Twig's hand. "Can we be real sisters? I think we need each other."

Twig smiled warmly at her. "Yes, of course."

"Oh, there's just this." Anna held up a sash made of royal-blue fabric.

"What's that?"

"Ada—Father said he had it made for you. For today."

Twig flinched. She tried to recover quickly, nodding as Anna wrapped it around her waist.

Avery came out of the bathroom fully dressed. She took Twig's hand. "Are you ready?"

"Yes."

"Do you think you can make it through this?" Avery whispered into Twig's ear.

"Yes." Twig paused. "If I just keep going and don't stop to think."

"Okay, let's go," Avery said, adopting a practical tone. Twig was thankful. Any display of emotion right now, and she might crack.

The three women walked across the compound to where the stage had been erected. Twig noticed how bare things looked. There was no music or lanterns. There was no joy.

People sat quietly in white chairs that flanked the aisle Twig would walk down. It seemed everyone was in attendance except one person.

Thomas.

Twig would find him. When her father came, they would go find Thomas.

Avery took her elbow to steady Twig, who had started to falter. Twig bit her lip to quell the nausea rising inside her.

Twig looked down the aisle. Adam stood beaming on the stage beside Doc, who would preside over the ceremony. Adam was clearly excited. Twig wondered what exactly it was about all of this that excited him.

She shuddered to think.

"Looks like we're on," Avery said gently into Twig's ear. She put her lips to Twig's cheek. Twig closed her eyes to keep from crying. She turned and kissed Avery gently on her mouth.

Twig took a deep breath, straightened her back, and started the march down the aisle toward Adam.

And then she heard it. Or felt it. She wasn't sure which came first.

The earth seemed to be lifting, folding into itself around her. A wild, whipping wind pulled her hair from its bun, blowing her skirt. It sounded like a thousand knives chopping violently at the air, as if the earth were being ground up by some giant machine. She covered her forehead and looked up. She remembered what her father had said about the security team arriving by helicopter, and his words.

Don't be afraid.

She was getting out.

She felt Adam's gaze on her. There beneath the blinding wind, through the sound, Adam was glaring at her, shaking his head. He began to run toward her. She felt Avery grab her hand and pull her in the direction of the forest where the helicopter was landing. Together they ran, faster than they'd ever run before. They sprinted toward the helicopter, which was now just a few feet from the ground. Several men dressed in black with helmets and large guns jumped to the ground and began to run to Twig and Avery. The air screamed all around them.

As Twig ran, she whipped her head back for one last look.

She didn't mean to. It was ludicrous after everything that had happened, but part of her was aching to turn back. It was the only world she had ever known. It was the family she'd grown up with. It was Ryan, her closest confidante. It was Sophie, whom she'd played with while she was still in diapers. It was Rose, whose color was a soft pink, who'd been nervous and excited on her wedding day. It was Farriss, looking at Sapphire with tears in his eyes. It was Anna.

Anna, trapped in a Family she didn't sign up for. And that's what Twig would always be here if she stayed: trapped.

So she kept running. She was no longer running away from her life. She was running toward it. Toward her father, whom she'd finally get to meet. Toward painting with real paint on real canvases. Toward music and Cohen Lip-Synch Nights. Toward Hazel, Alicia, and Jeff.

Toward Leo.

One of the men stuck out his arm. She felt the leather of his glove as he closed his hand around hers. She felt her feet, one by one, lifting off the earth, defying gravity, defying the magnetic pull of her former life.

She was getting out.

About the Author

Marissa Kennerson received her B.A. in English Literature from the University of California at Berkeley. Before earning her master's degree in psychology and art therapy, she worked for *Wired* and *Glamour*. She lives in California with her family. The Family is her first novel.

Visit Marissa on her website,
www.marissakennerson.com

36109725R00183

Made in the USA
San Bernardino, CA
13 July 2016